Peck's creativity and imag ... sails into the ozone with words and ideas. The novel is generous with the human condition and the fact that all people have weak knees at times. I very much liked the contrast between the weaknesses of his characters and their surprising strengths. This book is an act of love for the frailties of humankind, for the very deepest meaning of being human. The writing is marvelous, and Peck's sensitivity to his characters is impressive. I fell "in love" after I read the book and felt like celebrating the frail yet beautiful persistence common to us mortals. This is also a first-class treatise on nothingness and whether or not any God can arise from such.

—Phyllis Barber
Author of *The Desert Between Us* and
To the Mountain: One Mormon Woman's Search for Spirit

Only Steve Peck would meld elements from Mormon romance, the Book of Mormon, crime/psychological thrillers, academic prose, and nature writing and wrap them in theological speculation that is both universalist and uniquely Mormon. The result is challenging, heretical (in surprising, wonderful ways), redemptive, propulsive, and full of abundant, profound love and empathy for all living things, especially for us messed up, complicated, sometimes even murderous human beings.

—William Morris
co-editor of *Monsters & Mormons* and
author of *Dark Watch and other Mormon-American stories*

Wow wow wow! THIS is the kind of Mormon novel I knew somebody had in them.

—Angela Sweat Hallstrom
Author of *Bound on Earth* and
editor of *Dispensations: Latter-day Fiction*

Heike's Void gapes open with humility, horror, hurt, and something somehow heartwarming, demanding answers of Mormonism's most pressing question, a question too infrequently posed in contemporary Mormon literature, the question of Christ's infinite forgiveness. It does so with onslaughts of ontological argument, tender questions of social justice, the caprices of natural disaster, the tiniest neural complexities, and nose to nose conversations with naughty dogs. These currents come together in what amounts to a page-turner of a harrowing family drama told with the earnest curiosity and fine, earthy detail of Peck's alternately gentle and devastating prose.

—Jennifer Quist
Author of *Sistering, Love Letters of the Angels of Death*, and *The Apocalypse of Morgan Turner*

Never has The Void been more abundant.

—Michael Hicks
Professor Emeritus of Music, Brigham Young University and author of *The Mormon Tabernacle Choir: A Biography, Spencer Kimball's Record Collection*, and *The Street Legal Version of Mormon's Book*

heike's void

BCC
PRESS

By Common Consent Press is a non-profit publisher dedicated to producing affordable, high-quality books that help define and shape the Latter-day Saint experience. BCC Press publishes books that address all aspects of Mormon life. Our mission includes finding manuscripts that will contribute to the lives of thoughtful Latter-day Saints, mentoring authors and nurturing projects to completion, and distributing important books to the Mormon audience at the lowest possible cost.

heike's void

A NOVEL FROM STEVEN L. PECK

For information contact
By Common Consent Press
4900 Penrose Dr.
Newburgh, IN 47630

Cover art: Leslie Graff, "Night Aspens," lesliegraff.com
Image of parameter plane and Mandelbrot set for $f(x) = z^4 + mz$ by Adam Majewski
   (https://commons.wikimedia.org/wiki/File:Parameter_plane_and_Mandelbrot_
   set_for_f(z)_%3D_z%5E4_%2B_m*z.png)
Cover design: D Christian Harrison
Book design: Andrew Heiss

This novel's story and characters are fictitious. Any resemblance to actual
persons, living or dead, or actual events is purely coincidental. The historical
moments in which the story is embedded are real and listed on the page "Events
Relative to Story," Certain long-standing institutions, agencies, and public offices
are mentioned, but the characters involved are wholly imaginary. The book is
not autobiographical except in the sense that it all comes out of my peculiarities,
perceptions, and experiences in life, and how I imagine life is for others.

www.bccpress.org
ISBN-13: 978-1-948218-55-9

10 9 8 7 6 5 4 3 2 1

With love to the
Cosmic Microwave Background Radiation
for making this world possible

Contents

Significant Events Relative to Story

Electroconvulsive therapy first tried (1938)

Third major epidemic of Sleeping Sickness transmitted by tsetse flies begins (1970)

Baader-Meinhof Gang Bombing of Frankfurt Officer's Club (May 1972)

Fall of Saigon (April 1975)

New York Times first mentions AIDS Epidemic (1982)

"I Want to Know What Love Is" released by Foreigner (November 1984)

Monticello, Utah Temple dedicated (July 1998)

PART I

Apostle Holmberg
in Canyonlands

The void is an unimaginable place. Unimaginable because to imagine it is to negate its possible non-existence by creating a reference to it. One cannot paint it, write it, or put it in film. The empty space flung about the universe fails as a simile because it is filled to the brim with districts of effect, like electromagnetic fields, strong and weak nuclear forces, quantum foam, dark energy and its like. Not so the void. It is a country without borders, contour lines, or designations—no measure can be made there to quantify (or qualify) its extent or content. It dances beyond the edge of knowing. I can talk about it, as I am now, but it does not bring me closer. I can only give suggestions and intimations—gestures that convey a general direction, but not its elevation from some base or its latitude or longitude.

—Frau Professorin Heike Marquardt,
On the Void: The Theology of Nothingness

There are those God hates. He just does. It is as inexplicable as his love. He hates them passionately and with all his heart—which is an immense heart loaded with both the spaciousness, transcendence, and the closeness of infinite imminence. So this hatred is just as large and pure as can be imagined. Or, frankly, more than *can* be imagined: The Platonic form of hate. An Ideal of hate so glorious it can only exist in the ethereal realms of the One. It is often hard to convince people of this because they are conditioned to think that "God is Love" means there are no bounds to that love. The confusion seems to come from the New Testament scripture that offers this exact phrase. However, if you are going to take the whole Bible seriously, you have to take other scriptures that promote an alternative point of view. For example, in Romans 9:13, just a few books over in the New Testament from the "God is Love" scripture in 1 John 4:16, we read, "As it is written, Jacob have I loved, but Esau have I hated." There it is. God hated Esau. And it is not like He's going to change his mind. I think if there is one thing we know about God it is that he is steady and true. No flighty changeable being is He. If God hates you, you are stuck with it. This doesn't mean you can't go to heaven? No, no, no. God is not a monster. He recognizes His eternal hatred is irrational and not fair, but the fact is He just does—and you shouldn't be surprised. If God made everything, it stands to reason that he made hate too, and hate needs an object, and it turns out that object is indeed some people. He really does just hate some folk. That is that. He'll still use them for good, still blesses them when they plead unto heaven for His blessings, still prospers their posterity and all that. But when push comes to shove He just hates those that He hates. Not for what they've done or haven't done—they came into this world and it is just a fact that God just hates them. Of course being omnipresent, He knew He would, and one must ascribe a kind of infinite resignation to God because when an infinite being hates you, He really hates you. It just has no effects. It's just a condition of God's relationship to you. Sure you might sense it in moments of profound prayer, but on the whole you're unlikely ever to find out.

One person God hates is Elder Holmberg of the Quorum of the Twelve Apostles of the Church of Jesus Christ of Latter-day Saints. I will introduce him below, but remember just because God hates him, does not mean you must too. Look for his good side. Get to know him a bit before you let him have it with your despising. I personally think there is much to recommend him. But God? He really does hate him. With all His heart. Not for any reason, of course. It is just part of His nature to hate some.

⊃ ⊠ ⚹ ⊠ ⊂

Elder Holmberg stood at the cliff's edge looking down on the muddy brown waters of the Colorado River far below him. He was wearing a conservative royal blue JC Penny suit that his daughter helped pick out. A wide, amber tie found itself nestled snuggly in his vest where it was unperturbed by the stiff wind blustering all around him. His Italian leather wingtips and white socks contrasted against the rusty orange of the sandstone on which he stood—stalwart. A vision of authority. He was standing too close to the precipice, which worried his secretary, Alma Lune, a man in his 40s. He locked his arm around the apostle's, solidly anchoring him to this fallen world.

They were on their way to a stake conference in Blanding where a new stake president would be installed, the previous one having served faithfully for twelve years before succumbing to the frailties of age and other natural accoutrements of senescence.

Elder Holmberg stopped here in Canyonlands National Park in memory of a scouting trip he had taken at age fifteen during which he had gained his first testimony of the Book of Mormon at this very spot. This spot where he had come to pray after finishing the ancient work for the first time fifty-five years ago. He came here often over the intervening years, each time receiving solace and direction.

"This is where I received my testimony of Joseph Smith," he said to the wind, and to the brown river broken by white traces of rapids far below. And to Alma Lune.

"I know, Elder, but let's step back a bit, shall we? You make me nervous standing so close."

"Alma Lune! My what a worrywart you are," He said smiling, nevertheless heeding his secretary, and taking a step back. He then added, "Such a peaceful place. Balm to a troubled heart."

They stood silent listening to the sound of the wind fashioned and framed by the surrounding canyons and sandstone formations, allowing the air to glissade over the sage. Elder Holmberg rubbed his hands together to ward off the cold then breathed into them for some additional warmth. Scattered flakes of snow were falling, though Spring had arrived several weeks ago. Alma Lune glanced back toward the car—a subtle gesture indicating the direction they ought to be heading. The older man, however, did not budge.

"Alma Lune. I don't know what to do," he said, his tone matter-of-fact. Even so, Alma Lune, his long-suffering assistant, heard a tension in his voice that not one in a million listeners would have detected.

Alma Lune let the pause hold for a time, letting the cold wind play around them then asked, "How can I help, Elder?"

"I have to call a stake president."

"Yes, that's why we came... And?"

"I really feel like there are only two choices right now. The excommunication of Bishop White has caused some deep hurt, and also a bit of rancor because the people he swindled are all blaming their up and down lines. I need a good man. One not involved in any way. That leaves me with two to pick from."

"Is there any inkling from the spirit on which..."

"That's just it, isn't it? I have an absolutely clear feeling to call Brother Stout."

"Then call Brother Stout." Alma said in his best Groucho Marx impression.

"I can't. I can't do it. He confessed something in the interview, I can't tell you. Something that happened years ago. When he was a young man in the Navy. And well, it's disgusting. I can't get it out of my head. I'm horrified that this happened. I know he repented long ago. He was told not to go on a mission but to marry, which he did, and they've brought four wonderful daughters and two sons from the pre-existence, but... Do you think there are things so horrible that they can't be cleaned up? I know the Lord has forgiven him, but has it been forgotten? I don't know. I believe there are reasons people should not do things— even once, because that once reverberates down throughout your life. Should what he did be forgotten? If I call him won't it acknowledge there is nothing beyond the pale?"

His companion was silent a long time, but finally added in almost a whisper, "But if you feel inspired?"

"Am I though? Maybe I've got my tongue playing over a missing tooth so much I'm becoming attached to the hole itself. Do you know what I mean?"

"I'm sure you'll do the right thing." Alma Lune said, while gently trying to steer him back to the car.

The wind was picking up and Elder Holmberg relented to Alma Lune's nudging. They walked back to the car in silence. Before climbing into the passenger seat, the old

Apostle looked back at the large gouge cut in the Earth by the Colorado River and thoughtfully turned to his companion.

"Some cuts run deep." He said.

"Yes," said Alma Lune.

⊃ ⤬ � ⤬ C

They were now speeding over the high-desert chaparral between Moab and Monticello on Highway 191. Scattered red-rock sandstone formations jutted from the sagebrush flats in domes and fins that evoked a sense of age and wonder.

"My dad used to take me rabbit hunting down here," the Apostle said looking out the side window, a sense of melancholy gracing his words and face.

"That's quite a drive from Price? Weren't there similar places closer?"

The older man nodded, "Yeah, but this is where his dad took him. My grandfather moved to Carbon County from Paradox, Colorado, while my dad was on his mission to Sweden, so this place was a part of who he was."

Elder Holmberg was silent for a few miles as the landscape passed by. He suddenly started talking, as if he were talking to himself or relating a story into a tape recorder. It was clear he wasn't looking for comment from Alma Lune.

I was hunting with my dad when something happened I will always remember. I was ever cold, even frozen it seemed to me, on these hunts. Especially my feet. We'd put on one pair of thin socks, then a plastic bag, and over them both a pair of warm, thick wool socks. It didn't really do any good, and I always felt like my toes were on the verge of frostbite. But I loved rabbit hunting with my dad. We would awake long before dawn, eat some cereal, then my brothers and I would groggily get into the car with our .22s and my dad would drive us out into this country. He'd park along one of these access roads, and we'd scatter into the landscape. Dad never worried that we'd get lost, or not make it back to the car in a reasonable time—I suppose he thought the cold would drive us to the car sooner or later. Or maybe he just kept an eye on us without us ever being savvy. Well, anyway, this one time I'd seen a rabbit dash under a big sage. I could see it sitting near the scraggy trunk breathing hard, its nose twitching, and, well, it looked so helpless and vulnerable, you know? I just did not want to shoot it. I'd shot two already and, well, it just seemed so small and harmless I couldn't bring myself to take the shot. I just didn't feel right about it. Suddenly, there was my dad beside me.

"Are you going to shoot it?" He asked.

And I said, "Why don't we let this one go?"

He looked at me and said, "That's fine. But tell me why? We've got enough today to fill your ma's cook pot, but it might be nice to bring one over for Farmor and Farfar to enjoy. They always love rabbit stew."

Well, I hesitated and said, "I just feel like I want to let this one go."

The rabbit was still hunkered down there, not kenning we saw it. My dad told us once every time we hunt we pass hundreds of rabbits, but we only see those that break from cover, and those would end up for dinner either for us or a coyote.

Dad always took these moments to teach, "So feelings are important to follow if you think it might be the spirit. Do you think it is?"

I just shrugged. "I don't know, maybe."

My dad put his hand on my shoulder, "It might be. It also might be that it looks really cute sitting there and it's put you in a mind where your hunting lust is bled out. If that's the case, don't call it the spirit. But it is hard to tell. Sometimes untangling the spirit from what you feel inclined toward is really hard to pull apart. But do learn. The Lord don't mind mistakes, but I'm partial to erring on the side of making a mistake thinking it is the spirit when it weren't than missing something the Lord wanted done in this world."

We watched the rabbit a while and my dad said, "What do you want to do?"

"Well," I said, "Let's let this one go."

But you know what? Two days later Farmor died.

The Apostle fell silent for a minute, staring out at the passing scrub oak and cedar.

"And I always regretted that my grandmother never got to taste a bit of rabbit stew before she passed on. And I realized that my Dad was wrong about what he said. Following the spirit that ain't the spirit is just as bad as missing following the spirit. You know?"

He turned to Alma Lune and looked at him. Now he wanted an answer.

Alma Lune just nodded.

Elder Holmberg went back to looking out over the landscape, saying, "Wouldn't some rabbit stew taste divine right now?"

Now remember, despite the Elder's good heart, God still hated Elder Holmberg. It was part of the Almighty's nature to do so. Not that he had anything against the apostle.

Arrow Captures
a Hedgehog

Does the void exist? What could that mean? Is it a transcendental thing like π or ∞? Something whose existence can be used but cannot be found floating about in space, or hidden under rocks, or singing sad songs on the island of misfit toys? Nothing. No-thing. No thing. Nothing.

—Frau Professorin Heike Marquardt,
On the Void: The Theology of Nothingness

Arrow Beamon sat with his friends on the bank of a small stream that ran through the outskirts of Schweinfurt, Germany. Due to a yearlong drought, no water splashed down the creek. The dry, smooth-stone bottom glowed in the cool moonlight like the gravel of an aquarium lit by incandescent light. Or so it seemed to Arrow. The exposed riverbed even had a slight bluish cast like the colored rocks of his twenty-six-gallon fish tank in Moab. The ambience was so familiar he even cast a glance to his right with half an expectation that a Plecostomus suckerfish would dash out of the small trees lining the side then flee back to its cover just like his favorite fish still swimming in its aquarium back home in the States. He and all his friends were dressed identically—olive green pants bloused into highly polished black leather boots, a similar colored shirt with two buttoned pockets and patches on their shoulders marking their attachment to the First Armor Division. They were also all wearing black berets that identified them as belonging to the Calvary. The 3rd of the 7th. Indeed, the same one wiped out at Little Bighorn under the command of General George Custer. But none of that mattered because right now they were just four guys who wanted to get a buzz on.

All were silent, all staring down into the dry stream. A little drunk. Before making their way here, they had stopped at the Base Enlisted Man's Cantina to get a beer can in order to fashion a makeshift weed pipe. After one drink, however, things had not seemed as pressing and they stayed for a couple of rounds of draft. Even so, this smoke off post away from the barracks was the main event.

Arrow opened the beer can and took a long guzzle to empty it fully of its contents, then passed it to Killer, the guy next to him, who did likewise. While it was going around, Arrow removed his rank insignia, a teardrop-shaped Spec 4 pin, from his collar and waited for the can to return. There was just a smidgen left when it circled back to him, so he drained it, then shook out the remaining droplets onto the ground. He needed to get the inside as dry as possible. When he was satisfied that he had emptied it thoroughly, he gave the can a little squeeze, fashioning a dent in the middle to form a flat, shallow depression. Arrow pressed the can with his fingers here and there, shaping the surface of the divot into a flat surface. He then used the thick collar pin to punch seven holes into the can—not six or eight, seven. From his shirt pocket, he took out a small square of hashish wrapped in light, thin foil. He broke about a fifth off the brick and crumbled it into their makeshift bowl. Using a beer can was safer than trying to hide a small pipe in the barracks, especially because for the last couple of months they had been running dogs through their rooms almost every weekend looking for drugs.

After a few flicks of his thumb on flint-wheel, he held his square metal lighter up to the hash and sucked thick blue smoke through the triangular opening of the can down into his lungs. He held the toke for as long as he could, then exhaling passed the can to his neighbor for a hit.

Everyone was quiet. Not because the Sarge came in that morning and told them about the Fall of Saigon and that he was all busted up because his Gook wife was weeping madly because she had friends and family die there. The Sarge was even all teary-eyed because it was all for naught, and it was the first war America ever lost, or so said the Sarge. And he had gone on with that kind of shit for like a half-hour. No, they were quiet because they were leaving soon on a training mission in Fulda on the Czech border, and they would not be back to Schweinfurt for two months and it sucked that they would likely not get good dope there the whole time because they would run the dogs through their bags on the train and their tanks on the railcars, and who knew what the situation would be in the camp there, so this was their last blowout before they left. No one felt much like celebrating or talking. This was a drown your sorrows high. They all knew in their hearts that there would be Krauts hanging around selling shit, but you didn't want to assume it and get your hopes all up and then find out that there had been some sort of Polizei crackdown and there was nothing around.

Smithy, smaller than the others, but known as a scrapper, pulled out his own stash and crumbled some more into the ad hoc bowl. It made it three times around before everyone settled back into a deep, easy buzz. Killer had fallen asleep. With Big Man it was hard to tell.

From the open window of a nearby apartment building, the sounds of a violin could be heard leaking into the night. Arrow did not know the piece; of course, that is not saying a lot as there were very few pieces he could have identified. Growing up in Moab, Utah, he had taken few music lessons, played on no sports team, done very little in school, and spent most of his time wandering in the canyons near his home. He did find the violin more beautiful than anything he'd ever heard; maybe it was the dope talking, but tears were forming in his eyes. The stars, the music, the warm earthy smell of the hash, all combined to produce a contented sense of joy. No—not joy as much as magic and enchantment entering into the world. No, not exactly that either. It felt like the dawn of a new place, a new universe. The colors were softer here, and not because things had been recolored but because things in this new place were different all the way down. The glow of the world came from inside some hidden center that flowed into our reality from its depths. The guy next to him was nudging him with his arm, offering the bowl to him. He took a hit and passed it on. He looked up, and the trees were swaying in the breeze to the music of the violin. He knew that no harm could touch him here. It was safe. He could feel the bending and bowing trees looking down on him, smiling secretly from the core of their abundant wooden hearts. Nodding to his existence. And theirs. They were with him in this. Come what may. He glanced up, and the stars were in agreement with the trees and their branches and their twisting and turning leaves and the movement of the squeaking and groaning bark, twinkling in time to the vibration of the strings, proclaiming bliss to the radiant world all around him.

He remembered feeling like this when he and LeRoy Stout were up in the La Sals the week he was joining the Army, and his buddy was getting ready to enter the Navy the week after. They were in a meadow up near Don's Lake off of Taylor Flats road. A full moon was lighting up the aspens like the woods in a fairytale, and the dark shadows of the trees playing against glowing leaf litter made it seem as if there were magic in the air; drawn out—no doubt, by the weed they were smoking. And here he was half an earth away from his friend, and that same magic descended on him here in Germany. It all meant something. He was sure. Probably something very funny. And deep. Funny and deep.

Someone was hitting his arm, and he realized that Killer, awake again, had relit the bowl and it was coming around again. He took a hit and held it until a rush climbed up his spine, nearly causing him to lose his mooring in the waking world. The trees were singing something he could almost hear. This new world was filled with mystery. He could feel it in the trees and shrubs that lined the river below him too. Everything. Was. Everything.

He laid back for just a second and for a moment fell into a dream or a vision. He was still there, sitting on the bank of a river, but the little river had filled with water. Above the moonlit water hovered a heavenly being. In it was an angel, Nephi from the *Book of Mormon*, Arrow was somehow able to intuit. Nephi? Why not Moroni, the same who appeared to Joseph Smith and showed him where the *Book of Mormon* plates were hidden? Well, Nephi would have to do. A little disappointing actually, Arrow thought. Like he was getting sort of a second-rate angel.

Nephi looked put out, maybe sensing Arrow's disapproval. A large scowl marred his otherwise handsome face.

He was dressed according to angel fashion in a loose robe exposing his chest. His feet were bare. He floated only inches from ground, and he held his hands lightly away from his legs, palm out as if he were trying to calm a bank robber.

Hearken! For I am the Angel Nephi, yea, even he that is mentioned in the scriptures. Arrow, Arrow, Canst thou not see that thou art on the road to perdition? Thou must repent! Behold, think on thy dear Mother, and think on her broken heart, and think on....

Arrow was distracted by a slight disturbance in the bushes below on the bank of the dry creek. He looked down. There, lit up in the moonlight below, was a hedgehog nosing about in the leaf litter among the shrubs marking what would have been the river's edge.

His vision of Nephi had no power in the face of this level of distraction. His buddy Conner was already sliding down the embankment to try to capture it. It was a fast little bugger. Quicker than Conner was ready for, but that did not matter much because, in his rush to seize the creature, he had slipped and tumbled headlong into the vegetation below. Arrow watched with growing joy at his companion's demise, but he was no less interested in getting the beast for himself. Of course, he did not know why he wanted a hedgehog, but he knew he had to have one or his life would never be complete. He needed this hedgehog. He jumped up to better assess the situation. Nephi disappeared. A hedgehog he wanted, so a hedgehog he would have. He leaped into action.

Dashing down the embankment, he saw the fleeing beast making a rush in what would have been the downstream direction had there been any water flowing. He followed. The magical little creature was making for a thick patch of brambles that abutted the dry riverbed. If the sly thing made it to cover, the chase would be over. So Arrow, living up to his name, burst into a sprint as if shot from a bow.

People say that cannabis makes you lazy. Not so. It gives you powers. The ancients knew this, and that is why Magadha warriors would take it before entering a battle. Whether there were Persians to defeat or hedgehogs to capture, the power of weed was a force multiplier. He caught up with the little critter and swept it into his hands. It did not try to get away, but rather curled into a ball and exposed its prickly spines. Unlike the North American porcupine, which would do all in its power to embed one of its quills in your flesh, the hedgehog would simply trust its evolutionary design to do the work. For all Arrow could tell, it might have just been napping—its eyes closed. Under the influence of the hashish, he could sense that the calm critter was resting comfortably in its existence. It had no need to worry. The hedgehog's Zen was total. No violent struggle to get away, just trust that if it kept still and quiet, all would be well. Peace would reign. It was sure that this too would pass.

Nephi Considers His Charge

Does the void exist? Ha! You see the folly of the question. You see the trap laid out by trying to wrap some existential quantifiers around it as if a 'there exists' can capture a set so empty that the null set, $\varnothing$, is not even found there (for every set A, according to wise priests of set theory, contains the empty set $\forall A$: $\varnothing \in A$, (and note it is all the same empty set for: $\nexists\, A$ such that $\varnothing \notin A$ without which there is no way to add more sensible elements). As if the empty set holds open the possibility of a set until some element can slip its way inside. The void is such that even this little symbolic tittle is absent. The absence of absence.

—Frau Professorin Heike Marquardt,
On the Void: The Theology of Nothingness

The angel Nephi watched as Arrow clambered after the hedgehog. He shook his glorified head in sorrow as he watched him tumble-slide down the hill in a frantic exuberant display of drug-infused joy.

Nephi did not feel angelic. He set down in the gully on a large rock and put his face in his hands.

"I'm still a wretched man. I'm an angel, and I'm still a wretched man."

He sighed. He had been feeling nostalgic of late about his time on Earth, lo, those nearly 2600 years ago. There were so many amazing memories. At the insistence of those who loved him, he'd been trying to focus on those recollections of the good things about his mortal probation. Not the fiasco with Laman and Lemuel, certainly, which still hurt, or his loss of Asilah. And no, no, no, not the slaying of Laban. And there were a number of little annoyances as well as the big blunders. Like his allowing himself to be crowned 'King' by his friends and cousins that followed him into the new world. No, those things were behind him. He was trying to focus on things that had been positive. Remember that cool turn of phrase, "the Lord giveth no commandments unto the children of men save he shall prepare a way for them that they may accomplish the thing which he commandeth them"? Well, that would have to include his own task of making a better person of himself.

The building of the ship! Now those were the days! Think on that—working the timbers, his chest filling with the fresh sea air. How he fashioned axes, and other woodworking tools, on a forge of his own make. And the sound!

The ring of the hammer on iron and brass and bronze. The sound of the saw cutting long Lebanon cedars into fragrant planks. Squaring large beams to act as ribbing for the frame of the ship. Even with his resurrected nose, the smell of that wood resin still filled him with an ache for those earthy days on the beach.

Sigh. He had been somebody then. He'd made small plates of gold. He'd fashioned swords after the manner of that brigand who stole the family fortune, someone he had to kill to keep certain secrets safe. And... he had written on the plates. Still, the doubts crept in. Why had he not been the one chosen to appear to Joseph Smith, descendant of his own ancestor, Joseph who was sold into Egypt? Why Moroni? Was it because he was a General? I was a King! It seems like Mormon would have been the logical choice. Why Moroni? He was always surprised that these little petty thoughts would pop into his head, and he didn't even see they were coming until it was too late. Nephi shook his head thinking about Moroni. He really was a good post-mortal friend. Why the doubts? Just leave it alone, he thought. Even so, he felt silly when the other angels, Gods, or spirits mentioned in jest that he had been made a king by his cousins and kin. It had never even felt like it counted in the right way. Real kings were born into it. He was the son of a local merchant. Still.

And Sam. He always thought about Sam when he was in a low mood. His older brother Sam had been Nephi's best friend on earth and had taken care of Nephi when he was a toddler. Sam was always there. Always supportive. His other older brothers had been too old to have much to do with him, but Sam was always there for Nephi. All his life, even at the end when things had fallen so low and they had fled into the wilderness of the promised land because Laman and Lemuel had become so dangerous. Sam followed Nephi, even though Sam loved his older brothers, and they him. Sam made the choice to follow Nephi's leadership. He remembered Sam limping away from his home with his weeping wife and family, gesturing to Nephi in that way of his that things would be all right. They never really were. Not ever again.

He sighed. And now this. Trying to get through to this lotus-eater. Nephi struggled to rein in his confusion about Arrow. He had had a number of assignments since his resurrection during the time of Christ's own emergence from the tomb. What a moment of joy that was! He found himself with his newly formed bones sinewing-up right before his eyes (after they reformed, of course). He'd been giddy with joy! Blessed day. He'd been made anew! The land around the place of his transformation looked like a wasteland exposing huge swaths of damage from earthquakes and floods. He had been resurrected near a river that ran through the land of Lehi, under a gigantic cashew tree. Of course, nothing looked the same; he had died nearly 500 years previously. But still, the air! It felt, and even smelled, the same—rich and verdant, humid and tinged with the lush loamy smell of rotting leaves turning into soil. On the breeze there had been the hint of the kelpy Pacific. Did he remember smelling the sea during his mortal sojourn? Back then it was nearly seventy miles west from this his home to the ocean, so he inferred his resurrected body had capacities his earthly frame did not. It was a wondrous time with a new body, trying to remember what his earth life meant and how he had fared. It had not been the hero's welcome he expected.

Unfortunately, when his resurrected memory had been restored, some of the scenes he had written about in mortality had not quite been fully the way he remembered them. Indeed, the account inscribed on the small plates of gold he fashioned, and in which he recounted the killing of Laban, had not quite happened the way he remembered the events in his old age. As he looked back on the scene with his resurrected body, and his recollection was clear and shiny, he recognized that it played out quite differently. How could he have reconstructed it during his lifetime so badly? Mortal memory was a strange and fraught thing. So much of it had been a work of imagination. So much a reconstruction of what he wanted things to have been, rather than the way they were. Yes, he found the fool drunk and passed out in the black darkness of the alley. But there had been little debate in his mind. He had been so incensed when Laban had taken all their gold and silver and precious things that thoughts of revenge had been his constant companion. He was a teenager after all! When it came time to claim that recompense, he was ready to act. He was sure at the time that that was what the Spirit wanted him to do, but perhaps he had been a tad hasty. He remembered clearly now that he had Laban's head off before the rash youth in his memory had time to even think about it. He pulled out the sot's razor-sharp sword glinting in the cool starlight peering down from above—the only light in a still and silent Jerusalem. As a smith, Nephi still remembered the beauty of that blade appreciatively. It cut the head off cleanly. Well, clean was not an adjective you could use after that beheading—the blood had been copious. It had flowed from the drunk's neck like a stream coursing through a small wadi in the rainy season. Laban's cloak and clothes were saturated in blood—so much that he had slipped on the red sticky ooze gathered around Laban's body, which lay headless on the cobbles of the street. He saw his mistake immediately. He and Laban were both men of stature, and if he had donned his clothes before slaying him, he might have been able to get into the thief's treasury and get their goods back. But now the clothes were drenched in blood. No matter. There were things to do, and he would do them. The Lord had opened the way, he remembered thinking. And perhaps he had not been wrong in that despite the fragility of memory.

He undid the fastenings of Laban's clothes, and with some care, he was able to get them off the body. There was an ass's water trough at the top of the ally, and Nephi carried the clothes up the hill and tossed them in. Nephi thoroughly scrubbed them free of the blood, wrung them out as best he could, and then with the garments still soaking wet, put them on as his own. He wrapped his face in the turban to disguise it and then walked to Laban's nearby dwelling—leaving a stream of water trailing behind.

When he arrived at the powerful man's home, he stood on the stoop, dripping wet and shivering. He pounded on the door violently. Laban's household slave Zoram, not fooled whatsoever by Nephi's attempt at disguise, asked what had happened to his master. Nephi explained with some reluctance that Laban was dead. Zoram, not displeased at the turn of events, helped him raid the treasury and promised to go down with him into the wilderness. He was about Nephi's age, and by promising the slave his freedom, Nephi convinced him to help get the treasure back down to his father in the wilderness. He also pointed out his father was a prophet and should be listened to because Jerusalem would be destroyed. Zoram was thrilled with his new prospects.

Nephi followed Arrow back to the barracks. He lost the hedgehog when he absentmindedly set it down so he could rest on a bench and look at the stars. He was sad now the adorable little beast, whom he named Cute Nacho, had gotten away. He was near tears. Nephi shadowed his charge, but the angel knew the routine by rote. Arrow would fall face down on his bed and sleep like a corpse. And then Nephi would be left to brood that he was not high in the angel hierarchy (not that it mattered). He'd unjustly killed a man. Luckily, unlike the murderer King David (he met the sad little spirit once at a post-mortal gathering), Nephi had retained a measure of exaltation. Still, he was fortunate to be an angel at all, mostly because circumstances mattered. He had been young. A hothead. It was a dangerous time in Jerusalem. And maybe, just maybe, it was better that one man should perish than a whole generation dwindle in unbelief (he was still proud of that line too). There had been enough ambiguity in the slaying that the counsels of the Gods decided he should be forgiven. If he made amends. As he was doing now. With Arrow. Sigh.

He lifted himself off the rock for a moment, took a deep breath, then sat back down. He looked into the night. It had gotten darker as thick clouds drifted overhead from the east and a light rain began to fall. Nephi could use his angel powers to stay perfectly dry, but the rain seemed like a good metaphor for his feelings at the moment. Tears watered his eyes. He let a sob escape. He was not feeling sorry for himself, really, he was just sad that things had turned out so badly for someone who really, really, loved the Lord, and had tried so hard to serve him, even with his very human mistakes and failures. He had tried. He knew that. He loved the Lord. Isn't that what mattered? He bowed his head and prayed, letting, by an act of will, the rain reach him, soak him. Wetting his hair and clothes. Somehow that seemed appropriate. He was feeling less and less a part of bigger designs. Nevertheless he prayed with all his heart that he could do better. And he would. He really would. He always had been highly favored of the Lord.

Nephi looked up, and the Goddess Asilah was sitting nearby watching him. He looked down at his rain-soaked robe, realized his hair was streaming water like a hippo emerging from the Nile, and dried it with a thought.

"I didn't see you."

She just looked at him.

He looked as if he wanted to offer more explanation, but gave up and said simply, "How is my brother?"

"Laman is good," she said.

Nephi looked away. Then looked back, "Godhood suits him I think."

The Goddess Asilah did not reply but looked at Nephi.

"Why are you here?" He finally asked.

"Worried about you. So are Laman and Sam. We all are."

"Why would Gods and Goddesses worry about me? I'm doing my angelic things just fine. Did you see my charge? I'm sure he deserves a better guardian angel, but I'm the only one they could find."

Nephi was angry at himself for sounding so resentful. Asilah seemed to have this effect on him. Making him sink into self-pity.

Even so, he couldn't seem to stop, "Have you seen Arrow? A real winner. Going places, that one."

Asilah smiled, "You never know, do you?"

Nephi turned away abashed. His best friends in the universe were the Gods Alma and Amulek.

"Point taken."

She stood up as if gravity were really acting on her and looked down the gully in the direction Arrow had gone carrying his hedgehog.

"Good-bye, Nephi. Go visit your brothers. They worry."

"Good-bye, Asilah." Nephi said, not looking up.

⊃ ⋈ ⚴ ⋈ ⊂

Three Days Later, Nephi was still watching his charge.

It was rumored there was no dope in Fulda. Two guys from an artillery unit had just come back from the duty there, and they said it was bone dry. Who knew why? Arrow had gone to see Henrik and Astrid to pick up a few grams of hash for tonight—their last night before Fulda. The two Germans were sitting in a room breaking up kilo bricks into little pieces they were wrapping in foil and weighing on a science-y looking scale. Despite being laid-back, they were very businesslike when it came to product and would never toke up with the soldiers they were sell-ing to. They were listening to Arrow lament the coming dope fast.

Astrid commiserated. Her English was better than Henrik's, so she did most of the talking. She was lovely. She was wearing a tank top and jeans, and Arrow could not keep his eyes from noticing her breasts as she bent low to pick up another kilo brick.

"Nah ja, bummer, Arrow. It will be hard for you I think," she said without looking up from her work.

"Yeah. I'd take some with me, but they will run the dogs at the railhead and then again when we arrive. Can't chance it." He shook his head and took another deep breath of the rich spicy scent of hash that perfumed the room. "It's going to kill me though. I swear. I can't even stand the thought."

"Yeah, too bad for you. We are getting some nice fine grass from Thailand next weekend, you are going miss einige sehr gute Scheiße."

Arrow nodded sadly, "Oh man."

Suddenly, Henrik looked up and stared hard at him, then started speaking rapid German to Astrid. The conversation was animated and Arrow could follow nothing of it. He knew enough German to order a beer and ask where the train station was, but that was about it. Suddenly, Astrid looked thoughtful and nodded to Henrik.

"Arrow. Maybe we could bring you a brick of hash and a couple of keys of the Thai?"

"Bring it up there? To Fulda?"

"Ja, to Fulda. No problem."

"You'd have to front me the whole load, but I'd be good for it. There would be no problem selling it, as dry as it is. I could even charge top dollar. I mean there will be a bunch of people doing training up there we could make a bundle you know, so yeah that would be amazing." He was speaking like a machine gun.

"Anyway we don't want money—it would be all yours. We want to trade you for something we need for a customer."

"A trade?"

"Sure. No problem for you I think but very hard for us."

Arrow was feeling suspicious but was very anxious to get a hold of that much dope. He would make a killing. And he'd have an unlimited supply for this own needs over the next few weeks.

"I don't think I have anything worth trading for that much dope."

"Maybe you could get it."

"What do you want?"

There was some discussion in German. It sounded like they were negotiating with each other and finally came to some agreement.

"OK, here's what we want: two pounds of C4 explosive, fifteen meters of detcord, and two hand grenades; for that we will give you two keys hash and two keys Thai Gold. Possible?" She said so nonchalantly it took him a second or two to process what she was asking.

"Are you crazy? I can't get that kind of shit. It would be madness. No way!"

"You said you drive the ammo carrier back and forth to the range. Won't you be handling that for practice shooting?"

"Yeah, but they count that shit."

"I bet when things are busy it gets hard to track."

Arrow was silent. He knew that was true. Things went missing all the time. And when they were on the tank firing range, tracking became really hard.

"Arrow. Possible, you think?"

Arrow looked up. "Maybe. But I won't know until I get there and see what we are doing and what things look like at the range. But maybe. But what are you going to do with it? I don't want anyone hurt. You know?"

Astrid said, "Of course, of course. It's for our colleagues in East Germany to help fight Soviets. Anyway, they need to blow up a bridge the commies are building. At night."

"It's for a bridge the Russians are building?"

"Ja. Commie Russians. In East Germany."

"Well maybe. It might be possible."

Both Astrid and Henrik looked at him pleased. Henrik said suddenly, "You will like Thai Gold sehr. Very much."

There was more conversation between the Germans, then Astrid pulled a big piece off the scale and wrapped it in the light foil they used and handed it to Arrow, "Here. On-the-house as you say. So we will meet you at the *Der weiße Hase* in Fulda, it's a small Gasthaus as you come into to the city from the North. American GIs don't go there much. OK? If you have the things we asked for we'll give you what we promised. OK?

Arrow nodded, "No guarantee, but I'll try."

"Ja, try hard." Said Henrik.

Arrow walked out onto the cobblestone Schweinfurt street and pulled out the piece Astrid had given him in the light of a streetlamp. He felt its size with his fingers. They were going to get wasted tonight.

⊃ ⋉ ✦ ⋊ ⊂

Why me? Nephi thought. Not for the last time.

Heike Sorrows

If no set contains this nothingness how do we get to the void I seek? A void so complete it will collapse all our theory? It holds nothing open. It resides in no set, so those who want to hold it wide open with brackets marking the set, such that an existential qualifier can be used to say, 'There exists a set such that…' are out of luck. No, the void will allow no such promiscuity because the null set is not there to even allow a set to be formed. Alas. There is no sound. No noise. Not even any silence.

—Frau Professorin Heike Marquardt,
On the Void: The Theology of Nothingness

On early autumn mornings just as the dew-misted landscape was unmasked by the sun, Heike would walk through the forest on that little two-rut path that runs between an old stand of beeches and a collection of fallow fields that attentively pattern the contours of landscape.

From a distance, the crop fields look like a counterpane blanket thrown over a lumpy collection of rumpled sheets and pillows. Mind you, she would not have described it thus. Her mind was far away, and the subtleties of landscape, forest, and field were not among the things that could find place among her concerns. Her dog Georg, a vizsla (yes named after that philosopher famous among hermeneutic horizons), however, did take delight in the rolling drop and rise of the hilly patchwork of ecotone, wood, and grass—hunting vigilantly by sight for a rabbit or a squirrel to which he could declare his lifelong devotion. At least for the moment. Then he would tear off at a sprint toward his object of desire, never tiring until his good master Heike would whistle him back to her influence (though, to be fair, she was usually so distracted that the return of the hound also barely registered within her consciousness, which was focused intently on the one thing that concerned her—Nothingness).

But not today. Today she sits in her car. Grips the steering wheel. Georg looks at her, then outside, then at her, back and forth, questioning why they do not get out. She tries hard to breathe, but her lungs feel constricted. Not enough air is coming in. Not enough air. She looks out the front window and all the colors look wrong. Uncanny. As if someone has moved her from her familiar world where all is known and comfortable and where she is at home to a different world of blighted hues. Tainted colors that have no meaning—stripped of hope. A world in which everything has been replaced by a simulacrum, identical in aspect to the old world but like a changeling that does not belong to her. She thinks about James and gasps for air. There is not enough air in the whole world to fill the emptiness of her lungs. Her world is a vacuum of empty space. He has exited her life. He will no longer appear at her door. Holding flowers. Smiling. He has utterly fled. Stripping it of everything that matters. She feels the sob ripping through her body violently. It has replaced her heart so completely that she knows it is gone. Her chest is hollowed out like a beech struck by lightning and there is no organ beating in her center moving blood. There never will be anything there again; it has been burned away leaving only coarse ash and waste.

Suddenly there is a tongue licking her face, allowing her to draw breath. Again. The remnants of her heart find a beat. Air enters the world. She is parked near a forest that holds dear living trees and birds and things Georg can chase. The colors have lost their foreign aspect. Her world returns. She can think about 'nothing' again. She opens the door and steps into the fall day. Georg tears from her car like a bullet aimed. She lets her mind turn to things she knows; things she does not want to forget.

⊃ � ⊂

She understands thoroughly that the Gods spring from the void. Where else was there to spring from? In every myth they leap from some state of chaos, darkness, or other metaphor for the pre-formed state that exists prior to their "becoming." On this fine morning as the sun rises above the dew-covered blades of wild grasses on the fallow fields beside which she walks, she ponders the ancient Pyramid Text and its depiction of the nothing that started it all. She asks this question along the path she follows.

Question: Why is there nothing instead of everything everywhere?

In the beginning—the void. It was everything, and there was nothing that was not the void. How big was the void? What were its limits? What was its center? Circumference? How can these questions be even approached when everything was nothing? What does it mean to ask what is beyond nothing? Was the void sentient? No of course not. Was it all-knowing? Don't be silly. It knew nothing. All-powerful? Nothing cannot be put into terms of power or powerlessness. It had no power. Did it float in…? No, it floated in nothing. It was nothing. Could something exist outside the void? There was no inside or outside. The void was Everything. And Everything was nothing. But nothing was everything and everything was something. The void was full of nothing but it was also everything. To call nothing a substance would not be inappropriate, if by substance you mean nothing, or at least nothing like matter, or light, or fields, or anything that you could divide into parts, or find its components, or cut into finer and finer slices until you reached a point you could slice no more; in the void, you could cut forever (ha! if you found yourself in the void with a knife honed as sharp as a single cosmic string stretched out to form the edge of this voidish blade, there would be still nothing to cut). How long did it sit in silence and fullness? What a question. What could you possibly mean? There was no time, no space, no measure, no logic. Did it have potential? No. It was nothing and nothing was everything and that everything was something. This was not Plotinus's ONE floating about endlessly contemplating itself in its beautiful omniscience. There was nothing to contemplate and no one to contemplate the nothingness. Did it love? What would it love? What is love if it has no object? No. It was nothing. The substance of void through and through was void. No inside. No outside. No left. No right. No over, under, against, on, near, between, before, behind, or below. It was not growing or shrinking. Or doing. There were no verbs needed to describe it, no nouns it contained, no prepositions to place its position. It was pure undifferentiated existence. And existence was nothing. Everything that existed was nothing. No Thing.

Heike reaches a place in the road that dips to follow the landscape into a little depression in which a small permanent stream flows calmly under a makeshift wooden bridge someone made long ago. Alas, it is little more than two stout young pines laid across the stream with rough-hewn planks bolted to the trunks—it would hold no vehicle. There are ruts from tractors or small trucks that occasionally drive down into the creek a little to the right of the bridge because it cannot bear their weight. The tracks from the tires of the small vehicles enter the shallow water on one side then reappears on the other, but I describe this for your benefit. The truth of the matter is that Heike steps onto the bridge without seeing it, or the truck tracks to the side, or anything but the thoughts of her inner eye; she is seeing the Pyramid Text—which introduced the nothingness of the void in the creation myth—placed on the walls of Heliopolis that goes something like this:

> Long ago, there was a time when nothing existed, when the sky had not yet come into being, when the earth had not yet come into being, when death had not yet come into being and when the gods had not been born. There was nothing at all but Nu, or Nun, the father of the gods, the primeval waters, which stretched out without beginning and without end, a limitless ocean of inert but chaotic water. Darkness reached everywhere. (*Myths of the Near East*, p. 105)

Beyond the bridge the path turns right into the woods where it winds among the low branches of the gold, amber, and even dark brown leaves still clinging to the twiggy termini, weaned from the nourishing sap that quickened each leaf through the bright, dry summer days. The doomed little sugar factories nourishing the deciduous trees finally yield to chilly nights and shorter darkening days. Soon, whatever biological programming conditioned their response to daylight and temperature will condemn those no longer useful machines to becoming soil to bless the tree anew and allow the mycorrhizae fungi to help support the tree's growth again.

But does she see the glories of the autumn show of bright colors? Does she watch the leaves dancing and twisting on the terminal branches creating an animated filigree of motion and light? No. She does not. The void has captured her. It turns her eye inward toward the darkness, save for a moment when a long-antennaed cerambycid beetle stands menacingly on the bark of a birch, ready to start eating the tree's soft cambium through which the sap flows life up to the leaves and branches moving to the wind. In that flicker of an instant her eye blinks into awareness, and much like the striking beak of a woodpecker, Heike, the once would-be forester, attends to the adult form of her enemy, and pinches the hexapod monster between her finger and thumb. After wiping the sticky hemolymph from her hand with a clutch of low-growing forbs, she returns to her contemplation of the void. Empty again of awareness that there is a world around her.

⊃ × ⊀ × ⊂

She thinks of other creations: the shamans of the Kogi, the Tairona peoples of the Sierra Nevada de Santa Marta Mountains in Colombia, tell the stories of the time before Aluna made the world:

> In the beginning there was blackness, only the
> sea. In the beginning there was no sun, no moon,

no people. In the beginning there were no animals, no plants. Only the sea. The sea was the
mother. The mother was not people—she was not
anything. Nothing at all. She was when she was.
Spirit. She was memory and possibility. She was
Aluna....

—*The Heart of the World*

"The mother was not people—she was not anything.
Nothing at all." Nothing at all. How apropos—nothing at
all. She was emptiness. She was void. But this was not
enough. Heike knew her own myths and the tales they
told when all was darkness and void. But this void seemed
to contain God hovering over, and this would not do. For
the void she sought had no God yet to hover. Not in the
beginning. Eckhart knew this. Meister Eckhart understood
that the ground of God was this void. This nothing. Did he
not say this of the Apostle Paul?

Paul rose from the ground and with open eyes
saw nothing." I cannot see what is one. He saw
nothing, that is God. God is a nothing and God
is a something. «As is the void and here Heike
nods her head in agreement as she walks among
the wind tossed beeches.» What God is, that He
is entirely.... A master says whoever speaks of
God in any likeness, speaks impurely of Him. But
to speak of God with nothing is to speak of Him
correctly. When the soul is unified and there enters into total self-abnegation, then she finds God
as in Nothing.

*The Complete Mystical Works
of Meister Eckhart,* p. 140.

⊃ ⋈ ⊹ ⋈ ⊂

Heike's eyes tear, her pace quickens as her breath becomes rapid, and the panic that has gripped her for three years wells up and pushes the air from her lungs. She wants to breathe but can't. Her faithful companion trotting beside her notices that all is not right with his charge. He glances up, assessing her needs, because he has seen many tears and knows that her world has lost some luster. Faithful, he joins her mourning and heels beside her—watching the effects of her thinking about her lost lover, James, who pulls her from her thoughts of nothing to thoughts of everything. That person who takes up all that she is, and all that she wants to be, and is the great not-nothing, the everything that now fills her existence with its horror, because he is no more. So she starts to jog, trying to drive out the everything. The everything that was James, "was" James, because now James, like the void, is nothing. All that she was has been sucked out of existence and into this void.

⊃ ⋈ ⊹ ⋈ ⊂

She feels the familiar panic starting to return. She pushes it away, but it comes of its own accord. Who can communicate properly the depth of what she feels? That depth she feels on this fall day. As she wends her way down a forested path. Who would dare try? I will just let her walk, and jog, and cry. Until after a time she cannot face the terrors of her own void, and she pulls away from the abyss. There will come a time she will find calm again. When she has cried over the envoidment of James so often that some small rational part of her brain will watch these manifestations of sorrow and anguish with some patience, for she will have grown familiar with its face and will know well its habits and moods; at some point she will tremble at some intake of breath and her body will relax and she will breathe again more easily. Of course this is some imagined future. But not one imagined by her.

⊃ ⋈ ⚹ ⋈ ⊂

So she thinks of Jakob Böhme. He too knew God was grounded in nothing. In void. The *Ungrund*, he called it. The nothingness from which all things emerged—including God himself. God was still bragging about his emergence eons later, taking upon himself the name that defined Him clearly as not-nothing: I AM. He was something. Shelling picked this up from Böhme:

> God has in himself an inner ground of his existence that in this respect precedes him in existence; but, precisely in this way, God is again the prius [what is before] of the ground in so far as the ground, even as such, could not exist

if God did not exist actually.... Since, however, nothing indeed can be outside of God, this contradiction can only be resolved by things having their ground in that which in God himself is not He Himself, that is in that which is the ground of his existence. If we want to bring this way of being closer to us in human terms, we can say: it is the yearning the eternal one feels to give birth to himself. The yearning wants to give birth to God, that is, unfathomable unity, but in this respect there is not yet unity in the yearning itself. Hence, it is, considered for itself, also will; but will in which there is no understanding and, for that reason, also not independent and complete will, ...

*Philosophical Investigations into
the Essence of Human Freedom*, p. 28.

However, Heike the theologian, Heike professor of Theology at Leipzig, Heike the graduate in theology at Eberhard Karls Universitat, Tübingen, does not think this notion is right. The nothingness had no will. Schelling was correct: there was certainly no understanding in the void, nor was there a lack of understanding—it was nothing and that was it. The Ungrund was just nothing, or this something that cannot be distinguished from nothing. How did then the multitude of somethings we know come sliding into existence? If all there was was undifferentiated something qua nothing qua something, then whence the multiplicity?

Randomness. The nothing shattered. How? It is a mystery. A causeless act. Can we not allow this one mystery? It is certainly less unfathomable than a vast God-thing floating there in need of something to worship it, with attributes of intelligence (what made it so?), loving (before creation there was only itself to love), and all powerful (from whence?), and all knowing (what was there to know? a long list of potentials? Why bring things from virtual to actual?), infinitely possessed of every virtue we humans like to embrace? That seems a little much, don't you think? Compared to the randomness she is positing be granted? One little mystery is all she asks, rather than the BIG one you demand. True randomness. A blip of chance, and newness sallied forth.

So something of the nothing shattered, and the absolute emptiness was fractured into an infinity of little nothings (to be whispered sweetly in the ears of beloveds for eternity perhaps?). Then there were many. Even a shattered nothing, a fragmented nothing, cannot attend to the fact that it is fragmented. So each piece prehended the other. A sea of shards each aware. Windowed monads. Nay, not windowed—flat out glass-housed. Nothing but windows. Apprehension from each to each. But with the shattering came the possibility of relationships—left and right, up and down, me and not me, near and far. With the shattering came joining and the possibility of coming together, confederations and assemblages, the ability to form directed links. But not only that, the slivers could spin. Wave. Sashay. Rumba. The shards could writhe, wriggle, waggle, and squirm. They could rotate round about one another.

One's riffling could inspire (not consciously, mind you) another's tzim and tzum. Withdrawing here, expanding in excess there. And in this chaotic motion, driven by the infinite energy of the rending of nothing, came the birth of physicality. And this physicality of motion, and this prehending substance of nothing, join together in a kind of physics that together allow the unfolding of novelties unimaginable. If my wriggle causes your wrapple, then suddenly there is the potential for cause and effect, for bindings and loosenings, a cosmic chemistry all based, not on the substance of the nothing, but on the motion of the dance. A tangible world, based, like the honeybee, on the excellence of the waggle dance. And those who are successful will survive. Laws form. Regularities ensue. And suddenly there is in this mindless mass of motion a selective regime where things can evolve.

ꓔ ⋈ ⚹ ⋈ ꓛ

Heike is now far away from her parked car. The sun is high and starting to descend toward the west. The sky is deep blue, and she knows she must start back. She sits now on a log long ago fallen, and Georg licks her hand. Reminding her that he is there. With her. She is calmer now. She thinks about James without panic. She remembers his face. His caress. Absentmindedly, she strokes Georg's head. And she thinks about how when it came down to it, she could not kill the woman. The woman who had selected the target in Frankfurt. She had commissioned the device that would kill her beloved James. It was this woman who had planted the bomb that sent James into the void. And while Heike had not been able to pull the trigger, next time she would. She would yet *ungrund* this woman. But she needed practice at ungrunding. The woman had been too doe-eyed, too ordinarily human. Too much Levinasian other and not enough Lovecraftian Elder. The murderer answered the door wearing a Mickey Mouse t-shirt, holding a toddler on her hip, smiling sadly at Heike, apologizing for answering the door with applesauce spilled over her front and matting the young child's hair. "*Kann ich Ihnen helfen?*" the woman said. Heike pulled out the Glock .9mm and pointed at the woman's applesauce-stained chest and meant to say, "You killed James." Then she meant to empty the entire clip into her *Dasein*. Ending it. Making her consciousness void. But what she did was turn around and run. So she would not start with this one. She needed more practice at envoiding people. Before she killed a woman holding a toddler on her hip, she would end a more odious vermin. It had taken her two years to find Astrid Winter, leader of the August 4th Faction, an independent RAF wannabe, and when she was finished with the others she would visit Astrid again. And when next time she asked, "*Kann ich Ihnen helfen?*" Heike will answer, "*Nein.*" and this time pull the trigger and tear her heart apart with unforgiving metal.

She would start with the 'Bad Mormon.' The American who gave them the explosives. The cowboy. He would be harder to find but would teach her the art of ending others. A negation in totality.

It will take her nine more years to find Erhabenes König, as the Army man fancied himself. But like Schelling's God, she had will. And she was determined to birth her vengeance in his becoming void. Then she would finish with Astrid and the other six terrorists. If theology had taught her anything it was the joy of praxis, and this would be the ritual that would define her life.

Elder Holmberg Assuages His Guilt After Setting Apart a New Stake President

If we cannot imagine the void, or reference it, how is it that I am talking about it? Can we come to its border? Do the suburbs of the void contain enough real estate that we can climb to the uppermost chimney of one of the higher tract houses and attempt a glimpse of its true edge? Like the event horizon of a black hole, but within which is… there I am, at it again, 'is?' Can I use a verb of the form 'to be' in a place in which it makes no sense?

—Frau Professorin Heike Marquardt,
On the Void: The Theology of Nothingness

Elder Homberg is on his knees pleading with the Lord. He is in agony, having just set apart the new Stake President for the Blanding Stake. It went down like this.

He made the decision between Monticello and Blanding that he would set apart Bishop Jimmy Wendell. He was a good man. He ran the Purina Feed Store and knew most of the community pretty well, especially on the farming and ranching side of things. He had not served a mission, but was well known for his fifteen years as bishop of the Blanding Second Ward. Much beloved, hard-working. His wife, a stalwart of good pioneer stock, was known for her compassionate service and her work among the Lamanite school children. A fine couple. Yet. There was that, 'Yet.' He wrestled with whether he should call Bishop Stout instead. He almost felt like he had been inspired to call him, but he decided it was his own love of the atonement and his kind and forgiving nature. Not the spirit. No. When he interviewed Brother Stout a couple of weeks ago, he had confessed to a heinous sin committed during his days as a Navy seaman. That awful thing was still haunting the apostle two weeks later. He just could not do it. He could not call him to be a Church leader. He just couldn't. Brother Stout had become a fine man, certainly. There was no question about that. He taught physics in the high school and ran the San Juan and Colorado River as a river raft operator during summer break. Was liked well enough. His wife was a little too educated perhaps—a master's degree in mathematics, of all things. She sometimes took over the high school physics classes in a pinch—a little too much outside the home for his tastes. It was a fine thing for a woman to get an education just in case her husband left his mortal coil early. Even so, he had no real complaints to make about the couple, nor was there any question as to their worthiness such as it would disallow Brother Stout from being called as the Stake President. But that damn confession he made! It was ugly and just plain nasty in every way. Just horrible. Did all sailors behave so? He had been in the Air Force in England during the War and certainly no pilot would be found doing such things. Ugh! He rubbed his face in his hands to try to get the thought out of his head.

Admittedly there had been that tug that had *seemed* to indicate that Brother Stout had been the man for the job. That is why he was now on his knees. When he set apart Bishop Wendell, it had been strange. The day's meetings had gone well. The stake unanimously raised their hands in support of their new stake president's call. After some beautiful talks, including his own on 'Charity and the Pure Love of Christ,' he had gone into the stake offices to set the bishop apart, but nothing came. He stood there too long, but nothing. Finally just out of awkwardness and a sense of decorum he started talking and giving the usual advice and counsel. It was not until he was well into his admonitions on righteousness, the covenants that he was taking upon himself, and the blessings that would follow for unrelenting obedience, that the spirit took over and started

51

to give him voice. He promised the bishop that the Lord would be with him, that God loved him, and that, when all was said and done, he would be remembered as a great Stake President. But it was short and to the point. Maybe even too short. But there was no going back. He had issued the call. What was done was done.

⊃ ⋊ ⚡ ⋉ ⊂

On the way back to Salt Lake City, good Alma Lune noticed that his beloved Elder Holmberg was a troubled man. He was fidgeting in his seat—a sure sign he was bothered about something. He was also sighing repeatedly, thereby revealing himself to be deeply unsettled.

"Are you OK?" Alma Lune asked, beginning the long process of extracting his friend from what was pestering his peace. It took a while—repeated probes, redirections, reading between the lines, coming from the sides, drilling down—but after nearly a half-hour he suspected he might just have hit it.

"So you feel like maybe Bishop Wendell might not have been what the Lord had in mind?"

"I may have let my own feelings influence things—yes that is likely it. I don't know what to do," Elder Holmberg said with some relief. Confession was good for the soul.

"That's the risk of acting, Bonhoeffer says…" Alma Lune is interrupted.

"Bonhoeffer again? You said he was a minster of some sort? I like that he fought the Nazis; I have that in common with him, but he died by them as you've told me, whereas I was preserved of the Lord; and well, frankly, I don't like the way you bring in works from outside the Restoration…"

"Hear me out."

Elder Holmberg was quiet, granting Alma Lune permission to go on, albeit with a frown on his face.

"It's about risk, Elder. To be human is to take risks which means mistakes are made. To try to avoid risk is to deny freedom. You faced a complex decision. You acted, and in acting risked a mistake. But that is OK. God will deal with it. See?"

Elder Holmberg harrumphed. "You just don't get what straight and narrow means, do you? God has a plan. You fall off it, you are no longer following God's plan are you?"

"But no one is perfect… "

"Yes but we ought to be striving for it don't you think? You might remember the little scripture that goes BE YE THEREFORE PERFECT!"

"What are you going to do then?" Alma Lune often resigned himself to the force that was Elder Holmberg.

"I don't think I can go back and undo what's been done. That would destroy everyone's confidence in the brethren. We can't have that. But maybe a good chat with Bishop Stout, let him know he's a fine fellow. You know, soften the blow. My worry is that he might be feeling low not being moved into the Stake."

"Do you want me to turn around and head back to Blanding?"

"Yes. Turn around," the apostle beamed. "Let's see if we can undo what the Lord's weakest servant has wrought, shall we?"

⊃ ⊠ ⊁ ⊠ ⊂

No one was more surprised by the appearance of the apostle, 5th in the line of succession to the very Presidency of the Church of Jesus Christ of Latter-day Saints, than LeRoy Abraham Stout. He was just getting up from dinner when the elder arrived. He invited him in when he finally got his mouth working. His wife, Jezzy, called all the children from their various places and activities into the living room of their Charwood doublewide trailer to meet this Prophet, Seer, and Revelator who had arrived to bless their humble home like it had never been graced since it rolled off the factory in Michigan.

"LeRoy, I just stopped by, to let you know what a fine fellow I think you are. I was very impressed with the leadership of your ward and just wanted to encourage you to keep it up."

LeRoy was honestly taken back; tears were forming in his eyes. He didn't find his voice, but his nod was touchingly complete and heartfelt. That was clear.

"You know," the apostle continued, "I came about this close to calling you to lead the Stake." He held up a gap between his forefinger and thumb to show exactly how close he had come. It was a very small distance.

Jezzy popped out with a nervous, "Oh my! Where are my manners! Can I offer you anything? I have a peach pie sitting in the fridge that I could microwave up with a scoop of ice cream. Would you like a slice? With a glass of milk perhaps?"

"That sounds delightful! Thank you."

Jezzy raised her eye expectantly at Alma Lune offering him the same, but he declined with a slight wave of his hand.

They all retired to the kitchen table from which Jezzy hurriedly cleared the dinner and replaced it with small bone china plates that had been neatly stacked behind a glass-windowed door in a maple corner cabinet. The plates had been unused since their wedding reception so many years ago. This was the perfect occasion for their debut. She called the children over to meet the apostle and introduced them one by one. The old elder, bending low for the little ones, gave each of their hands a warm and friendly shake. Then they all took their seats around the large table. Jezzy quickly wrapped the three gallon tub of Neapolitan ice cream in her best dishcloth and brought it to the table and then set the pie nearby.

They all sat there with nervous smiles. Jezzy looked at LeRoy. They could convey entire chapters of information by the smallest of facial gestures: She suggested that he should ask one of the children to say a blessing on the pie; he hesitated because they had never prayed over their dessert before, but then they had never had an Apostle over for pie before either; so she responded to his silent request and asked five-year-old Samuel to say a prayer.

"It's not my turn." He said defiantly.

"Say it anyway, Sam," his father patiently stated with resolve, "we have a special guest with us."

Sam shot a semi-resentful glance Elder Holmberg's way but quickly relented and said the standard family blessing on the food, but gracefully added a request that the Lord would make it so there was enough pie for everyone—not an unreasonable request in a house of six children all under ten.

Everyone agreed the pie was fantastic, and when after his second slice Elder Holmberg said it was the finest he had tasted in years, Jezzy beamed. He folded his napkin and addressed the children.

"Children. You have fine parents. You listen to them, and your days will be long in the land. You remember I said that. Listen to your parents and your land will yield its fruit to you. You have a virtuous mother and a fine father. I almost called your father to be the stake president. Did you know that?"

It was Samuel who piped up again, "I heard my Mom tell my Dad that she dreamed he was made the new Stake President."

"SAMUEL! It doesn't work like that."

"But you said it was one of your special dreams. Like Lehi got."

LeRoy just laughed and ruffled the boy's hair. Jezzy looked embarrassed. But most odd of all was the look of horror on the apostle's face. Clearly, her having that dream had upset him.

"Samuel," she said quietly, "it was just a dream. Just like the kind you have where you can fly; it doesn't mean you really can."

LeRoy laughed again, kindly trying to cover his wife's embarrassment. Then said, "You know, Elder Holmberg, you ought to join us on a river trip at the end of this month. The river will be high and mostly smooth. You told that story in Stake Conference about running the Colorado when you were a lad, and well, we'd be honored if you would join us running it this spring. It's a two-day ride and, well, frankly I'd love to help you relive some of your early joys."

LeRoy looked from the apostle to his secretary, who was looking at the older man with what was obvious concern, then back to the apostle who seemed to be distracted and weighed down.

"It would do you good," the secretary said somewhat strangely, as if there were some chastisement in his voice. "Give you a chance to get to know Bishop Stout a bit."

The old elder nodded, "Yes. As you say. Maybe. Let me think on it."

The secretary held out his hand to Bishop Stout and said, "I'll have our office contact you about the details. But plan on us. Plan on us both."

The apostle seemed to come back from some care he was attending to, smiled, and slowly rose to his feet. He again shook each of the children's hands, praised the pie again, and shook LeRoy's hand saying, "I look forward to going down the river with you, but let's not finalize until I check on my availability." Then added almost to himself, "It is a shame that Sister Holmberg is no longer with us. She loved adventure and would have liked very much to shoot the rapids in a raft. Perhaps she will enjoy the proceedings from afar." His eyes moistened, and he walked over to Sister Stout and held her hand and smiled sadly.

The entire family watched from the porch as the apostle made to climb into his car, but then at the last minute paused and stood up again and took out his white handkerchief and waved it at the gathered family. They all waved enthusiastically back, especially some of the younger children. Then he climbed back in, as did his secretary, and they pulled away heading for Highway 191 North to make their way back to Salt Lake.

God hated Elder Holmberg. Again, certainly not for any reason, such as this mistaken Stake Presidency call, and certainly not for any character flaw in the old man. It was just an eternal fact of His existence. God ignored His own hatred completely. His Beloved Son had taught him how to love in the face of His nature.

Interlude—
Arrow Beamon's Tale

It came to pass that Arrow was sitting in the military base's enlisted-men's bar when he learned about the death of the American officer in Frankfurt. Colonel James Fields.

Arrow was having a beer with his three buddies, celebrating their return from the field maneuvers in Fulda. There had been one of those natural silences that come when a topic peters out. Smithy and Big Man had just been discussing whether Hendrix was a better guitarist than Carlos Santana. The moment was decided when the spirits of fate intervened and *Oye Como Va* came from the jukebox as if declaring which side of the question the powers of the universe came down on.

Killer, who had not gone to Fulda with them because he was with the AG, had been looking in his beer during the Hendrix/Santana debate, suddenly looked up and said quietly, "You guys hear about the Red Army Faction killing one of ours in Frankfurt last week?"

"The who faction?" Smithy tried a little harder to focus on Killer through his beer haze.

"Red Army Faction. They've been blowing up Krauts for a while, who knows why, but they just bombed some of our guys in Frankfurt. The dude that died, Lieutenant Colonel Fields, I knew him. Sort of. I met him once anyway when I went up to Command to drop some shit off. Nice guy. Real fucking hero. Did time in Nam flying a chopper. Comes back from Asia and fucking shits waste him middle of downtown Germany. Crazy, huh?"

"What kind of bomb?" Arrow was suddenly pasty white.

"*Stars and Stripes* is saying it might be one of ours. Looks like *plastik*. Investigation is on-going…. Man are you OK? You are shaking like's it's 20 degrees in here."

"Yeah, 'course. Just um, yeah, I knew the guy too."

"Seriously?" Killer wanted to be the only one to know him.

"Maybe. My mom has a cousin out here named James Fields. That's my Mom's maiden name."

"Shit, that's the guy. So you knew him well?"

"No. I never met him. My mom said to look him up if I ever got to Frankfurt. But…" He was really shaking violently now, "Thinking about my Mom. I got to go."

With that, Arrow made his way shakily to the door.

Killer, Smithy, and Big Man never got to have a drink with him again. He was arrested at morning formation. A goodly bit of detective work went into convicting Arrow.

The bomb was set off by members of Baader-Meinhof Red Army Group, and through an informant that had regrets about the bombing, the investigators were led to the person who drove the bombers to their target at US Army V Corps headquarters. She did not know them, but she spilled on Astrid and Henrik, who then, under some sort of legal deal-making, narced out Arrow and told how he had given them the *plastik* and det cord in Fulda for a bit of hash. That wasn't enough to arrest Arrow. It was their word against his, but they found on an undamaged portion of the *plastik* wrapper, a piece of the serial number, which allowed them to trace the source to the arms depot in Fulda and then to the weapons master, Sgt. Francis Gattelli, who gave up Arrow while literally driving from where they picked him up at his depot office to the interrogation center and told everything about how Arrow had given him some hash for just a little bit of plastic and det cord that he said he was going to just go fishing with on the river (a "little bit" turned out to be 5 kilos). That was enough. The witness of the German hash dealers and the sergeant in charge of the arms depot on the day in question was enough.

Normally, of course, Arrow would have spent the rest of his life at the military prison in Ft. Leavenworth, Missouri, but the Germans really, really wanted him because of his connection to the Baader-Meinhof Gang. There was an Army captain who had been arrested by the Germans for running dope using his company's Cobra helicopters and, well, the Army really wanted him in Leavenworth, so it was a you-scratch-my-back-I'll-scratch-yours match made in heaven. The Germans wanted Arrow, and the Army wanted the drug runner. Everyone was happy. Except Arrow. And one supposes the Cobra commander.

Arrow was sent to a prison near Munich. He didn't hang out with the other imprisoned BM Gang members. It became apparent in his trial he was just a derelict know-nothing drug addict and dealer and not really the political prisoner they were hoping for. He was sentenced to 7 years to life for his role in the bombing of Frankfurt HQ. During his trial he became known as "The Bad Mormon" for being from Utah, or "The Cowboy," just because so many westerns had been made in Moab.

During Arrow's time in prison, Nephi became discouraged. Not since his mortal life had he felt so dispirited. He helped Arrow in prison stay encouraged, kept his hope up about his future life. Despite his mistakes, he could still live a full productive life, Nephi whispered in his ear. He helped Arrow avoid the coarser and more dangerous elements in prison, and inspired the warden to give him meaningful and productive tasks and classes to keep him actively engaged in his rehabilitation. But the more he worked to help Arrow, the more despairing, and if he dared think it, depressed he became about his own angelic life. Certainly, he was never bored or fatigued, nor did he feel the infirmities of age, but the obvious fact that he was tending to someone who had assisted in a murder began to weigh on him. And the irony was not lost on him either; here was Nephi, slayer of his cousin—rich, drunk Laban—being the guardian angel of a man who had (indirectly) killed his cousin James Fields. And people said the divine had no sense of humor. Still, he began to feel somewhat bitter about his assignment, although he fought it off (and a visit from John the Beloved had been a momentary act of grace in a particularly low stretch). The daily monotony of being the guardian angel of someone with such a simple range of daily activities began to wear on his soul.

While in prison, Arrow worked on bachelor's and master's degrees in Animal Science. He worked in the prison dairy farm and became one of the most well-liked managers on the premises. After he was released in his seventh year for good behavior, he could not go home. He had killed his mother's beloved cousin, a war hero, and he was not welcome in the family. So he decided to stay in Europe. Upon his release he was fluent in German, so he went to University in Wien and worked on a doctorate in African livestock problems in the developing world, focusing on genetically-based attempts to breed varieties of cattle resistant to tsetse fly attack, the cause of the animal disease Nagana.

He was working in Ethiopia when Heike discovered his whereabouts.

Asilah Comforts
Her Charge

Ah, perhaps there is the hook we need. It may be that the way into the void (if you'll pardon the expression) is through the techniques of negative theology. There does seem something right about divine aseity serving as a mirror into the void, for it too has an aseity of sorts—it is its own foundation, self-existent, eternal, and causeless.

—Frau Professorin Heike Marquardt,
On the Void: The Theology of Nothingness

The Goddess Asilah, messenger of the Mother, sits next to Heike on a bench in one of the many Berlin dog parks. As the mortal woman watches her Vizsla try to free a Frisbee from the mouth of a blocky Labrador, the owner of the black dog smiles and waves at Heike, signaling he's OK with their dogs having a little fun testing their strength in a harmless game of tug-of-war. Heike waves back and pulls a thick book from her bag, *Das Buch der göttlichen Tröstung**, by Meister Eckhart. She reads for a few minutes then sighs and closes her watering eyes. Asilah knows where she is going. To the darkness. To emptiness. With her hand Asilah pulls back her own hair as an errant breeze teases it playfully about the Goddess's brown face. She leans over and whispers into Heike's ear.

"Think on the Mother, dear heart, remember when she came to you in Sweden in the light of a midnight sun in the forest meadow when the birds of late summer sang their joy at abundance? Of insects playing in the nearby wetlands? Remember her radiance and voice, and remember how she spoke words of peace and purpose into your heart? Think on the joy of finding your vocation. She sent me with her greetings! Do not think she, or even I, cannot know the pain in your heart from the loss of your love James? Even I, a lesser Goddess, am capable of feeling the pain of having those we love torn from us by violence. Do you think I cannot weep in anguish?" And suddenly the Goddess' frame begins to shake, and her voice becomes unsteady and broken and, though a Goddess, she has to pause to catch her glorious breath, and recall her mission of comfort to this damaged soul. She gathers the spirit of love about her. She puts her arms around Heike and pulls her spirit close to hers and weeps. "Please dear beloved, what is eating your soul will canker and whither you. You

---

* *The Book of Divine Consolation*

know the void. It is more hollow than that. It is emptiness without mercy...." Suddenly Heike reaches into her handbag and pulls out a small pad of paper and writes into it, "An emptiness without mercy" and underlines the words several times. She takes a tissue from her bag and wipes her eyes. "An emptiness without mercy," she says out loud, "That is it."

Heike gathers her things and starts calling Georg back to her. Asilah knows she has an appointment with her committee chair and knows that she will pull herself together for the meeting. Then she will go out for dinner and drinks with two of her university friends from the theology department. Afterwards, Asilah knows, Heike will be fine for a couple of days. The Goddess, however, will be ready when she is needed again. Heike is loved by God, who hopes to make her a blessing to many. She was broken, though, and still needs help. She is dangerous and vulnerable right now. When Asilah watched her pull a gun on the other woman, her heart almost melted in fear. It was OK now. She hopes anyway. She knows Heike's heart is still full of violence and thoughts of revenge, and she can feel the whisperings of the spirit saying, 'Stick with her. No matter what." And she will.

The Goddess watches as Heike puts the leash on Georg, and pulls him, protesting, toward the gate. The man who owns the black lab speaks a few words with her, and when they part the two give each other a smile and a wave as they go their separate ways. It makes Asilah smile too. Such kindness lives in this world!

An emptiness without mercy. The Goddess remembers hers. She recalls when she walked the holy planet many years ago and her son was killed by someone she had loved her whole life. It was during a skirmish. A war. The ugliness of greed and power. An emptiness without mercy. But the thought no longer darkens her. Her son is with her now in glory, and many of the terrors of earth have come to an end. Though the pain of betrayal still bubbles up from time to time, she has forgiven the killer. Justice has been served. But she will never, ever, forget. Of course. How could she? She has a divine mind after all. Nothing will ever be forgotten.

Elder Holmberg is Guilted into a River Trip

Are voids so null that not even negative properties can be assigned? Even in the richly populat-
ed real numbers, zero has a place and properties.
Can a void even be reached? Observe: $\varnothing - \varnothing = \varnothing$
still leaves the null set floating around, by what
operation do we remove the null set from our set?
Again the impossibility of even formal conversation seems obvious. We can assign neither positive or negative properties. One can try, certainly.
but the contradictions pile up so quickly that it all
falls apart.

—Frau Professorin Heike Marquardt,
On the Void: The Theology of Nothingness

Alma Lune found Elder Holmberg staring out of the window of the Church Office Building looking rather glum.
His eyes seemed to focus on nothing—distracted enough
not to have even noticed Alma Lune had entered the office.

The office was lavishly furnished with a beautiful dark walnut desk, a matching bookcase, a massive framed Arnold Friberg painting of a thin, bare-chested Abinadi before King Noah, and a thick, noise-muffling beige carpet that added an ambiance of seriousness and purpose to the room. Not all of the books in the bookcase had been read, but most had. A staff member dusted them weekly, kept them nicely lined up and in proper order. Talmage's complete works were there. *The History of the Church.* Even a full set of the *Journal of Discourses* took up a couple of shelves. In addition, Cleon Skousen's First through Fourth Thousand Years were there. Bruce R. McConkie's *Mormon Doctrine.* A proper assortment of books published by Deseret Book and Bookcraft by colleagues in Church administration made up the bulk of the tomes. A few years ago, Lowell Bennion had gifted him a collection of his books. While he intended to read them, he hadn't gotten around to them yet. Someday he would when he had more time. A few non-LDS volumes gave a sense of balance, including *Strong's Bible Concordance* as well as a book about learning biblical Hebrew. The latter book was taken down at least once a year, or at least every other year, when Elder Holmberg was inspired at least for a day or two to magnify his resolve to learn Hebrew just as Joseph Smith had modeled, but it never lasted much beyond that, even though it filled the good apostle with regrets that he had not yet mastered the ancient tongue as his patriarchal blessing had promised.

There was also an artificial ficus tree in one corner which had a single Christmas bulb hanging from one of its branches. It had been placed there by one of his granddaughters and he had proclaimed that no one should touch it. It was to hang there until the second coming. A nice Baptist hell awaited anyone who dared try to remove it.

Alma Lune was surprised to find the elder so pensive. Usually he was a beehive of activity and rarely paused from his demanding schedule long enough to even eat a hurried sandwich from his bag. To see him looking out of the window was very un-Elder Holmberg-like to say the least. The secretary walked over to the window and joined in staring down into metropolitan Salt Lake City.

"Are you all right, Elder?" Alma Lune said placing his hand on his shoulder.

He looked at his secretary as if seeing him for the first time, stared for a moment, then patted the hand on his shoulder. He sighed.

"Brother Lune. I can't get it out of my head. Something is wrong. The Spirit isn't happy with me."

"What's bothering you, Elder?"

"It's that Blanding business. I'm just not sure what the Lord wanted me to do down there. It still feels out of kilter."

They were silent a long time. Then the apostle asked, "Is that offer to take us down the Colorado still open? You know when Brother Stout offered to take me on one of his river trips?"

Alma Lune smiled. "I'm sure it is. It seems to me that was pretty much a standing offer."

"Good," Elder Holmberg said resolutely. "Look at my schedule and book us a river trip. I need to spend some time with that man. I just want him to understand I'm not holding a grudge about the despicable and heinous things he confessed to me. I'm sure he has thoroughly repented, so there is no more reason for him to dwell on it."

Alma Lune went out of the office to call Brother Stout. Elder Holmberg was overcome by the sins of the world. He knew it was his burden to bear, but even so. The weight of the mistakes and evils people perpetrated on one another from time to time. Even though the atonement helped people repent, the weight that it must have imposed on the Savior astonished him. He was lucky, he supposed. He had never indulged in any of the misdeeds that seemed to afflict his fellow saints. He supposed that in the preexistence he demonstrated such a high level of faithfulness in defending Heavenly Father's Plan of Happiness that he had been blessed with extraordinary parents who guided him in the ways of righteousness, in ways that kept him from falling into any major sins or foibles. He was not perfect, and he gave a slight chuckle at the thought that so many thought him so, but no, he had committed his share of misdeeds and errors. Perhaps he was inclined to have too demanding a demeanor toward others; and he did like the extra piece of cake when one was offered, but all in all he had kept himself as clean as might be expected. He had, for example, never smoked or taken a drink of alcohol, or even partaken of caffeine of any sort; he had never looked at pornography; or masturbated, even as a young man; he had not stolen, nor spoken evil of the Lord's anointed; he had not lusted after other men's wives, nor had he been especially quick to anger. He had done his home teaching almost every month for years. It had been over a decade since he had last failed to do his duty that way. He kept that Sabbath day as well as he could, given the occasional ox in the mire, and had not even allowed his children to watch television on that holy day (how sad it made him feel that his son Gerald who had gone inactive for many years would watch football even on the Lord's day!). No, he had tried with his might to serve and do his duty as best he could. By any measure he had succeeded. Was he not an apostle? One of the Lord's anointed? He had much to be proud of.

And yet he could not help but ask himself how it was that Bishop Stout, a seemingly upright man, could have been involved in such scandalous crimes against his own manhood. What had happened that he could do such evil?

Alma Lune interrupted for a moment. "Elder, Bishop Stout says he's got a trip planned on the Colorado this weekend, it's sort of a training run before the season begins, so it won't be filled with tourists, and he'd be glad to have you along."

Elder Holmberg was about to tell him to cancel, as the bishop's crimes were in front of his mind's eye, but he realized that he really needed to walk among the sinners,

like Christ, so he relented. "Tell him that would be fine...
no wait, ask how many people and who would be going
with us? I would rather it not be with gentiles who will be
drinking or smoking."

Alma Lune ducked back into his office. He was back in
seconds.

"He says besides you and I there are only three others: his wife, an old buddy of his from Moab, and he's a
Mormon, and a Swedish woman, and he's explained to her
already that there is no smoking or drinking allowed on
his trips. It sounds like a great opportunity to go with a
small group. What do you think? The run goes from a few
miles above Moab all the way past the confluence of the
Green...."

The Apostle smiled. A small group floating down
through some of the gorgeous canyon country. This is just
what he needed. Plus, being alone with a Swedish woman
might be just the ticket for his bashful secretary to meet a
future wife.

"Yes. Tell him yes."

It was a rare thing that he did not have to attend a Stake
Conference. It all looked meant to be. This would be fun.
He turned his eyes upward and gave a small prayer of
thanks to the Lord for his kindness and tender mercies.
Yes. This was just what he needed.

And the good Lord did have great kindness and tender
mercies. And this despite His divine hatred of the blessed
elder. God knew how love acted.

Interlude—Heike's Tale: 'Her First Loves,' Written for an Autobiographical Chapter of Her Dissertation With Details Added for A Later Project

My life has been a series of love stories. I grew up in Antenbichl. A small hamlet in Bayern. My mother owned a small basement tavern called *Die Schleiereule*, about eleven kilometers from our home in Berchtesgaden. She also sang there on the weekends. Of my father, she would not speak. Although as a teenager I pressed her hard, she would tell me nothing, whether I was the accident of a one-night stand or the child of an early marriage, I do not know. From her reaction to being asked about him, it is clear that there was some pain involved, and although I am curious, I have been able to discover nothing. While growing up my mother would never bring home her lovers. I knew there were many because sometimes she would not come home, and those times I knew she was dating someone. I would only get to meet them when it was becoming serious, but that rarely happened and never continued more than a year.

I was given a great deal of freedom. Near my house there were many trails that wandered through the surrounding mountains. I found it so beautiful, and at times even sublime, that it led me to believe in God. Later, this area would become a national park, but then it was my private backyard. My mother taught me how to camp in the woods, and from age twelve, I was allowed to spend many summer nights alone high among the meadows and forests of those celebrated alpine habitats. This was my first love: the great peaks of my homeland. I would walk among mossy trees, listen to the songs of the birds among their branches, and feel the power of living things.

My first love, then, was the manifestation of God as Goddess. There in the montane timberlands, I would walk in transcendent wonder at the vast scope and power of a providence I could understand only as a mothering deity— or so I supposed. I would haunt glades far off the trails where few, if any, others walked. The well-worn paths of others meant little to me. I was a friend to the marmots which sang to me in their meadow homes. The chamois were my friends, as were the wise goats. They did not fear me, I think, because I was infused with the Goddess's love.

Networks of feathered creatures delighted me. The tril-ly-high-caw of the alpine chough worrying the verdure above the timberline. The multiple joyous voices of the meadow water pipit. The sweet conversational chirps of the alpine-accentor hunting for insects. The welcoming song of the goldfinch. All these I knew as friends. The creaturely soundscape was as rich as the landscape. Creation's flourishing floral and faunal diversity. There I came to know the smell of each kind of tree, the scent of mint, anise, and timothy. The rich fragrance of deep forest soils gladdened my heart and seemed to imbue my entire being with a sense that I belonged on this earth and was part of something that ran deep into the geologic strata of this planet and its attending surface presences. From mosses and ferns to butterflies and beetles. And its skies made new every day by clouds soft or frantic in their arrays. And the stars. Everything. Being and non.

Rivers and streams were friendly too—the sound of turbulent water over ancient stones, sparkling playfully down the mountains to the lower hills where they merged with other streams to form the cold rivers along which towns and villages were built—their banks harboring aged battlements, castles, and sometimes still functioning monasteries and convents. I loved the feel of a cold mountain stream running between my toes when I dipped them into the clear clean water. I adored the scent of the river, or not so much a scent as a presence and clarity that infused the air around it. Its ethereal pleasure would tempt me to taste, then sip, then drink the river's glacier-gifted offering as I knelt to refresh myself. I was a child of this unique planet and all her processes—water, air, fire, earth.

My spiritual roots burrowed deep in those folds of ancient rocks and hardened seabeds. I learned to climb up rocky faces and boulders free hand, never fearing that I might fall. I learned from the goats how to make my way by finding tiny protuberances, minuscule knobs—small imperfections that would allow a single finger to find purchase. But always, no matter how high I'd climbed, I felt the cradling arm of the Queen of Earth. I'm sure if my mother had seen what I was doing she would have been horrified and forbidden me to ever set foot alone in the mountains again, but what little supervision she gave me centered on the mundane chores and tasks of typical modern existence. She never encroached on the me developing from my acquaintance with wildness and the untamed beauties of forest, fen, and meadow. My mother demanded excellence in my studies, and I excelled, not to please anyone, but because I was blessed with an insatiable curiosity and an eager stubborn commitment to understand the workings of the cosmos. I excelled in English, mathematics, and science. I fell in love with Goethe, Schelling, and the other romantics because I felt they understood and spoke the language of my soul. This was my second love. Still, my greatest teachers were the massive *Berge* that enveloped my home and provided the context and meaning for my life; the ecology of my being. The life of the mind, which engendered a curiosity never satisfied, for one puzzle led to another question that opened up galaxies of thought where more mysteries orbited around my heart's yearning to understand the comings and goings of all things—the ecology of existence.

In all my love of the creatures that made the woods speak with the music of birdsong, or provided movement of insects and mammals, it was the matrix in which they were embedded, that secured that love—the trees. I planned to become a forester. I wanted to study the beeches, firs, and pines that so defined the substance and essence of the little knot of complexity that was me—what Thoreau called "a parcel of strivings." I arranged to work in Sweden for my *Freiwilligendienst* with a conservation group working in Tyresta National Park near Stockholm. It was a year of hard work, constructing outbuildings to house the new visitor center, but there was time to explore the beauty of the northern forests.

It was there I met Per Fulgesang. My third love. He was beautiful. Long dusky blond hair. A strong Viking build. Siegfried reincarnated. More important to me was that he loved the landscape and its inhabitants. Like me, he lived much of his life outdoors. His father had been a lumber master, and Per spent much of his youth among the trees. There is something about an acquaintance with forests that bores its way to the soul like an ichneumonoid wasp bores into a tree. Or maybe better, as if the mycorrhizae that curl among the roots of these great trees also enter your bloodstream and enmesh you in that world. You become an elemental creature who knows the moods and dispositions of growing things—connected to the woods and its denizens.

Because both of us were spirits of the copse and grove, our roots entangled almost upon first meeting—and with our roots, our bodies soon followed. He was working there for just the summer and my *Freiwilligendienst* was to last a year, but he stayed on to be with me. After my service ended, we decided to hitchhike north and visit the boreal forests that stretch across the Neoartic, as if the Earth were wearing a great scarf, as Per once described it.

Then a single night under the endless arctic sun changed everything. We were camped in a patch of forest by a beautiful lake near Gällivare in upper Sweden. With the intent of being alone, we hiked to a lonely spot deep within ancient trees. In Northern Sweden, it is not hard to find places where such isolation is easily available. It was mid-July; the weather was beautiful and unusually mild, with a soft breeze reminding us not to take the warmth for granted. A man at a local pub had given Per a small bag of psilocybin mushrooms that were found locally growing wildly in cattle shit. He told us to take one cap with a strong draught of a particular dark beer bottled in a nearby village.

We lit a fire, mostly an attempt to drive off the flies and gnats emerging into the warm spring evening air—having becoming a nuisance almost everywhere as we moved further north. By firelight we talked until the sun was readying to bounce off the horizon and resume its daily course through the indigo sky. We then opened the beers and swallowed a couple of the mushroom caps each. The beer was good: stout, bitter, and sweet. The evening seemed to pass on. Nothing was amiss. Nothing could be amiss, the low, clear sun seemed to say.

I became aware that a great peace settled on me, reminiscent of the carefree days of my childhood, my romps through the mountains of my home region. It felt profound. Complete. The colors seemed to soften. I felt an enveloping love that gathered around me and seemed to lift my body into the air. I was as light as a helium balloon. The wind captured me and blew me toward the horizon. Even though I was not in control, I was not afraid—a complete trust infused me. I was being cradled toward something warm and cozy. Something like home or what I imagined home should be. It was as if I were being cared for by the mother of all mothers. The ur-mother. Someone who cherished me so completely, and knew me so thoroughly, that despite my many flaws, loved me more deeply than anyone ever had or could. A sense of the sublime infused what can only be called my soul—as if every electron in my body suddenly reversed direction, and every proton had become a neutron star and vice versa. I note the contradiction in that 'vice versa,' but it was true nonetheless. I was a new creature modified by this feminine power that lofted me toward something so grand and sacred that the matter of my being was being transformed into a manifestation of love. True light. Grace. Becoming.

I came to the edge of the horizon, and unlike the Earth bounded by space and void, it ended like an island. An ocean stretched before me, not of water, but a seething, writhing dance of light, substance. It was chaos; it was the substance that presupposes matter. Its depths, I knew, were unfathomable. Yet I saw moving under the waters something enormous and of import proportional to its size. Leviathan. Uncreated monster of the deep. It breeched like a hunchbacked whale, suddenly stretching to the stars, then arching back, falling to splash the universe itself with chaotic ungrund. I was drenched in an intensity of love so profound I thought I would cease to be. A light so penetrating that I expanded to fill the immensity of space and existence. I was remade. Unmade.

"Who are you?" I asked. I felt no fear in asking. I knew I was in the presence of something that loved me so profoundly and so wholly there was nothing I could do to change, tilt, or upset that love. I was protected in this place. My questions would be answered. All unease was swept away by an acceptance so total that my only comparison is a mother's gaze upon a newborn child.

Suddenly, the leviathan arose from the water straight and tall, its fins held horizontal, its great snout pointed to the sky. It began to transform, to transmogrify into a young lady, naked and beautiful, and without question powerful beyond imagination. Her silk hair was blowing in a wind I could not feel. She looked to be someone my own age, but with a freshness and maturity that no human could ever mirror.

"I am maiden and mother. I am crone and child. I am everywhere love and wisdom. I am lover and warrior. I am Goddess of chaos and void."

She reached out her hands and took my own. And in her eyes I saw the birth of universes and planes upon planes of existence beyond what my brain could contain, but not my body. My body held it all. It was my body learning.

"Will you help me?" she said.

"Anything." I meant it. I would die should she command it.

"Find me. I am hidden in the texts. I am obscured in the rituals. I am cloaked behind a thousand masks of order. I am screened by the churches. The smoke of a thousand agonies has obscured my presence. Find me."

"How?" I whispered.

She smiled, "I will send one of my daughters to guide you. Look for her. A messenger."

Then, becoming leviathan again, she rose as if to swim into the stars—but instead, as she reached the apex of her flight, she fell over stiffly, creating another mighty splash, then disappeared, powering to the depths of chaos. This was my fourth and greatest love.

But the experience of the Goddess burned as fierce as a welding arc, saturating my mind and heart. I knew what I had to do. We finished our trip, by the end having fallen out of love. Perhaps my encounter with the Goddess turned to new explorations, or perhaps we just ran out of things to give each other. We remained friends, but each returned to our separate lives. I knew exactly what I was to do as if it were implanted like a map on my heart. I applied and was accepted to Tübingen's theology school. There I would find the Goddess' presence again and again. I would reveal her body to the world. The mother would be known again.

The following was added later as an addendum to a book idea Heike was working on. Attached here to give more details.

Things were not easy in University. My feminism was seen as radical. I was ostracized and often felt lonely and afraid. From time to time, especially when I was among my old friends—the mountains and forests—I would sense the presence of the Goddess embedded in the chaos of the deep. I worshiped with a group of Wiccan hedge witches because they worshipped the Goddess. But I became disillusioned. They saw her as a kind of Greek or Norse deity whose aspects captured nothing of the sublime. My attendance became sporadic as my dissertation work took me in new directions.

My theology became more sophisticated, more formal. I learned logic and became aware of the great Japanese continental philosophers like Suzuki, Nishitani, and Nishida. I replaced Goddess with the Nothing. *Das Nichts.* The Nothing is not gendered. The void became my passion. No sea of chaos. Instead, absolute emptiness. I started practicing Zen meditation.

I graduated with honors and began to do dissertation research on the feminine divine again, after a powerful dream of a Goddess weeping in the dark wood. I could hear her. I knew this was the promised messenger, but I could not find her among the trees of the moonlit forest. An owl sitting high above me on a branch looked out into the night and said, "She is lost." I awoke with a sense that I needed to return to my fourth love. I was still captured by the void and intended to draw out the feminine again, exploring the work of Keller who argues for the void as womb, when I met James. And I fell in love again. My fifth and last.

Asilah is Crushed
by the Darkness

But wait? Can we even be concerned with contradictions—that omniscient presence appearing from logic itself? When there is no middle, can it ever be excluded? If there is no x can not-x ever be framed? If there is no 'either' nor 'or' and there is not an 'and' to be found snuggling with a 'both' why should the void participate in logical necessities at all? There is no logical constraint. No physical possibility or impossibility. What a frightening beast that knows no law or restraint!

—Frau Professorin Heike Marquardt,
On the Void: The Theology of Nothingness

Asilah screamed when she saw the vicious wound. She reached down and touched the hole in his torso with her fingers. She sensed his life ebbing away. His eternal spirit was readying to depart the broken mortal body. She had failed. This was her fault—a botched responsibility she could not bear. She fled to the darkest regions of the solar system. For her lack of attention she screamed and wept and wished the rocks to fall upon her agony and bury her glorified body under a planet-sized ball of debris. She willed to be forever hidden. But the Spirit said, "You must not leave her." She returned. Nothing had changed. Nephi looked at her, his face a study in confusion hidden beneath a veneer of calm indifference.

Heike Shoots Arrow in the Heart—1st Time

The void seems to partake of a perverted type of nonexistence, one floating free, haunting us like a ghostly presence from the great beyond. Like a floater detached from our retina that flees our gaze whenever we try to get a glimpse, never to be captured but always there to mock our attempts to bring it into focus. Perhaps we are left with Wittgenstein's injunction: "What we cannot speak about we must pass over in silence." Although, I'm not sure we can ascribe silence to the void. Sound requires a difference from some other noise. Silence stands vis-à-vis sound. Where no vibratory note is possible, can the lack thereof be thought?

—Frau Professorin Heike Marquardt,
On the Void: The Theology of Nothingness

The flight to Arba Minch from Adis Ababa was not crowded, so Heike had both seats to herself. The loud hum of the engines caused a low vibration that could be felt up and down the seats lining the single isle of the small commuter plane. Heike, seated near a dirty window, looked out at the green patchwork of fields and forests below. She arrived in Ethiopia right after the rainy season, which meant that abundant, verdant greens of various hues dominated the landscape below. Nature's lushness was in full display this season of the year, and only the coffee brown of the rivers branching up into the highlands indicated that colors other than green existed in the world.

A tear rolled down her cheek, which she quickly dried with her hand.

Below her passed the Rift Valley. She could not keep herself from thinking about Lucy, the little Australopithecus whose human-like bones she had read about in a science magazine. The little hominid and her kind had roamed this land over three million years ago. What had her life been like? Heike was not interested in the little pre-human's material culture per se, or the day-to-day grind of making a living on the unforgiving plain below. Neither was she curious about what dangers the little ape faced or how it communicated with its compatriots. Nothing of these facets of her life held any interest for Heike. Rather, she wondered who Lucy had loved? Had there been someone in her life she cared about more than life itself? Was her brain large enough to think about that person endlessly? Did this person enter into each of her electrons and cause her subatomic particles to spin and weave in new directions after they met? When he returned from foraging, did they run together and embrace? Did they look into each other's eyes and, with grunts and gestures, promise that they would never leave the other? Did they raise children together? Did they make love under the stars of the expansive Serengeti plains, and did they press their bodies together breathless in that moment that has been enacted again and again since creatures crawled from primitive seas? In an explosive orgasm of ecstasy, did their cries pierce the night with a voice of love and passion?

Another tear rolled down her cheek, and she wondered if her ancient grandmother had experienced someone stealing a loved one of her own? Did some beast take him away? And then, in rage, what did she do to that beast? What vision of destruction did she harbor in her sorrowing heart? Did her days seem empty and vain but for her visions of the suffering she could, indeed would inflict on that beast?

Heike's mind wandered as her tears flowed. She thought of the Barrett M82 sniper rifle dismantled and resting in her suitcase among her panties, blouses, and slacks. She had purchased it in Norway from a man selling them from his farm. She did not ask him how he had gotten it.

She was now ready to kill the cowboy. It had been nearly ten years, but that was no matter. Love is timeless. Her theology training engrained that. And like love, revenge was conditioned on such endless durations. She was ready to kill this beast. As the plane descended into Arba Minch, she regained her cold control and dried her eyes. It was time at last to start to set the world right again.

After picking up her baggage, she walked to an area crowded with people entreating her with offers for taxies or to help with her luggage. She waved them away then found a short Ethiopian man holding a sign that said, "Ishigarro." He did not speak German or Japanese, so they spoke in English. She refused his offer to help with her only bag—an unusually long medium-sized carry-on—as they walked to a small parking lot in front to the terminal. He led her to a four-wheel drive pickup truck that she had made arrangements to hire. The vehicle was ready and fueled. The man from the rental agency continued to spend some time trying to get her to hire him as a guide.

"Many dangers and roads treacherous, much better you let me drive you, you enjoy the beauty of Park," he said as if pleading to save someone's life. He was right of course, she thought smiling, but taking a guide on *this* planned execution was probably not a good idea. Still, she regretted not letting him help her to the hotel. Making her way to the Arba Minch Spectator Hotel took her much longer then she thought it should. The dirt road into the city was muddy from recent rains, and there were numerous people walking near the sides trying to keep from stepping into the muddy pools that seemed as ubiquitous as craters on the moon.

The entrance gate to the hotel had a tall, handsome guard, who, when he saw her white face, waved her in.

Tourist hotel indeed, she thought. The room was squalid and dirty. In the corner was a bucket of water for washing and a shower head attached to a hose that drained into the tile floor of the room. The toilet stood in the other corner, again with a bucket and hose to flush the waste away. The hose leaked and had to be kept in the toilet to keep it from flooding the room. She could not imagine that there was a sewer system in this town, so when it was flushed the shit likely ran directly into a small stream she'd both seen and smelled as she came to the Hotel.

Over her bed was a moth-eaten mosquito net with enough holes that she had a hard time imagining that it would protect her from anything smaller than a bat. Luckily, she had brought her own just in case the hotel did not have one at all.

She took her clothing from her bag and unwrapped the disassembled pieces of her Barrett sniper rifle. She assembled it quietly sitting on her bed. She had become quite proficient at this. After learning from the man who sold it to her how it operated, she had spent hours taking it apart and putting it back together again. With the permission of a friendly farmer, she had spent a great deal of time firing at targets at various distances. She learned to clean it thoroughly after each day's practice. She was a very good shot. To Ethiopia, she brought only four rounds, each harboring an evil-looking steel-cased sabot. She didn't need an arsenal. Given the practice she put in, she was pretty sure she would only need one of the four rounds to complete her mission.

The gun felt good in her hands. She sat on the bed and aimed it out of the window through a slit in the curtain mostly covering the window. The sun was bright enough she thought it unlikely anyone could see her in the shadows of the room, so she scoped in on a monkey swimming in the fountain of the common area. With the scope, she could see its eyelashes glistening from the water. This would do.

She put the rifle under her mattress; then, placing the Do Not Disturb sign on her door, she walked over to the hotel's bar and restaurant. She sat down and ordered a glass of wine, a plate of local fish, rice, and some fried plantains. The wine was not very good, the plantains tasted starchy and overcooked, but the fish was delectable, and she liked it well enough she asked for another. Afterwards, she ordered a Heineken and sat and listened to a group of tourists from Taiwan singing karaoke covers of Elton John, Carol King, and James Taylor standards. To her surprise she discovered she was enjoying it. After four more beers, they coaxed her onto the stage where she offered a fairly decent rendition of Pat Benatar's '*Hit Me with Your Best Shot*,' which got her giggling at its current relevance. During the remainder of the evening, she was having such a good time that for a little while it slipped her mind that in the morning she was going to kill a man.

Although they spoke only English in common, she had a great time with her new friends. By the time they broke up to return to their rooms, they made plans to get together the next day. But when she got back to her room and saw her bed, she remembered what lay under the mattress, and the smile drained from her face. She would not be staying long enough to party with them again.

In the morning, she felt like shit. Her travel alarm went off at about 4 AM, but she could not drag herself out of bed. She stood up and felt a little queasy, so she stumbled groggily over to the toilet and vomited violently. She felt a little better so climbed back under the mosquito net and slept a little longer.

Before dawn's light she awoke to strange and breathtakingly beautiful music. And even though the music was clearly coming from a rooftop PA system, its power could not be distorted by its conveyance. A deep, passionate voice resonated through her little room. She gathered that it was coming from a nearby church or mosque, but she could not even guess the tradition from which it came. The sound contrasted with the smell of burning wood that seemed to seep into every space in this city. It sounded otherworldly and exotic, but one thing was clear—it partook of Holiness. The sublime. It reminded her of chapel when she was in divinity school. She had joined a choir, and they practiced several times a week before dawn. On winter mornings the chapel seemed cool, almost cold, but for some reason she especially loved it then. It felt more medieval, as one of her classmates accurately described it, and maybe that was it—it brought her closer to her favorite composer, or really, second favorite because Bach would ever be solidly first. But her second favorite was nearly as dear: Hildegard von Bingen. As she had sung these songs in the deep darkness of January, there was a sacredness about them. The void was thick in Hildegard's music—an unaccountable, hollow center that she had decorated with such tonal beauty that it penetrated to the core of Heike's soul. And this even though she did not believe in a soul of any kind.

How strange then to be here in Ethiopia, more than slightly hungover in an uncomfortably warm room, with the smell of burning wood mingling with a trace of sewage all around, and the otherworldly music coming from an unidentifiable source, to find that same holiness that she knew from Germany. She crawled onto her knees and recited the Lord's prayer to God the Mother. She felt strengthened, even though she had renounced a formal deity in favor of the Nothingness of the Void. Sometimes she forgot that she had, and the music had drawn this spontaneous and unexpected response out of her. It helped that she was not a dogmatist about any of her beliefs—able to roll with the flow of her spiritual inclinations. She still remembered the visit of the Goddess so long ago in Sweden, and she held to this, even though it conflicted with her reasoned theological commitments. What was it that the American poet had said, "I am multitudes?" and "If I contradict myself, then I contradict myself?" The beautiful song continued for nearly an hour then stopped abruptly, leaving a rich contemplative stillness.

As in the fabled princess's confrontation with the pea, she could feel the presence of the gun beneath her under the mattress like a ghost—felt but not apprehended. She did not question her resolve to end the life of the cowboy, but she wondered what changes it would make to her psyche. She knew there would be effects and that she would suffer them, and these she would endure gladly. Still, it was unclear to her what they would be.

A rooster sounded nearby, so she crawled from beside the bed. The music seemed to have restored and rejuvenated her from the effects of alcohol last night. She gathered her things quickly and packed them away. She stepped out of her room's porch and looked quickly around to see if others were about. No one was. She ran her suitcase out to the truck, then checking again for others, she ran her now fully assembled rifle back to her vehicle. The first glow of the rising sun was starting to appear in the eastern horizon. She hurried into the lobby and banged wildly on the desk bell until a sleep-addled man appeared in the doorway from a back room and stumbled to the front desk. She explained that she was leaving and wanted to check out. He protested that it was too early, but an extra 1000 birr added to her bill persuaded him that it would be worth his trouble. In the name of expediency, she paid nearly triple the price she told him she paid for her dinner and drinks because the restaurant had not brought over the bill from last night, but she had other things to attend to and was not willing to quibble. So she paid the amount despite it being higher than any individual could even imaginably eat and drink. Even so, it took nearly a half hour to get checked out. The sky was glowing brightly when she exited from the hotel's green steel gate.

She headed north on paved Highway 7 following the shore of Lake Abaya for a while but then took a dirt road toward Chencha, a very small town in the foothills above the lake. The land was covered by small agricultural plots, still being plowed by oxen. She pulled off the road to get her bearings and check her detailed topo maps. She began making her way to the site where the Cowboy would be dousing cattle with pesticides to control tsetse flies and ticks. It was her luck that the paper in Wien had done a write-up a few months ago about the Bad Mormon's work helping African ranchers control cattle pests. The paper had given enough details to figure out that on the first Thursday of every month, Arrow Beamon personally supervised the spraying of the cattle. It only took a couple of phone calls to the Ethiopian office of agriculture in Arba Mench pretending to be a reporter to get the location for today's spraying. It was located near a village called Shara Shara in a large field below a steep escarpment. Herders would bring their cattle from many kilometers away to get this free government insect treatment for their animals.

She did not really notice the patches of thick forests with tall trees emerging to capture the abundant tropical sun. She did not notice the variously colored butterflies flitting about flowers blooming from the verdant ground. The varieties of green were stunning, so many shades and nuances of color, from emerald to dark lime. These she missed as well. She did not notice the expansive homes in the villages of the Oromo people made completely of sticks. She saw these things, and knew peripherally that she should notice them and actually felt fairly guilty that she was not engaging with them as she should, but now was not the right time.

On the dirt road, she climbed the large escarpment in the truck. She noticed an expanse of forest below her and decided she had better test her weapon before she tried to end James' murderer. She had not passed another vehicle since she left the highway. A few times along this road, she had passed occasional pedestrians carrying loads of firewood, or barefoot children dressed in worn pants and well-worn t-shirts, but it was only a few. She wanted to think about this too, so earmarked it for thought later, after her deed was done. Poverty, inequality, and injustices that placed her in a Bavarian home living in comparative luxury and these children born into poverty of a kind she knew she could not comprehend. But again she thought, not now. She pulled off the road and waited to be sure that she was alone then pulled her weapon out of the truck.

She unfolded the two-leg stand attached to the front of her rifle and lay down on the forest floor. She sighted in on a small hole in the trunk of a large umbrella thorn acacia about 1000m away on a dry patch between two gullies. She pulled out her range finder, and sure enough it was 1030m away. The gun was accurate to 2000m, so this was a good test.

The hole was situated high up, just below the first fork, which then expanded into the characteristic flattish canopy of this tree. A shot like this would let her see if she had put the gun together correctly, as well as ensuring that the scope setting was still sighted-in properly after the rifle's long trip from Europe. After a couple of hairline adjustments, the scope magnified the hole nicely and she steadied herself for a well-practiced shot. Her brain had committed her to the shot, and she was already pulling the trigger when she registered movement in the hole. But it was too late, the bullet was on its way already and she could not change her mind and communicate it to her finger in time to change the fated trajectory. Before the kick had thrown off her view of the hole through the scope, she saw an explosion of feathers in and about the bole hole. She quickly sighted back on and could see a few feathers decorating the sides of the hole and on the ground at the base of the tree. She had killed a feathered thing.

She stared in horror. She had shot a bird of some sort. She stood up. Then she got back down and looked at the hole through her scope again. Then she set that gun down on a log, stood up, and ran to the truck, but then realizing she shouldn't leave the gun, turned around and went back to the weapon. Then she went back to the truck, unlocked it, and put her rifle in the cab. Her hands were shaking. She wrung them and then squatted on the ground moaning and crying. She had not meant to kill one of the Goddess's creatures. Finally she got the gun back out and looked through the scope again; then she took off down the hill, running and tripping, toward the tree. It took her nearly 45 minutes to reach it. The vegetation was not so thick as to impede her progress except in short patches, but the tree was a little over a kilometer away, and the terrain was steep. She kept sliding. When she finally reached the tree her pants were torn. One knee had an ugly gash. Both elbows were skinned, mostly because both times she tripped she protected the gun more than her body.

The hole was about four meters up the trunk, and there was no way to reach it. At the foot of the tree lay several feathers. She picked up a soft wing feather, brownish grey tinged with green. Her eyes glanced up at the dreadful sound that greeted her—baby birds clamoring to be fed. Her hand began to shake, and she sat against the trunk and sobbed. Of course the bore hole had a bird in it. It would have as well in Germany. If she had been there she would have assumed it was the home of a woodpecker, an owl, or a cuckoo. It might have had a red squirrel or any number of inhabitants. Why had it not occurred to her that it would be true in Africa as well? She looked at the feather, then up to where the baby birds were making such a racket; there was nothing she could do.

"What kind of bird were you?" She asked the feather sobbing. In Europe she could have named every bird that could have shed a feather. She could have named the species if she'd heard even a snippet of song. But here, she was helpless.

She had to go. The hole was too high, and there was no more time. She'd lingered already far too long. She had something odious to kill. Something that deserved death—not like this bird.

She marched back up the hill, tears streaking her face the whole way. She did not mean to kill the bird. Once again, the harm from this slimy GI had even reached out to take this bird's life. The tendrils of his crime continued to spread like arms of some mythical cephalopod—from her beloved James, to a harmless African bird. She would end his reach today.

When she got to the truck, there was a small boy, maybe 10 or 11, standing beside her truck. He greeted her, then tried to ask questions, but she did not understand what he was saying even though she was pretty sure it was English. When he saw what she was carrying, his mouth fell open and he began to back quickly away. She tried to signal him that she meant no harm, but he was obviously scared to death. She smiled at him and in English said in a soothing voice. "Hallo! Hallo! I have this to protect me from lions! Do you understand? Lions." But he kept backing away. Suddenly he bolted down the road. She did not wait for him to return. She got back in the truck, started it, and continued to her rendezvous.

It was only about five kilometers to the top of the escarpment. She thought she had better not leave the truck out in the open where it could attract attention. She found a small two-track road that headed south. She followed it a hundred yards into some dense vegetation in a thicket of trees that, with a little rearranging of some branches, did a passible job of camouflaging the truck. She grabbed the gun, a canteen, and a bag of dried fruit and nuts and climbed back up to the road that she had come in on. She crossed it and made her way to the edge of the embankment, which looked down on the large area where the cattle would be brought for treatment. She found a nice rock outcropping that made a wonderful stand from which to take her shot. Providentially, it even had a flat rock on which to rest her gun to steady its aim. It was all going to work out.

She took the rifle out of its case again. She set up her shot on the rock and watched the activity gathering below through her scope. She could see the large hoof-trampled, vegetation-free field to which the herders were driving their cattle for treatment. A fairly large crowd had already gathered but there was no sign of her American. He wasn't due for another half an hour, so she had been told, so she settled back to wait. She took out her topo map and planned her return to Arba Minch. She did not want to chance driving by the child that had been standing by the truck. It was unlikely, but she didn't want anyone to see the license plate when she left. He might have recruited some of his relatives, and when word of her killing the monster spread they might try to detain her. She'd been seen with a gun by the child. However, there was little to worry about—the place was filled with unimproved roads. Finding a way out by means of another route was trivial.

She watched the people arrive with the large, mostly reddish or white, cows. Some were the same kind of soft blond cattle that might be found in Switzerland grazing in an Alpine forest. Others resembled a kind of dun Brahman with a large hump topping its shoulders, and high, thick half-moon horns rising from its head like a cherub's wings. A white beat-up compact pickup truck pulled into the area—the only vehicle she'd seen. Her heart skipped a beat thinking this might be him. Three men, all black, climbed out and set up a small table at the edge of the field in front of which people formed a queue. The man opened a large ledger and began, apparently, to take names.

The place had a festive air. There were children playing. And even the cattle seemed rather playful and excited, some lowing and mooing loud enough for her to hear. She could see the road leading up to the field. She saw another vehicle approaching. That would be him. Surely. But no. Two more Africans got out of the truck then took several large white carboys out the back, donned yellow elbow length rubber gloves, and began mixing things. They took a large backpack sprayer out of the truck and loaded it with the chemicals they had just mixed.

She took out one of the steel-coated armor piercing rounds she had selected for the cowboy, pulled back the single action bolt, placed it on the guide, and chambered it by pushing the bolt forward, fixing it in place by then pushing the bolt action down. It was now ready to enact her revenge.

Heike was starting to panic. Where was he? He was at least fifteen minutes late now, and things seemed to be proceeding just fine without him. The article that had given her this idea claimed he was always there to help supervise. If so, where was he?

The man with the sprayer walked up to a large cow and placed five parallel lines of white pesticide down the beast's back. She thought about the bird she had killed. She thought about James and his death. This can't be happening. She had made meticulous plans for this, and now they were about to be ruined. The treatment of the cattle was going on. And there was no cowboy.

Then he came riding up on a donkey followed by a group of laughing children. This was her first actual sight of the man who had done so much harm, but she had seen his picture many times. Even so, she expected a larger man for some reason, as if his size should have been proportioned to his evil. He was of average build, not skinny or fat. He had had on a cowboy hat, jeans, and a white shirt. His hat had fallen off as he entered the field, allowing her to confirm that it really was him. She had memorized his image from photos—now she was face to face. A child brought his hat back to him, He put it on, hamming it up a bit with a goofy face. His hair was dark brown and he wore... really could it be? Cowboy boots. He lived up to his name. She was surprised how handsome he was. He had that easy, rugged, confident air exuded by American film cowboys from the 50s. He rode up to the men who had come earlier and dismounted. He tied the ass to the window frame of one of the trucks and began a conversation with the man wearing the pesticide sprayer.

But he was surrounded by children. They seemed smitten with him. Of course, he was a real live American cowboy. She supposed, like her, they had managed to see a western or two in their lifetimes. She screamed in rage. She was too far away to be heard, and her voice was carried away on the wind. But the people below must have felt her sorrow and despair and anger from here.

She had not pictured children present. In fact, westerns never had children on cattle drives. Somehow, similar to her failing to think about the possibility that there might be a bird in the bole hole she had fired on, she had never even considered there might be others present. If asked, she would have supposed there might be a few herders about, but she had not pictured it this way. Not so festive. Not children. Not little boys and girls laughing and thickly gathered around him like pigeons to a spilled popcorn bag. He was now passing out tootsie rolls like a Fasching

Narr. She screamed in rage again. All her planning. All her preparations were wasted. She would not shoot him in front of the children. What that kind of violence would do to them was too much for her to contemplate. Scarring them so was not in her nature. Tears poured down her face again. How could this have happened?

Then a miracle. As she watched through the scope, he said something to the children. They all laughed, and he walked away from them. They all remained with the man who had started again to spray the cows. The killer was walking toward her. Walking toward the edge of the field. She knew instantly he was going to take a pee. Her mind exploded with joy. She counted down the distance. He was 30m from the edge. 20m. 10m. He had entered the thick vegetation at the edge of the field, but he was still perfectly visible from her angle. Still facing her, he pulled out his penis and started to pee. She could see the thick urine stream glistening in the sun. When she had arrived, she had used the range finder to measure the distance to the center of the field—about 980m from her. She estimated he had come 50m closer. She centered the cross hairs on his chest then made a field adjustment based on her estimate of the distance. She'd done this a thousand times in practice. There was no wind, so she did not have to add the windage. This was an easy shot. Just as he put his business away, she squeezed the trigger. The kick was violent enough it took her a moment to look through the scope again and find him to see what happened. After locating him again she saw him lying straight back on the ground, his head resting amicably in his felt cowboy hat. It annoyed her that his arms were spread wide like a Christ figure. He was no Christ. But there it was, and she smiled as she noticed a moist red dot centered on his chest expanding through his clean white shirt.

The gunshot had not really attracted any attention. Guns were not uncommon among the herders who used them to kill predators that might desire a quick meal on a young calf. No one had come running over to help the Bombmaker, whom they could not see lying on the ground.

She stood up and quickly made her way back to the truck. She had scouted out a new way back to Arba Minch on another of the dirt roads that crisscrossed this country. As she approached Highway 7, she crossed a small log-and-plank bridge. She quickly took her rifle apart and tossed the parts into the stream running under the bridge. Then she got back into the truck and went directly to the airport. Her plane didn't leave for six hours so she would have time to do a little reading. Then she remembered the bird, and tears sprang to her eyes, and she could not help but let out a sob on its behalf. Then she smiled, remembering who else had died.

Two Divine Failures

Nephi stared at the man lying on the ground. There was frantic activity all around him and lots of hurried and frantic conversations as they worked to cut the bloody shirt away from his body.

"Is he alive?"

Nephi turned to see who had addressed him. His face became a tragic mask of surprise and hurt and despair and frustration and doubt.

"Asilah," he finally said, "Have you come here to mock me? Nephi fails the test again? He's given one charge: watch over a drug rattled ex-con, and he can't even do that. The simplest of tasks. What a fool."

"Are you done?"

"Yes Goddess. I'm done."

"Is he dead?"

Nephi stared silently at the still figure on the ground. He finally answered, "Who can say. The wound is very bad, and he is far from help."

"What have you done to help?"

Nephi watched another minute before answering. Then he said, "The usual. I inspired those around him to draw on their best medical knowledge. I gave a heart surgeon in Adis Ababa an impression he should go to the hospital early in case he was needed. I lulled a helicopter pilot into a longer sleep when he should have left twenty minutes ago, so he's still here. I've sent the Comforter to a few of the children who loved the cowboy and found him distorted and bleeding on the ground. And now I'm waiting for a glimmer of consciousness from my charge to offer comfort, hope, and the will to live if he should awake. Did I miss anything? Isn't that why you're here, because someone said the Angel Nephi has failed again and now his charge is on the ground dying? Send a Goddess to straighten him out. Is that it?"

He was surprised she was weeping. He had the impression it was not about him at all. Something was wrong.

"Goddess Asilah?"

"You did not fail, Nephi. It was me. My charge has done this."

"I don't understand?"

"She was the lover of James Fields, your charge's second cousin."

"He's repented of that. It's not remembered. It was an accident."

"She has neither forgiven nor forgotten."

Nephi stared at her. He didn't know what to say. She was a Goddess. How does an angel help a Goddess?

"You were supposed to stop her from doing this?"

"I didn't know she planned it. I thought she had made progress, and I was letting it flower. She did this so suddenly. I didn't...Stop her? Who stopped you?"

Nephi turned away sadly, his mouth tight and bitter. He did not respond.

She was weeping harder.

Finally, Nephi said with some softness, "You are a Goddess."

She looked at him, her eyes set in anger. She then said curtly, "Yes I am."

And with that she was gone.

Interlude—
Alma Lune's Love Story

I saw him first in my weightlifting class at BYU. I had just returned from my mission in South Dakota, and this was my first semester since my return. I'll never forget my first view of him standing before the big mirror in the back of the classroom doing curls with an over 100-pound straight bar. He was wearing the bluish-gray standard BYU athletics-issue t-shirt with its matching blue shorts. His bare calves were strong and well defined. He was sweating slightly, his short hair muffed like he had just gotten out of bed. After that I could not keep my eyes off him, and occasionally I would catch him looking at me. He would return a half smile then turn away demurely. About half way through the semester we started talking, and after a while we were spotting each other on the bench press and hanging around after class to chat about this and that. He was a returned missionary too. He had served in Italy. We started meeting for lunch and dinner and then going to the movies. The first time he reached over and took my hand we were watching *E.T.* I remember the fear. I remember the excitement. I remember the sense of terror that this was a sin, and the absolute conviction that I would never love anyone like this ever again.

We kept our love a secret from both our families. Mine lived in Bountiful and his in Salt Lake, where his dad served as an Area Authority. We lived a double life. We were at BYU, and this was the 80s—and what we were doing was considered a perversion. We moved into a small basement apartment. To the world, we looked like a couple of clean-cut students living like thousands of the Mormon archetype all over Provo. But in every sense, he was my husband and I was his. We made love endlessly, and it was bliss. I don't remember what happened exactly. It was the church though. I still believed in it. I wanted to be good again. I wanted to feel the spirit I felt on my mission. He would have none of it. And suddenly, almost like the snap of a twig, he was living in New York, and I was in Boston working on my MBA. Although we were not geographically far from each other, we did not communicate for almost a year. A horrible year. My only solace was the church. I was in a great ward, and they made me the elder's quorum president in the single's ward. I loved my work. I felt like I was doing good things. It felt important. I knew the things I did for people mattered.

Then one day I got a letter from him. I could not even breathe. I set it on the table and started to cry. I was afraid it would be what I wanted it to be, and scared to death that it would not be. Finally, my hands shaking, I opened it. It was a cautious letter. Newsy, chatty, careful but hopeful. He was living in NY doing odd work, mostly as a waiter, or sometimes doing retail of various forms. He joked he was the NY stereotype, trying to land a part in a play, just like everyone else. I returned a similar letter, and soon we were exchanging letters almost every week. They were simple, and we talked around what I think we were both trying to find. Then they stopped. I wrote a few times more, but they remained unanswered and, sorrowfully, I gave up trying. I thought about taking the train down to New York. Just to find out what had happened to him. But I never did.

Then one day I got a phone call. He said his name was Mike and that he was a friend of Kye Holmberg. I could hardly talk but learned that Kye was very sick. Dying, he said. He said he kept asking them to contact me. I said I would be there in the morning, and they gave me their address.

⊃ ⋈ ⚹ ⋈ ⊂

I found him blotched and hollow-eyed, his skin pallid and dank, his arms covered in violet sores. I found his mouth covered in wounds and his soft hair falling out. His voice was weak. His breath like the wisps of a bicycle tire pump, broken as if on each word the pump had to be lifted and pressed to get the words to hiss from his mouth. When I arrived, I reached out and took his feverish hand and stroked it softly, like the head of a purring cat. He was burning up. Despite the smell, I leaned in to kiss him but he turned away and rasped out a firm No. "I have the disease." I knew he did. I didn't care. I just wanted to hold him again, but he cried and said it would destroy him if I came down with it.

Days of horror followed. I stayed in his room on an old green cot we picked up at the Army and Navy thrift store. His good roommates hired a nurse to dress his bed sores and change his linen. We took turns reading to him from *Middlemarch*, his favorite book. We sang him songs, sometimes with the guitar accompaniment of his transvestite queen flat mate, Sylvia Stench, whose voice was angelic, sultry, and sad. Nevertheless, he began to hollow out, and his spirit just barely clung to a pile of ragged flesh and bones and seemed more and more often ready to flee him and abandon the cause of keeping him on this side of the veil. It was like watching him being burned alive by a very slow fire. I thought how this was happening all over. All over the world. People were being burned slowly to death, and other people thought it was a just punishment for their sins. A slow, terrible, lake of fire and brimstone. And no one cared. They were just watching as bystanders as their children were being destroyed slowly by wretched flames.

On the day before he died, he made me promise to go see his mother and tell her that his last thoughts were of her. I chided him and argued that he could not know what his last thoughts would be about? He knew.

Early that morning, I awoke to a terrible smell and a sound I'd never heard a human make. A loud forced breathing, on the verge of gurgling, but shallow, as if the air were traveling through the hookah his roommates used from time to time. I jumped up, and he did not respond to my attempts to wake him. I don't remember if I called out for his roommates, but they were soon around him. One by one we began to tell him what he meant to us. How glad we were he came into our lives. We cried and held hands and then told a few jokes, then we all just waited. Not long. Suddenly, his breath became different and lost its rolling cadence and became choppy. Then it stopped.

⊃ × ⚹ × ⊂

It took five years for me to visit his mother. I told her about his last hours. They hadn't talked since he had come down with "that" disease. His mother cried and suddenly begged God to forgive her for failing to be the kind of mother who would have kept her son from the temptations that destroyed him. His father showed no emotion and seemed to not want to hear any details about his son's death. He asked how I knew him, and I explained we had not seen each other in years, but I was his college roommate. His father was high in the church and at that time an assistant to the Quorum of the Twelve Apostles. He asked what I did, and when I explained I was working in finance. He became very interested in that, and he suddenly offered me a job at the church under one of the lead financial managers. Out of the blue. I took it. I wanted change. I wanted the church back in my life. After his call to the Twelve a couple of years later, I became his assistant and grew, despite all his oddness, to love the old man. The father of my only love became my charge and care. So much of what I do for this apostle is to honor the memory of my husband and do for him what I think his son would want done. My husband, who, despite all doctrine to the contrary, I know waits for me in the next life.

Arrow in Moab

There is no terminology we can use. No set $A = \emptyset$ in which this monstrosity holds for

$$\mathscr{R}_1 \colon \forall \epsilon > 0 \; \exists \; \{U_n\} \; \left(A \subset \bigcup_1^\infty U_n \; \wedge \; \sum_1^\infty |U_n| < \varepsilon \right),$$

or sadly, for any $\mathscr{R}_2$ or $\mathscr{R}_3$ or on and on we go until... $\mathscr{R}_\infty$ or why stick to math? We can go further and say there is no set of fluffy cats or non-existing unicorns that will let us recover the void we are looking for.

—Frau Professorin Heike Marquardt,
On the Void: The Theology of Nothingness

Arrow sat on one of the chairs near the curtain at the back of the chapel that separated it from the cultural hall. No one sat near him. People were friendly enough in a false sort of way, but he had no expectation that he should be treated better by his fellow saints, because he did not treat himself any better. He had done a terrible thing, and most of the people in his ward had heard some version of his crimes. They all knew he had personally murdered, or participated, or at least helped in his mother's cousin's murder. His role varied from directly putting a bullet in his head, to pointing him out to members of the Red Army Faction because they were gunning for James—a true American hero. He didn't try to clarify things. Both his parents had died while he was in the German prison. Some claimed they died from a broken heart, and his mother's heart attack came when he was first incarcerated, lending some credence to the claim. His father had died of pancreatic cancer about three years later. He was their only son, so had inherited their trailer, and the small lot on Spanish Valley Drive where he was now staying. No one came to visit him, not even his home teachers, and when he passed a ward member at Miller's Grocery Store or City Market they pretended not to see him.

After being shot in Ethiopia, he had lost everything. It took almost a year for him to recover physically, but the panic attacks made it impossible for him to continue his research or teach his classes. At first it was believed that one of the rebel groups operating near Sudan had gunned him down in a random act of revenge against Western colonialism. However, the forensic analysis by a detective brought in by the University of Wien to assess the situation for the safety of their faculty discovered something odd. The bullet was from a high-powered sniper rifle. A boy from a nearby village claimed to have met a western woman, or maybe Asian, who had such a gun. The detective, knowing that the gun was likely disposed of, offered a $500 dollar reward to anyone that recovered it—an enormous sum in the local economy. Men, women, and children began scouring the countryside for miles around. Every river, cave, and patch of forest was searched thoroughly. On the second day, it was found by a group of six teenagers who, walking arm and arm down the local streams barefoot to see if they could find it, hit gold. The rifle was scrubbed of markings. Checking passenger manifests for the first few weeks they found eight people who seemed likely to have a connection. All of them had alibis.

Who wanted him dead? That it was someone targeting the Baader-Meinhof Red Army Faction seemed certain. Why kill him? He was a loser US GI who just wanted to get high and had done terrible things, but why kill him? He had not narced on anyone. He had not been involved in anything. It made no sense, but all the evidence, it seemed to him, pointed to a paid assassin sent to target him. Why?

Arrow partook of the sacrament. Several people were subtlety glancing to see if he would after Sis. Pine's powerful talk last week on King David and how he, because he murdered Uriah, had forfeited the Celestial Kingdom. She looked at him the whole time, her eyes daggers. As water passed his lips, Brother Pine gave a powerful "hmph" and visibly shook his head.

Arrow did not care. He had other things to worry about.

The panic attacks pushed his wife beyond what she could bear. It had not been a good match, and their year together as husband and wife alternated between chaotic turbulence and erotic delight. They had no children, and shortly after he said he was giving up teaching and research she told him she could not take it anymore and left. Ups and downs. Mostly downs, outside the bedroom. They had not talked since she walked out the door.

He spent another six months in Wien trying to salvage his career, but it was not working. He could not focus. He became afraid to leave his apartment for fear the assassin might strike again. About this time, his parents' lawyer called and said there was a buyer for the land and trailer and asked for Arrow's approval to have the renters removed to finalize the deal. It was then that Arrow decided to return to the place of his roots. He knew he would not be welcome, and maybe he'd be no safer from a sniper's bullet, but at least he could go out in wide open spaces where he could see them coming. He'd get a good watch dog, maybe a Doberman pincer or a mastiff.

After the sacrament, he left church. He came for that ordinance alone. He'd stay sometimes, but since he'd been subject to the 'King David' talk last week, he was in no mood to endure the boredom.

⊃ ⋈ ⊬ ⋈ ⊂

He went home and was greeted by his Scottish Terrier, Fritz. No Doberman, but a good watchdog, and a more comfortable fit for his Kenwood Trailer.

He cooked a can of Campbell's Bean with Bacon Soup and dumped in an entire sleeve of soda crackers then stirred them together into a kind of light brown paste. He carried the bowl out to his porch and set it down on a TV tray next to a recliner. His porch looked out to the wall of sandstone that formed the rim of the Moab valley, and afforded a limited view of the horizon, just what he wanted. Even so he pulled out his 30×10 binoculars and quickly scanned some of the ledges and vegetation that might harbor a sniper. Nothing there but a fine specimen of raven sitting on a ledge and preening her feathers. He put down his binoculars, picked up his bowl, and ate it up, his terrier watching every move.

"Not for you, boy. This stuff gives you farts that are against the Geneva convention."

When he was finished he took the bowl to the kitchen and placed it in the sink, gave his dog a mug of dog chow, grabbed his copy of *Lord of the Rings* off his coffee table, and went back on the porch to read. He gave one more quick scan with the binoculars then buried his face in the book. It was his fourth reading since the shooting. Somehow this book from his teenage years grounded him, providing a place to go that brought some comfort. In Middle Earth, at least, the bad people were clearly defined. Gollum. Orcs. Trolls. Balrogs. When you were bad it showed up in your body's shape and form.

When the sun had fallen below the rim of the west canyon he went back inside, washed the bowl, and turned on the TV to watch M*A*S*H reruns on Nickelodeon. Fritz joined him. Just as the third episode was starting, his phone rang. Fritz and he looked at each other. Who could that be? The only calls he got were from an old high priest secretary (seemed to be too out of it to realize Arrow was a monster) to check up on whether he had done his home teaching. It was only mid-month, so it could not be him.

It hit suddenly and fiercely. His heart raced, and the world took on that aspect of raw terror that enveloped his whole being. It wasn't like the panic, which was nothing like regular fear or terror or anxiety or dread. It was more like an emotion from another universe, an emotion and feeling that had never existed before Ethiopia. Like a color that did not exist on earth and then suddenly shows itself, its newness made the world feel strange, alien, and other. It was as if his mind were being sucked into a black hole that squeezed his spirit until it was ragged and raw. Every time it happened, he was afraid it would never end. That it would get stuck. Like the universe was imposing a suffering that no one could bear. More than Christ had suffered. More than could be suffered.

The phone was still ringing. He picked up Fritz and walked toward it. He could not let it go unanswered. If it were a wrong number it would ease his mind, and if it weren't, at least he would know.

"Hello." He sounded like a man about to be executed.

"Arrow Beamon, you old coyote. Why didn't you tell me you were back in the area!?

The voice was unmistakable.

"LeRoy!"

"Who else! One of our old classmates said she saw you coming out the church last Sunday and told me you were around."

"I can't believe it! Are you still in Blanding?"

"Oh yeah. Six kids in ten years—don't say a word, I know what you are thinking."

"LeRoy, LeRoy I can't believe it. It's been a long time. I've been through some shit, man, some real shit."

"So I hear. But listen. I don't want to rack up a bill. Sister Stout will kill me if I run up phone charges too high. But hey, I'm coming up there for some church welfare meetings. I'd love to see you."

"Yes! Absolutely. We've got some catching up to do. Hey, how did you get my number. It's supposed to be unlisted."

"Well you won't believe this, but I'm a bishop, and I just called yours, and he gave it up without being tortured. Seemed sort of like he was surprised I was asking after you. When I told him we were high school buddies, he sounded like he was about to give me a 'tsk, tsk, tsk.' You staying out of trouble there?"

"You have no idea, but I'll fill you in when you get here. It's been a wild ride. Hey... Sorry I never answered you letters while I was locked up. I just... I just... Didn't feel...."

"No worries. No worries. I figured you were going through things. Don't you dare apologize, you hear? Things are square."

"Thanks LeRoy. It's good to hear your voice."

"Likewise. I'll see you Saturday around three after my meetings. We can go for a drive down the river and reminisce, maybe get a bite at the Sundowner, Sound good?"

"Sounds amazing. See you then."

ɔ ≍ ≁ ≍ ⊂

LeRoy and Arrow met at the Dairy Queen. They had not seen each other for years and yet, after ordering chili dogs smothered in onions, they were soon chatting and laughing like they'd never been apart. There was no hint that they had matured a bit, and they giggled and snorted like a couple of high schoolers. When LeRoy started blowing bubbles into his shake like back in the day, Arrow completely lost it. He started guffawing enough to draw looks of consternation from the manager as well as some embarrassed but appreciative smiles from the few other late Saturday afternoon customers. LeRoy, despite being the dignified bishop of a Blanding ward, was still LeRoy. Arrow found great comfort in that.

Things took a serious note as Arrow caught LeRoy up on the last few years, leaving prison, his degree, his research, and the assassination attempt.

"Can I see it?" LeRoy said, and Arrow pulled up his t-shirt above his chest. There was the wound. A small star of raised flesh marking the point the bullet entered. He then turned around in his chair and showed him the exit wound. This was a larger wound, but not by much. Arrow pulled his shirt back down.

"It almost ended me."

"I don't see how you survived. I mean, it seems like you would have needed like EMTs and great surgeons. I mean, it just missed your heart by like... what?"

"Like an inch. It passed right between the lower right atrium and the left side of my lung. The shock waves alone tore a hole in my lung and softened up my heart good, making my pericardium leak out. If I hadn't gotten stabilized I would have been a goner even though it missed the good stuff."

"I have no idea what all that means, but, wow. So who stabilized you?"

"I was up there with a couple of Uni vets I worked with, studying the incidence Bovine trypanosome...."

"In English?"

"I was up there with some cow doctors."

"That's better, mister college... and they just hit you with a cattle prod, and you jumped up good as new?"

Arrow laughed. "Yeah, to them I was just another big animal, and they stopped the bleeding, had me stabilized. They had enough connections to call in the park anti-poacher helicopter patrol to fly me to the park airfield for a plane back to Addis Ababa. Four and a half hours from bullet in the chest to being patched up at one of the best hospitals in Africa. If you knew the condition of things in Ethiopia, you would see this as an almost biblical level miracle. Parting the Red Sea is a cinch compared with getting stuff done over there."

"The Lord must have a plan for you my friend. I believe in miracles, but they are rare and used only in special occasions. You are being groomed for something big I bet."

Arrow looked uncomfortable and his gaze turned to look out the window.

"You remember how we used to drag main? Driving up and down this street? Turning around in the A&W?"

"I remember it well."

"Remember that time we talked Ol' crazy Lucibell into letting us tie a rocking chair to the roof of Rob's Corvair, and we went driving up and down with her sitting up there rocking back and forth?"

LeRoy shook his head, "We could've killed her."

"That's what is so strange. THAT never occurred to us. It was only something funny. Now, I shudder to think of the ways it could have gone wrong. We were flying at over sixty miles an hour at one point. If our lousy knots had come loose…"

"Man."

LeRoy looked at his watch. "I'd best be getting back to Blanding. Jezzy will wait up and…."

"It's too bad you can't stay the night. Remember Professor Valley and how we used to hike up there and get high—not that that has any appeal mind you, but the hike would be nice."

LeRoy looked thoughtful. The big window of the Dairy Queen was opening to the last rays of the sun striking the east rim of the Moab Valley from the west, lighting up the assemblage of red rock cliffs that formed the eastern wall sheltering this magical city. The burger place was in full shadow, which cast an easy calm on the darkening city. He got up from his booth without saying a word and walked to the cashier, who was standing there with the manager looking over some things attached to a clipboard.

"You wouldn't happen to have a roll of quarters, would you? I need to make a phone call," he said producing a ten dollar bill.

The cashier smiled but the manager gave a frown and answered curtly, "Do we look like a bank? Zion's Bank is a block North." He turned back to the clipboard.

"It's not open on Saturday," LeRoy said.

"Not my problem."

LeRoy returned to the table and smiled at Arrow, "Hey, let me call my Old Lady and let her know I'm staying the night. We'll grab some stuff and head up Professor Valley like old times. Hey. How does that sound? I just need to get some change to make the call."

Arrow was beaming. As if a blessing on the plan, the cashier walked over, glanced back cautiously to make sure the manager, who had disappeared to the back, was not watching, and handed LeRoy a roll of quarters. He quickly pulled his wallet back out and handed her a ten. She smiled and nodded to the roll he was holding, "We've got a ton of those. He's just an asshole." LeRoy mouthed a soft, whispered, "Thank you." She smiled and walked away.

⊃ ⤬ ⤙ ⤬ ⊂

By the time they purchased some camping supplies (including two sleeping bags—which Arrow was glad to pay for), stopped to picked up Arrow's dog, and drove to their destination in LeRoy's truck, it was nearly dark, and the sky was half-full of stars. They parked at the end of an old jeep road at the trailhead to Professor Canyon. The place was empty, so they decided just to camp there rather than haul their gear further up the canyon in the dark. And besides. What they really wanted to do was talk.

Arrow got a fire started using some driftwood collected on the high bank of a nearby bend of Professor Creek, piled and tangled there last year during a monsoon thunderstorm. The wood was dry, and once the fire was kindled, it provided a lively flame that produced a nice bed of coals more quickly than either man would have guessed possible. They talked of trivia as Arrow emptied two large cans of stew, a pound of hamburger, a package of all beef kosher dogs, two cans of tomato sauce, two raw yellow onions, a lot of Tabasco sauce, and salt and pepper into a

Dutch oven. Standard fare. LeRoy talked about his family, the doings of his children, the ups and downs of being a bishop, having pie with an apostle, his contentment teaching at the high school, his river running business in the summer, and his explorations of some Anasazi ruins he had discovered up a canyon on the San Juan. Arrow in turn caught him up on his life since prison: his PhD, his love of Austria, his wife leaving him when she couldn't deal with his being shot and the ramifications of someone hunting her husband, his return to the church, and the trials that had ensued because he was rumored to have murdered his mother's cousin. By the time they had gotten these preliminaries out of the way, the full moon had risen and dinner was ready.

They ate with the same gusto they would have as teenagers. Something about this particular concoction brought out their old selves, including a string of fart jokes and lots of loud oohs and hums.

"*Lecker, Lecker, Lecker!*" Arrow crooned.

"Are you cursing in German there?" LeRoy teased.

"I'm saying this is the worst thing I've ever tasted, and you are a bastard for making me eat it," Arrow deadpanned.

"There is one word for all that?"

"German is very efficient."

Having downed the entire cauldron's (their word) contents, they threw their paper plates onto the coals' red dancing glow and watched them blacken, and then flare into flame. The remnants of their meal boiled and bubbled until it sizzled into nothing. Soon, only the coals again remained.

Arrow took some more of the dry river-churned cottonwood branches and put them on the fire. In no time at all they were sitting around a merry dancing flame. The night around them was cool, but not cold enough to make them wish for jackets. They sat for a while in a comfortable silence, listening to the crackle of the fire and the buzzing of insects.

"Life is strange," LeRoy said with a sigh.

"That, my friend, is truth itself."

There was another silence. The moon was starting to light the landscape with a soft beauty that disclosed the sage-covered undulations of the hills that ran up to the rock formations that separated Professor Valley from Castle Valley. The La Sals could be seen rising in the background, their still white peaks glowing softly in the moonlight.

"This is God's country, and I have to say I'm glad you are back here. It's where you belong."

Arrow didn't respond.

"Do you know what you are going to do? I guess your university pension will keep you flush."

"Yeah. I was doing university business when it all went down, so it wasn't hard to argue that that's what ruined my ability to teach and do research. But I feel sort of guilty. Anyway, I haven't made up my mind to stay or not. My ward wants me to go, and their constant silence is an argument that I ought to go back to Austria. I'll never fit in here. I need the church more than ever now, and they aren't going to let me have it."

"Come to Blanding. Make a fresh start of it. In my ward, we'd never let you slow down."

Arrow smiled at his friend. "I think you'd keep me too busy. And thanks. But I think it's either here or Austria for me. I've got roots in both places, and I'm thinking that over there is where I belong."

LeRoy looked uncomfortable, "What about the freedoms this place gives? Won't you miss those?"

Arrow laughed, "What freedoms do you think I won't have? I've only noticed things I gain, like my prison education. And all the usual constitutional stuff about pursuing happiness we get in spades...."

"Yeah, I wasn't thinking about those kinds of freedoms, I was thinking about the freedom that the canyon gives, to be among ancient things, to sit under these stars," LeRoy waved his hands skyward, "to breathe the sage-scented air and wander in the La Sals? What about the magic of the rivers?"

Arrow went silent for a long time staring at the fire. He finally said, "Yeah. I do miss it. I think Navajo sandstone is running through my veins, instead of blood."

LeRoy nodded. "Yeah, me too."

"And you know what's weird? Even though my ward wants nothing to do with me... I'm so comfortable there. These people—many I've known all my life. But I grew up here and… I know their ways. I know how to move here. I speak their language in ways I'll never speak German because I speak it with my whole canyonlands body. It's weird."

LeRoy looked at this friend and said softly, "That is why you have to stay. This is your home. Why else did you come *home* here?"

Arrow picked up a stick and began rearranging the fire, pushing half burned logs into the hottest part of the coals and turning over others that were just burning on one side. When he was finished, he sat down and said, "I suppose I was looking for healing. Forgiveness. You know. I wanted to confess my sins and move on."

LeRoy nodded, then looked over at his friend and said, "Well have you?"

"Confessed?"

"Yeah."

"I set up an appointment with my bishop, and I was going to do it a few weeks ago, but when it was time to go… I couldn't. I just couldn't. How do you confess to someone you're quite sure hates you with all his heart?"

"Are you sure he really…."

"Quite sure."

Both men were silent, this time less comfortably. Suddenly, Arrow looked at this friend intently, his eyes lit dancing by the flicker of the flame.

"You could do it? You're a bishop? Right?"

"Technically, I only have stewardship over my ward in Blanding... but it's not unheard of where the bishop was somehow one of the wronged parties...."

"He was. He is. He is also one of my mom's cousins, well second cousin, or third with a couple of 'removed's in there, but it's as you say. He at least knew James... Fields... the guy I got blown up. So you could take my confession right?"

LeRoy got up and began pacing back and forth in front of the fire. Then he said, "Look, technically I should get permission first, but yeah, let's just do this, and if we get in trouble then so be it.... Yeah, this feels right to me.... Let's just do it."

Arrow got up and formally shook his hands, in an odd way transitioning from being in the presence of an old and dear friend to standing before his ecclesiastical leader.

"How does this work? Do we have to pray or something? I don't remember except when I was a teenager confessing I had succumbed to 'the temptation of masturbation' and the bishop went out of this way to make me feel awkward and shamed."

LeRoy smiled, "I'll try to keep the shaming to a minimum. So why don't we walk? We don't have to sit across from each other like it's a job interview or something. Let's just walk back up the road toward the river."

Arrow nodded, and both men stood up. Arrow grabbed his water bottle and filled it from the carboy in LeRoy's truck and then sprinkled a little on the fire, not to put it out, but to cool it a bit. There was no wind, so little worry about it raging out of control, and besides, even if there had been a breeze, the ground was barren enough that it would have taken some serious blowing to get the flames to anything that would catch.

The moon was high now, creating a patchwork of shadows among the sage and large boulders strewn across the landscape giving the appearance of a garden of squat shapes and voids, fissures of shade among lumpy effigies of rock goblins—none of which seemed malicious, but rather ancient, deserving honor and regard. The road, well-lit by the moon, wound its way through the sage and seemed to be offering a path to a kind of hope.

They walked a good ways down talking of trivialities when Arrow asked, "Well how do I start? Do I need to confess everything I've ever done or just big stuff?"

LeRoy got very serious. "The atonement of Jesus Christ is very powerful, and most things are handled through your relationship with him. Let's not start with sins, let's talk about his role in your life. If this is to be a proper confession, I want to understand why it matters. Why *you* think this will do any good. Do you have faith that Christ can heal you?"

The question seemed to surprise Arrow. He walked in silence for a while, then said, "I read in the Book of Mormon about how bad the Sons of Mosiah had been. Alma the Younger. That. It gave me hope that God could still have use for me. I read about their conversion and...." His voice cracked and he had trouble going on for a step or two but then continued, "Well, their faith in Christ gave me something to hope for."

LeRoy reached out and put one arm around Arrow and gave him a small hug meaning to offer a little reassurance, but Arrow stopped and faced him and pulled him close in a sob. LeRoy patted his back, then pushed him to arm's length and smiled.

"You've got the right of it. Good. So, to the sins. Don't feel like you have to dig up every little thing you've done, but obviously there are things weighing you down. Those are what you need to confess. Not for my sake or the Church's, but for yours. There is something about speaking them that disarms them. Tell me about what you still feel guilty about. Be honest with yourself."

They started walking again and Arrow started, "It's strange. I think about it a lot and I feel such a mixture of emotion. I feel like I don't feel guilty for the right things, and hate myself for things I could not control. Like James' death. It's complex."

"Tell me what you mean. I'm not following exactly. Are you saying you don't feel guilty for James?"

"I look back, and I can see a kid really locked into drugs in a big way. I see him making some bad choices. I see him thinking he was getting some explosives to help fight the Soviets... and hell... that's what I was doing in Germany anyway. I get to get some good drugs to see me and my buddies through a rough time on the border, and as a plus,

I get to strike a blow for democracy and apple pie. But then James, my mom's own cousin, is murdered! By the explosives I procured. The direct line of cause and effect is from me to James' death, but that was never my intention. What if instead of James dying, a bridge in East Germany was blown up. How would I feel? I suppose if I repented I would only feel bad for having been involved in drugs. Maybe something I would not even need to confess to my bishop. But I was tricked by some bad people. I was a link in a chain of events that, without me, James would still be the father to his family, but I didn't mean for that to happen. It's like going too fast on a dark road and hitting a guy walking you never saw. You didn't mean it, but you were going too fast. Normally your punishment for speed-ing would be a ticket, but this one time you kill a guy. It's like that. And as strange as it sounds, I feel guilty for not feeling guilty about James' death. Everyone blames me, and I blame myself, but how do I repent of something that wasn't intentional? Taking drugs is bad, sure, but lots of people did it. Hell, you did it, but I get James hung like an albatross around my neck for life. I wasn't like the Sons of Mosiah, actively trying to destroy the church and the people in it. I just wanted a good time. And now James is dead, my mom and dad died in shame, and I'm cut off from what I know I need—the people of Christ. That's what I want to confess. I want to feel the weight of guilt for this death, but I didn't do it. Rationally, the fault I find in my actions isn't a murder."

LeRoy smiled, "So your confession is you have nothing to confess?"

"Well not exactly. I got drunk once and cheated on my wife at a party visiting old friends in Köln. She was mad as hell for a while, but we worked through it, until I was shot and then things fell apart. I think my screw up might've hurried her decision to walk away, but I'm not sure. We always had a rocky relationship, even when we were living together in Uni. Oh, I guess I better confess that I lived with my wife for a couple of years before we married. But I've never felt much guilt about that, just the fling at the party, and I pretty much worked that through with my wife. I don't think about it anymore."

LeRoy was silent a long time, and Arrow didn't push him to answer. They came to small shallow stream that cut across the road, but neither felt like getting their shoes wet. So they walked upstream a bit to find a spot with enough rocks properly spaced to hop-skip across the water.

LeRoy finally spoke, "You feel bad about James' death?"

Arrow, "I feel horrible to breaking. I'm so sad he died. I'm filled with anguish that it happened. I feel awful that I was involved. But even though I was a direct line cause, I never wanted him, or anyone, to die. It's a mistake. But I didn't murder him. I just didn't. I did not plan the bombing. I did not pick the target. I never would have given the explosives if I would have known they planned to kill anyone, maybe even a Russian. They were going to blow up a bridge. How can I feel guilty that they used the monkey on my back to manipulate me? It's not like I planned his death or even slaughtered him in a fit of passion. But I still feel guilty. I still feel it is my fault. In my heart I still condemn myself like my neighbors do, but I don't know how to rationally accept the deed as mine? Is this making any sense?"

LeRoy looked at his friend, "This *is* complex. Why do you think you don't feel bad about cheating on your wife?"

Arrow looked out over the landscape. No judgment came from it. It just was. Accepting what it was given. Why can't life be like that.

"I think because the aftermath has all been healed. It may have even kept my marriage alive for a little longer. We were bickering a lot before, and after it gave us something to focus on. A point on the landscape that drew our attention from the lesser things eating up our relationship."

"Sand in the shoes."

"Exactly. It was big and dominated in ways that made us work through the small stuff. And now she's gone and just last month she remarried, and by all reports from our friends, she is happy. They are better suited than we ever were. So while I felt guilty at the time, things are mended for her...."

"And for you?"

"Well my life is a mess. I'm suffering from panic attacks, from paranoia about being gunned down in the middle of nowhere, changes in life like losing my ability to do research and teach, and to live with the burden that knowing my actions ruined lives so badly it killed my parents and makes me a pariah. So yeah, I'm not doing as well. But I didn't kill anyone."

LeRoy looked at this friend and stopped him by grabbing his shoulders. He looked into his eyes and spoke straightforwardly, as if commenting on the weather.

"No you didn't. You have nothing to confess. Go and sin no more. God has forgiven all. You are whole."

Arrow stared at him for a second them burst into tears. They held each other only a little while. Then walked back. Talking of when they were young. When life was nothing but potential.

The Kripo Call

So we have no symbols. No representational
devices will do. Our only access is death. Wait?
What's that? Death? That seems a bit of a cheat.
Doesn't it? Like in George Eliot's novel *Mill on
the Floss* in which the relations among the characters become so insoluble she gives up and unleashes the flood, drowning the town lock, stock,
and barrel.

—Frau Professorin Heike Marquardt,
On the Void: The Theology of Nothingness

Hello.

Mr. Beamon?

Yes?

*I am called Halim Kaya, with the Kriminalpolizei sta-
tioned in Berlin.*

The Kripo?

*Yes. I am investigating your shooting in Ethiopia in last
years and there may be a connection for your shooting and*

a group of murders in Deutschland. Is this a good time to some questions ask, or can we arrange a time being more convenient?

I'm not doing anything. Now would be fine. It must be late at night there.

Yes, very late. {some laughter}

I'm at your disposal.

Gut. Thank you. If it is convenient may we speak in German. My English is poorer than it should be.

Ja. Das geht.

Danke.

<translated from German>

Have you heard of the Baader-Meinhof Butcher?

Yes. Terrible. Do you think I was targeted by him?

Very possible, yes. Like the others killed, you were convicted in the deaths in the Frankfurt bombing by the Baader-Meinhof-Gruppe; all of those murdered were similarly involved.

I read that in the paper. How worried should I be?

There may be reason for concern. However, we have no direct evidence that you are in danger. Your recovery from the shooting was not widely reported here in Germany. It would appear you were the first targeted, but you stayed in Germany for nearly six months after, and no attempt was made on your life, so the killer may not know you survived. Especially since the person killed two people in that six month interval.

I hope you are right.

I have your report of the shooting, but I have some follow-up questions as the connection with the Baader-Meinhof-Gruppe was not known.

If I can help in any way I will.

There is some investigative information we have gathered that you are not yet aware of, and we ask you to not discuss these with others as we don't want our case revealed.

I understand and will comply with your wishes.

We believe the killer was a woman traveling under a Japanese Passport.

Japanese?

Yes. The passport was from Japan, but the name does not comport with Japanese records, and we believe it was a forgery. We believe she was a Westerner.

Of course, that's consistent with what I know from the previous investigation.

We have more details. Airline records suggest the woman arrived in Addis Ababa two days before you were shot. Ethiopia Air does not require passport verification to travel within the country, so we do not know if she drove or flew to Arba Minch, but she apparently used a false name if she flew, as none match the passport. There were a number of Westerners visiting the hotels near the national park, and we have no leads there. Records are poor, and nothing in our investigation stands out as relevant. The Japanese passport was used the day after you were shot to fly from Addis Ababa to Frankfurt and from there we have no information.

There was the boy who saw her. With a gun, was there not? She must have rented the car he described.

Yes, but he was not able to give a useful description of the woman. And no rental agency would admit that they rented to a Western woman that day. We suspect they feared the attention that came with your shooting, and also likely were operating under the table. All dead ends. Do you remember meeting any person that you didn't know in the days before you were shot? Oriental or Western?

No, I was visiting other encampments in the area doing the tick/tsetse treatments. I saw only Ethiopians for nearly a week before the shooting.

As you know, we believe your movements in Ethiopia were revealed in a news report on your work with tsetse flies, but was there anyone who would have known your whereabouts?

Just the vets I worked with, and I trust they would have told me if a stranger had been inquiring after them.

Could you give me their names and contact information?
Yes.

Have you been contacted by anyone that you do not know?

No. You are the first, which seems...

Sounds suspicious yes. I will have a verification of my credentials Fed-exed to you in the morning. Please send me the names of your Ethiopian contacts in the envelope that I will enclose.

Could you also send some of the news reports of the other killings? I would just like to see what's happened since I left.

Of course.

Do you have any other leads? Is there hope that she will be captured?

I will be honest Mr. Beamon, it does not look hopeful. She is very careful and very smart. And we are not finding any useful leads. We are tracking down loose ends, but nothing seems to be allowing progress.

I'm sorry to hear that.

As are we. We want very much to catch this monster. I thank you for your time. If I have follow-up questions, do you mind if I contact you again?

I don't mind at all. Thank you.

Thank you.

Goodbye.

Goodbye.

Heike, Having Honed Her Skills

That will clean up the muddle. Throw them into the void 'from which no traveler returns? eh? But in the void there is no time, for what could change to mark it? And there is no space, for what could move to define its extent? It defies all hope of getting a single hook into its domicile—so complete is its voidishness.

—Frau Professorin Heike Marquardt,
On the Void: The Theology of Nothingness

Heike turned out to have a knack for killing. She had just killed the last member of the August 4th faction involved in the death of James: Thomas Liedtke. She knew what the papers would say. There would be a review of the August 4th faction (after the fourth killing the press made the connection to the bombing that claimed James Field's life). The paper would then point out how horrific Liedtke's death was. How he was tortured. How the perpetrator was a psychopath. How there are no leads (she was very careful). They would have nothing to go on. Her and James' affair had been completely secret. There was nothing to tie the lovers together. He kept no diary, and hers was safely in her possession. They would have no reason to scrutinize her whatsoever. There was just no visible connection.

How had she come to enjoy killing? It was like this: she felt a measure of disappointment at the Cowboy's death. One minute he was standing there taking a piss and in the next he had entered the void. He did not suffer. He did not see his death coming. On the plane ride home, she realized he had gotten off too easy. He had not suffered as he ought to have; he should have at least understood why he was being killed, who was killing him, and why it mattered that he die. Hence the reason that she devised a more satisfying revenge for the others. She wanted to teach suffering. Much like God? Perhaps that was the right comparison. Did He not create a world with suffering beyond measure? Why then, when she retaliated against those who destroyed her life, should she not do the same? When she came to kill the woman right before the Cowboy, she had chickened out. She had killed the cowboy and it had opened her to possibilities. Her second murder would be done better, she decided.

The woman marked for revenge lived in an old apartment building sandwiched between two identical structures. An old stairway climbed up to the fifth floor; each floor had four doors leading to spacious Viennese-style apartments with high, excessive ceilings, tall doors, and massive windows that stretched upward from near the floor as if the glass simulacrum of a cupola. A mid-century elevator with an iron cage that serviced all the floors rose beside the stairway but appeared to be used only by a pensioner on the fourth floor.

Heike spent three days watching her. Her husband left at 7:30 AM. She dropped her child at school at 8:30 AM, then worked out at the spa for an hour and a half. Then she returned home shortly thereafter, perhaps stopping at a small market near her home for dinner supplies and a bottle of wine. She remained in her apartment until 2:30 PM, at which time she picked up her child.

The apartment building formed one of the walls of a small plaza in the center of the building, which had an access door to allow the garbage to be hauled out. This was loosely secured, and she had little trouble unsecuring it, allowing access to the woman's apartment. Two days before she planned to do the deed she placed fliers in secured envelopes in all the doors save her victim's that instructed the inhabitants to plan on being away the Thursday two days hence when the apartments would be sprayed with insecticide to stop a roach and bedbug infestation.

On that morning at 11:15, Heike rang the bell. When the woman opened the door she found Heike smiling broadly, wearing nothing but a swimsuit (she had put a pair of jeans and t-shirt and sandals behind the garbage can downstairs), her arms hugging her chest and her hand hidden in her armpit.

"*Hallo. Kann ich Ihnen helfen?*," the woman asked with an amused smile at the nearly naked woman standing before her.

Heike laughed and said, "*Perfekt. Ich habe ein lang zeit gewartet.*"

She drew the gun from behind her back and shot the woman in the shoulder. She tumbled violently backward into the attached kitchen. Seeing Heike walking forward she scrambled to one end of the kitchen crying in agony and fear.

Heike considered the woman, cowering in the corner, the white ceramic tiles stained with blood, mostly from the exit wound. The hollow point bullet had mushroomed into a far more serious wound then a more conventional round—like the one she had used on the Cowboy—would have made. The woman's eyes were staring at Heike in rage and terror.

"This is what I missed killing your American accomplice," Heike said. "You need to suffer. You need to atone for my loss."

The woman was trying hard to breathe, but some blood gargled out of her mouth. She had probably bitten her tongue when shot. In desperation, she screamed as loudly as she could, "Someone help me. Please. Help!" Then she gave a long scream.

"No one will hear you. Your neighbors have all gone away."

Heike placed the pistol on the kitchen counter and smiled at the woman.

"Why are you doing this?" There was a pant between every word of this pleading sentence.

"Why?" Heike asked philosophically.

"Because you killed James Fields. The love of my life. Because you killed my heart and stole everything from me. We might have had children. You know? Like you," Heike said.

The woman was silent.

"What is your daughter's name?"

"You leave my daughter out of this. She has nothing to do with this."

The woman found some strength in Heike mentioning her daughter and made a move to scramble to her feet. The topic of her daughter roused something. But she slipped on the blood pooling below her and fell hard to the floor. She was weeping and crying frantically now.

"Oh, my good woman, I will harm your daughter. I'll harm her by taking away her murdering mother. You know. But no. I will not lay a hand on her. I'll even call the police after I leave, to make sure it is not your little girl who finds the mess I make in voiding you."

The woman visibly relaxed.

"Thank you."

"Don't thank me. I do it for her, not for you. If I thought it worth the life of a little girl to give you more pain, I would. But let's focus on your physical pain for now. Shall we?" And Heike pulled a fish filet knife out of a block near the stove.

⊃ ⋊ ⋌ ⋉ ⊂

She did not know if toe prints left something like fingerprints, but she pulled off the short socks the woman was wearing and put them on her feet. She had tracked some blood around the kitchen, and she used the harsh cleaner she used on the woman's eyes to mop it up carefully (holding onto the mop with a dish towel so she did not leave any prints there either). She wiped down all she touched and then padded into the shower and took a long hot shower. After carefully checking to make sure she left behind no evidence, she left the apartment with the few things she brought or touched like the gun and knife. She walked down the stairs, came to her clothes and put them on. The street outside the apartment building was empty, so she entered the sidewalk and strolled for about a mile with a breezy determined air, then used a payphone not visible from the street to call the police. Another four miles, brought her to a bus stop, where she waited impatiently before boarding a bus to the train station from which she took a train home. At a stop along the way, she disembarked and threw the murder weapons into a long, slow river, then boarded the next train for home. She knew she would never be caught. One by one she ended the other members of the August 4th faction and now she was done. She would return to normal life.

⊃ ⋉ ⊀ ⋉ ⊂

Several months later Heike watched her dog run through a new K9 park that had just opened. It was a small enclosed area with a fire hydrant for doggie bathroom stops, abundant grass, a few apparatuses for agility training, and a tall fence surrounding the area with double gates at three entrances to keep dogs from wandering out when people arrived or left with their pets. She smiled at his sense of abandon, his raw joy in movement. It warmed her heart to see him run so carefree and uninhibited.

She felt no need to stay near her well-trained Vizsla, so she strolled through the park, her head downward as she thought about the events of the last few months. She did a quick self-scan as she learned from Buddhists while studying philosophy with Kitarō in Kyoto. She found that she was more relaxed and happy than she had been in a long time. There were lots of reasons. Principally, she thought she didn't have to kill anyone else. The last one had been rough. She noticed she had become crueler and crueler after each murder, and the last one had been horrific—more so perhaps than all the others put together. The woman had been the ringleader of the attack that resulted in the death of James, and she had taken her time. It made her sick to think about it. At night when the images returned to her, she often had to run to the toilet to vomit. It was too much. Certainly at one level she accomplished what she set out to do, but it had not felt as good the last time. She had crossed some line, and this felt diseased and nauseating.

But it was over.

She would never kill again.

A shudder of relief passed over her. She sighed. The killers were all dead. It was time to move on. To begin again her work on void and nothingness, she had begun a translation and critique of Johannes Scotus' *Periphyseon*, and it was shaping up to be a book-length project. Her Medieval Latin was getting nearly as good as her Japanese, and she was feeling more confident than she had ever been that she was about to do theology that would have a lasting impact. She was idly playing with titles as she watched Georg play with the other dogs in the park, *Nothing. Ex nihilo. The Abundant Emptiness of the Nothing. Envoiding People: a User's Guide to Making Pain Linger?* Where did that come from? She shuddered for a different reason.

She watched as Georg introduced himself to a new dog. It approached with tail wagging, then placed its head alongside the other to maneuver over so they could smell each other's behinds. Apparently everything checked out, and the other dog lowered itself onto its front paws and barked playfully. Georg took the invitation, and the two were off playfully biting each other and tearing through the dog part like old friends. Heike looked at the dog's owner, an older lady, who smiled at her in a way that acknowledged that their dogs were playing together but offered no invitation to get to know each other further. This suited Heike perfectly. How annoying it was when some stranger felt that because their dogs had made a connection, they had one too.

Heike walked over to a bench and sat down. She was facing the sun, so she raised her hand to her brow to watch the dogs play. But soon she tired of it and turned away from the bright sunlight and pulled out an academic paper she wanted to read. While she scanned the paper, however, she was thinking, I have murdered six people, five of those cruelly and with premeditated planning to make it as horrific for them as I could. She purposely decided to bracket this series of acts, to carve them out of her life as if the events had not happened. She had given up on guilt after her first year of graduate studies in theology. She thought that, after letting these acts happen as they needed to for revenge's sake, she would be able to intellectually edit and excise what she'd done, and then go on. But the deed was turning out to be hard to elide. It haunted her. The images of the tortured bodies kept popping into her head over and over. And to her surprise, she did feel guilty. Even though she had come to believe that guilt was a useless concept intellectually (she had even written a paper on it, framed by Nietzsche's ideas on false consciousness). Still, the slaying bothered her. She found herself playing with ideas about whether she could have done things differently, and of course she could have, but she was surprised by how seriously her mind was taking up the question. When she was intent on carrying out her vengeance, she had not considered alternatives. She was focused on the task at hand. 'Purity of heart was to will one thing,' Kierkegaard had written. She had made that little saying a mantra whenever she had been tempted away from her project. She had kept her mind single to enacting the revenge she thought was needed to atone for the gangs' deeds. But now the alternatives that had never appeared during the last few months began to appear again and again.

Why hadn't she forgiven them like Jesus taught? They had all served jail time, why not let that be enough? Why could she not just have moved on with her life? But no, she went on a rampage of horror. Every newspaper reported it as one of the most inhuman crimes since World War II. The fact that it was terrorists she tortured and killed did not seem to matter to the press or the broadcast news. It irked her. These were not good people. They absolutely deserved exactly what they got. Couldn't they see that? But these doubts about the rightness of her actions were starting to creep into the forefront of her mind. She had to stop. She had originally framed a coherent strategy. She knew she was enacting some evil. Her theology included the ideas of compassion, grace, kindness, and other Christian virtues, and these she still embraced—except for this one act of vengeance. Hadn't the Lord God acted like this from time to time? Had he not vowed to kill every man, woman, and children on the planet in Noah's flood? (Not that she believed there had actually been a flood mind you). Vengeance was one of God's attributes, used sparingly, but used nevertheless. Many of the holy fathers had written on that. And never was there a person more entitled to vengeance and revenge than Heike. So why was she feeling so low about this? It was over now. Time to move on.

She whistled for Georg. He would not come, and she spent fifteen minutes chasing him around the dog park before she could snatch him by the collar. She sat down on the ground crossing her legs and pulling the dog's nose into her own as she rubbed the back of his head.

"You are a bad dog." She said rubbing his back vigorously with her hand. "A very bad dog."

⊃ ⋈ ⋆ ⋈ ⊂

Two weeks later, after meeting with two of her students working on a comparison of Nishida Kitarō's idea on the void and a French philosopher named Deleuze on the idea of virtual, she got home feeling tired. So slipped into her chair and turned on the news as she sometimes liked to do after a busy day. Near the end was a story that made her sit up. It was about her. Well not that anyone would know it was her: it was about the murders of the members of the August 4th gang. She'd watched these stories often, mostly to make sure there were no leads. But this story was different, and at its conclusion she was shaking so badly and hyperventilating so violently that the world was beginning to spin and go dark. Just before she lost consciousness in a faint she started to scream at what the story revealed— Arrow Beamon was alive and living in Utah. Arrow Beamon. The Cowboy. The murderer. Was. Alive.

⊃ � ⋏ ⋉ C

First she found a Russian prostitute who had the right kind of connections to put her in touch with people who moved people around Europe working as sex workers. Using them, she obtained a Swedish passport. Heike could not countenance what was being done to the woman, so she helped her escape and start a new life in Leipzig, anonymously turned in her handlers to the Bundesnachrichtendienst. This took nearly four months.

Then she went to Utah. She knew only that he was in Moab.

⊃ ⋉ ⋏ ⋉ C

She stayed in Moab twenty-two days before she found Arrow. He was eating at the Dairy Queen with a friend when she walked in to order one of those decadent but hard-to-resist American vanilla milkshakes they served. Over the course of her stay these had become a favorite.

Indeed, she had become fond of this high, semidesert landscape. The canyons, the valleys, and the sage suited her. The spring wind was cool and carried scents of old rock and new water. She loved the way the light played off of the canyon walls, changing the feeling of the place in subtle ways depending on little things like a cloud formation, the shape of the shadows of the cottonwood trees playing on the walls, or whether it had rained recently. The wildflowers spreading their fragrance. The sound of birds she did not know the names of. The calls of strange buzzing insects. The timbre of winds glissading through the canyon's rough shapes and rocky turns. The fractal hollows that wind and water had carved into vibrational devices made of earth and rock, trumpeted with the breeze, reeded with willows, and orchestrated with the photonic light from assemblages of night stars harmonically contrasted against the interpolating nothingness of black sky. All caressing her with holy magic and radical wonder.

⊃ ⤬ ⚡ ⤬ ⊂

She spent at least some of the day sitting in her car watching people move in and out of supermarkets—those strange American institutions based on a grotesque abundance of choices. Or driving up and down the streets hoping to find him. At last. At the Dairy Queen, when she had not even been looking for him. Of course. Quit looking and the God (or demon) appears.

She followed them to his house. The two men drove separate cars. She watched her enemy get out of his truck, and pulling the keys from his Levi's, he opened the door. So this was his place. They drove off in Arrow's truck, but she did not follow. This was enough information for her purposes. When they were gone, she drove to the hardware store and bought duct tape, wire, a set of filleting knives, a bicycle cable lock, a leather belt, and a large scarf to serve as a gag. When she returned to the trailer they had not returned, so she parked about a mile away and walked back with her supplies in a knapsack. Then she crawled under the trailer and waited. They did not return that night. But she was reluctant to leave the damp shade and earthy smell of the crawlspace under the trailer, so she waited. Around noon she was about to abandon her vigil when she heard the truck pull up. When they came inside, she learned four things:

1. The friend was named LeRoy and was from Blanding.
2. He was leading a raft trip with his wife down the Colorado River to test the equipment and 'runs' and wanted Arrow to go with him.
3. It would be a five day trip.
4. Arrow said he would go.

When the Cowboy's friend left she rethought everything. She wanted to go with them.

She would get to spend a short week with the killer, her last remaining enemy.

She could learn enough about him to individualize his death using his greatest fears.

She might find his personal pressure points.

She could design a death that would be a work of art.

She knew such an opportunity should not be missed.

It was not hard to find out the name of LeRoy Stout's company. He tried to explain that he was not doing commercial runs on the dates she wanted to go, but after she tearfully lied that she had always dreamed of running the great American Colorado River since she was a teenager in Sweden, and she would be leaving right after his first run and would likely never be back, and after offering him an unheard of sum and convincing him she would not expect the treatment most of the usual clients received because she understood this was a training run, he agreed. She wept with joy. Those tears were real.

River Preparations

The question that has occupied the philosophers
and flummoxed the great thinkers of both antiq-
uity and modernity is what is 'Being' as such.
That question has generated an industry of hand
wringing and speculation, with the writings
of philosophers on the matter providing a Ror-
schach Test in which devotees may twist their
arguments into whatever shape they wish to pur-
sue. But what if the question is wrongheaded?

—Frau Professorin Heike Marquardt,
On the Void: The Theology of Nothingness

Elder Holmberg

Elder Holmberg shook his head in sorrow. This trip
was off to a bad start. The foreign woman was wearing a
tank top with bare shoulders. Was he going to have to put
up with this immodesty the entire trip? This was not going
to be acceptable.

He motioned to Alma Lune to come over and whispered, "I cannot abide spending five days with a woman with such disregard for proper dress."

Alma Lune patted the old man's hand, "Elder Holmberg, I fear that on the river swimming attire will be standard so might I suggest that we just let this one go. I suspect that even Sister Stout will be wearing swimming attire."

Elder Holmberg sighed. "Ok. But I'm worried about you young men on the trip. Will this be temptation to distraction? Will you be able to handle the proper placement of your thoughts?"

Alma Lune assured him he would be fine. Elder Holmberg nodded, clearly not convinced. God smiled down upon the aged apostle. In all his hatred of him, he certainly made Him laugh.

Alma Lune

Alma Lune, however, found shirtless Arrow Beamon a beautiful specimen of manhood. He was in good shape, fairly tan. He'd clearly been through some things and bore a nasty scar on his chest and another on his back—to all appearances that he'd been shot straight through.

Alma Lune turned his eyes away and began to place the gear he had brought into the waterproof bags that Brother Stout had provided. He was feeling as buoyant as the raft itself. He had been feeling low of late, his duties with Elder Holmberg yoking him with the weight of the older man's apostolic concerns. This trip would be good for everyone.

Jezzy Stout

Sister Stout was helping in five directions at once. She had taken a liking to Regine, the Swedish woman. The Swedish woman was confident but not prideful, friendly, and eager to pitch in and help as needed. In her native land, she said she was a forester and was excited to see the great western drylands, with its giant rivers, canyons, and mountains. This was her first trip to America, and she was grateful for being allowed on this run, even though they had not planned for any tourists to come along.

Always watchful, Sister Stout could not help noticing how Regine seemed to have an eye for Arrow Beamon! In odd moments, she would catch the woman sneaking a peek at this rugged man. Sister Stout had to acknowledge that he was not unpleasing to the eye.

She was glad there was another woman along to help with cooking and cleaning. So often these trips turned into a nightmare of meal preparation and late nights cleaning up and preparing the next day's breakfast. Although she was a paying customer, Sister Stout felt like she was not one to stand around watching while Jezzy handled the bulk of the womanly duties.

As Arrow moved near Sister Stout, she could not stand the mystery of his scar anymore and asked, "How did you come by that scar on your chest? Were you in Nam?"

Everyone in the group looked up to hear Arrow's answer. LeRoy, the only one who knew, looked at his wife with a playful but serious reproach, then said to Arrow,

"Ain't no one's business but yours. So if you don't want to answer…"

"I don't mind. It's was all over the news in Austria anyway, so it's not a big secret." He stood up from the ropes and straps he was helping LeRoy stow away, and looked at Sister Stout, who also got to her feet with a shy, apologetic smile playing on her mouth.

"I was in Ethiopia sort of loosely supervising the spray of some tick and fly pesticides on cattle, and I went to take a pee, and someone plugged me in the chest with a sniper rifle."

There was silence. Regine went back to packing her stuff into the plastic bags, but Sister Stout looked at him in horror. Her mouth was trying to say something, but nothing was coming out.

"Yeah. Not my best day."

"Is there… you know permanent damage?"

Arrow laughed at Sister Stout's Question. "Well, nowhere but here," he said tapping the side of his head.

Sister Stout was fairly outraged. "Who would do such a thing!!! Did they catch them? I hope they are rotting in jail."

Arrow shook his head, "At first they thought it might be one of the guerrilla groups operating in the area near Somalia or Sudan, but now they think it might be someone taking revenge on the August 4th faction—a radical leftist anarchist group. There have been a string of murders…"

Sister Stout noticed her husband was standing behind everyone else making throat slashing motions, and shaking his head back and forth frantically. She realized she had just brought up something that was nobody's business but Arrow's.

"Well I'm glad you are OK," she said sheepishly, then added, "and hopefully this trip will take a load off your mind. Could you hand me that bag of cooking gear, dear." She said it in a way that she hoped indicated the conversation was over.

Jezzy Stout noticed that Elder Holmberg was looking at Arrow with narrow eyes, as if he were trying to work something out, inducing a panic that was starting to bubble up into her throat from her stomach. Alma Lune, having noticed LeRoy's signals to Sister Stout, distracted the apostle from further inquiry. She looked at him with gratitude.

Arrow Beamon

Arrow was glad that the conversation had turned another direction. He didn't feel like explaining to anyone the full story. He was also quite smitten with the Swedish woman. He had only known one person from Sweden—a young woman named Maja Jutvik. She was reserved, in the European way, until you got to know her. Then she was witty, playful, and fun. She was also very smart, which he enjoyed. He was interested in her back then, but all the time he knew her she had a boyfriend from England, so there was never any hope. But as he looked at Regine, he thought he could see some resemblance, and his interest in the Swedish woman seemed to transfer over. He knew it was superficial, but he kept stealing glances her way, and was pleased to note that she was occasionally glancing at him. She would quickly feign looking generally about, as if her random gaze just by chance had settled on him, but he could tell. She was pretty. She was neither thin nor heavy but had an athletic build. She looked toned with short wavy hair that brought out her dark eyebrows and handsome, slightly cleft chin. She was wearing red shorts and a sky-blue tank top that complemented her features. He could honestly say that it was the first time since his divorce that anyone had drawn this much attention from his monkey brain (as he liked to call it). He noticed that she did not smile when she caught him looking at her, and it made him smile because when Maja and he first met, she was exactly the same. Swedes. Stoic through and through.

This was going to be good for him, he could tell. He looked over at LeRoy and Jezzy and felt a wave of gratitude for their kindness. He knew Jezzy had given up some alone time with her husband for him, and quite likely Elder Holmberg, because they usually did this first test run as a kind of yearly honeymoon (LeRoy told him that at least two of their children had been a result of this run). Jezzy looked up and found him looking at him and mouthed, 'Sorry' at him. He smiled back and just waved it off with his hand, and she gave a forced smile and went back to her work. He did not know Jezzy well, but he liked her and thought LeRoy had been damn lucky to find her.

He was a little nervous about the apostle. It's not that he knew anything about him, as his return to church had been so recent; he had heard him in the Semi-Annual General Conference but could not remember a thing he said. It was one of those generic talks. Or to be more charitable, it had not been a sermon he needed, or connected too, so he had not really paid attention. He knew the old apostle had a reputation for having sort of a no-nonsense attitude about repentance. His presence made Arrow uncomfortable, like all authority did. He hoped he did not ask him about the shooting or his selling explosives to the August 4th Gang.

The apostle's assistant was just plain annoying. He was a little too neat. He was always fussing with the apostle, brushing his pant legs to get the sand off (like that's going to help when they will be camping on sandbars), and making sure he was sitting in the shade with a strange black parasol and was drinking often from an army canteen. Arrow was sure these were helpful and good actions, but he performed them with a single-minded devotion that rubbed Arrow the wrong way. He would just stay out of their way, he decided. This trip would still be amazing. It would just take a little management to make sure he was not near the apostle or his secretary.

LeRoy Stout

LeRoy was as nervous as a mouse on a basketball court fielding bobcats. He went from task to task making sure all was in order. Did they have the food, the cooking gear, Coleman stoves and lanterns, maps, the life preservers, the extra oars, the bailing buckets, the potable water in carboys, the medical supplies—everything from suntan lotion to snakebite kits, from calamine lotion to Benadryl for poison ivy, was the fishing gear ready, the foot pumps, the gas for the emergency outboards (the outboards!), the tents and canopies, sleeping bags in waterproof containers, his and his wife's clothes stored in waterproof plastic bags, knives, he felt like he was forgetting something? What was it? It had been nagging him all day. It might have been the coffee. Usually his clients demand a big pot every morning and decaf at night, and indeed the Swedish woman was incredulous that she would not be able to drink coffee for five days. She said she'd bring her own, but he explained that with Elder Holmberg along drinking coffee would be considered an insult, and he refused to allow coffee on his boats. In the end he encouraged her to buy no-doz to stave off the headaches from withdrawal, which she finally reluctantly accepted as the only way she would make it on the trip.

Elder Holmberg! He was taking an Apostle of the Lord Jesus Christ down the river on one of his boats. He couldn't believe it. It was almost like carrying an angel. Elder Holmberg! This was unimaginable and unprecedented. Suddenly he had a strange thought. What if Elder Holmberg gave him an endorsement! What if he could add on the bottom of his newspaper ads, "I've never had a better time on the river. Seeing the canyon country with the Stouts was the best decision I ever made. Elder Holmberg, LDS Quorum of the Twelve Apostles." LeRoy Stout literally sat on the ground at that thought. They could be as big as Mount Tukuhnikivatz River Tours if that happened. They'd get thousands more tourists from members of the Church. He could launch more boats, hire more people... he had better put in for permits as soon as he got back. This could happen.

One thing was clear: he had to make Elder Holmberg happy. This could be the game changer. Maybe both he and his wife could quit teaching and do this full time. Why not? This was an answer to prayers.

Heike Marquardt

Heike thought about the void. Principally, Arrow's being put in the void. She noticed that the bullet wound still seemed sensitive. Certain motions caused him pain. She would have to pay attention to the nature of that. It could provide a focal point for her planned ministrations. She looked up and found him looking at her. She couldn't help smiling back. Getting to know him a little was going to make her work (as she'd come to call it) so much better. This time she would get it right.

The Storm

What if the question, 'Why is there something instead of nothing?" is just a bad start? A lousy beginning. What if (and I hesitate to state it, for I can hear your protestations already) what if the void is substance? What if the substance of the void is not modeled on empty space, but rather on a pure and undifferentiated substance? An empty metaphysical sea of univocal something? If so, the real question is, 'Why is there nothing instead of something?'

—Frau Professorin Heike Marquardt,
On the Void: The Theology of Nothingness

Sometimes, not even Gods can predict the weather. There was only a 10% chance of rain, so there was little to worry about. Besides, LeRoy had packed rain gear for the trip, and a summer shower can be a pleasant experience on the river. In the summer, any relief from the relentless sun is a blessing, and the darkened landscape discloses its own treasures. If the wind is low, rain coming down in thick sheets causing the water to boil, it brings a soft beauty, creating an otherworldly ambiance as the soft white noise of falling rain stirs a pleasant contentment. However, when the wind picks up enough to be described as fierce, and the willows and tamarisk on each side begin to toss like rippling grass on the prairie, it can start to feel ominous, portending threat. But two tropical storms, one from the Pacific and one from the Atlantic, converging in Mexico and pumping moisture and massive thunderstorms into Arizona and Utah, were out of anyone's purview. The storms were supposed to go east, into Colorado and Kansas (hence the 10% chance in Utah), but weather does what it wills, and the little group of river runners was caught off guard. They had just entered the Goose Neck, just above the confluence of the Green and Colorado rivers, when two massive thunderstorms clashed above them dumping water in washtubfuls. Waterfalls were pouring off of the west Mesa, and by the time they got to Salt Creek raging flash floods from all over the Canyonlands were converging on its entrance into the Colorado river creating powerful currents and eddies in what is usually the most peaceful of stretches. LeRoy pulled them onto a sandbar on the east bank, and everyone set to work trying to set up some shelter to get some protection from the Noachian deluge pouring from the sky. Everyone was soaked. The wind was too strong, and nothing could be set up, so Sister Stout guided Elder Holmberg and Alma Lune under an outcropping of sandstone that provided sufficient protection from the rain if not the wind.

Meanwhile, the others tried to help get things off of the raft and onto the sandbar. They had only unloaded the kitchen when LeRoy screamed that they had to get onto the bank: the river was rising enough that it was being cut off from the shore, and LeRoy wanted everyone to move the stuff up higher on the bank. The sandbar would very shortly be submerged. He pulled the raft around to the end of the sandy river deposit in order to move the boat closer to the shore, when a large cottonwood with an enormous root mass pulled down by the flash floods scouring the canyonlands snagged the raft and pulled it down river. LeRoy's palms were badly rope-burned as he tried to hang onto the line, but it was torn from his hands. He stood in the storm watching his raft and all their gear save a few kitchen supplies float down river. Cataract Canyon, some of the meanest Class 5 rapids between here and the Grand Canyon, lay just a few miles downriver. Likely everything was lost.

LeRoy ran up to the overhang where the others were huddled. Elder Holmberg was soaking wet and seemed to be in a state of shock. His clothes were soaked through and clinging to his skin, and he was shivering violently. Alma Lune had his arm around him. No one could offer any clothing, as they were mostly wearing swimming attire or, in Elder Holmberg's case, a Hawaiian shirt and sweatpants. Regine looked at LeRoy and said, "It is important to get him warm don't you think?"

Arrow said he would try to find a better place to hide from the storm, while LeRoy went back to the disappearing sandbar to bring up the kitchen box which held a Colman Stove and some propane that he could use to start a fire and boil some water. He could at least make some Brigham tea from some of the local shrubs to contribute a little inner warmth to the group's cold bones. By the time he got back to the outcrop, Arrow also returned with news that, just up the hill a fissure was running through the sandstone that had produced a roomy cave that went back about thirty yards. It was dry and had a sandy floor.

Alma Lune literally picked up and carried the aged apostle like a bride. He followed Arrow and LeRoy through the sage up the incline to the slit in the canyon wall, a high-ceilinged cave offering shelter. The others followed behind, sagging through the relentless downpour and keeping close together because of the poor visibility. Lightning was flashing every few seconds, and the roll and boom of the thunder was relentless.

Once the people were inside, Arrow and LeRoy went to work setting up the stove, gathering some branches from a dead cottonwood tree and dry sagebrush branches that had gathered around the face of the cliff in which the fissure stood. Back in the cave, LeRoy lit the stove and held one of the small branches over the flame until it was burning brightly, while Arrow built a small teepee out of some of the other branches.

In no time they had a nice campfire going. LeRoy went back into the storm and ran down to the hill to where Salt Creek was raging madly into the Colorado. Large boulders could be heard rolling and bouncing down the wash. The roar of the flash flood was terrifying, and at the same time an awesome display of Nature's power and rage. He gingerly knelt near the bank fearful that somehow the waters would reach out and grab him as he filled two pans of water.

He didn't need to be careful marching back up the hill because, as water sloshed out of the pans, the torrential rain replenished the lost water nearly as fast as he lost it— not quite, but it was easy to trick yourself into believing it.

He found Alma Lune and Regine holding the apostle near the fire. The old man's demeanor looked ragged and tired, but his eyes were active, looking around at their situation more attentively than when LeRoy last saw him staring into empty air and shivering. Regine was rubbing his back and arms trying to get his circulation going, and Alma Lune was whispering encouragement to the elder.

The little space was warming nicely, and the narrow confines were soon almost comfortable. While the clamor from the stream below rumbled and boomed as loudly as the thunder above, there was a sense that they were beyond its reach

Jezzy Stout ran back out into the storm and in a few minutes came back with a few leafy branches of *Ephedra nevadensis* for Brigham tea. It was a well-known pioneer remedy for just about any ailment you could name. It grew abundantly along the river drainages of the canyonlands.

Elder Holmberg looked at what she was carrying with interest and said, "My mother used to gather that plant and we would drink its tea every morning in the spring when the buds were green and new." He chuckled and continued, "Deer and cows can eat it. But don't give it to horses. Bad for their bellies."

Alma Lune beamed at the voice of his charge talking sense again without his lips quivering from the cold. He smiled warmly at Regine, and she smiled back. Things were going to be OK.

LeRoy watched how carefully Regine was attending to the aged apostle's needs. She had warmed to him quickly, and nearly the whole of last two days had been in constant conversation about the Mormon faith. He found it intriguing that a botanist knew so much about religion in general. On the first night they stayed up till nearly midnight talking about the nature of God, the Mormon idea of Mother in Heaven, and the Mormon God's material body. A concept so new to her she begged for more information. She laughed often at some of the things he said—not exactly as if she was laughing at his ideas, but more that she found them delightful. Something about the language she used made him think that, like Arrow, she was college-educated and knew more about religion than she was revealing. She not only knew the names of some of the Protestant reformers like Luther and Calvin, but she would refer to Barn-hoffer, or Till-ick. He was glad she was keeping him busy, as obviously was Alma Lune, who seemed to enjoy the trip more since she had taken over entertaining him. He was genuinely glad they had brought her along.

And he was glad for another reason. Arrow was obviously taken with her. LeRoy caught him looking at her almost every time he glanced his way. He was watching her like a schoolboy smitten with his first crush. She seemed awkward around his friend. The time or two Arrow had tried to talk to her since the first day, she had seemed flustered and quickly left the conversation—if you could call it that. The first evening Arrow and Elder Holmberg got into a conversation about cattle, since that was Arrow's area of study. Soon the talk moved to branding cattle, which the elder had done a time or two in his youth. Arrow pointed out that in Europe they mostly used ear tags. Until that time, Regine seemed almost hostile to Arrow, but suddenly she perked up and started to ask questions about what cattle feel when branded. She seemed very interesting in how cattle experienced pain and what branding would feel like to a human. She even asked about where you could get brands and how they were heated. Elder Holmberg pointed out that you don't want the brand to be white hot, only red hot, otherwise it would burn too deep and cause too much pain. Regine seemed particularly interested in what it took to get the metal white hot. She was a very curious person, it was clear, but to his sorrow she did not appear to be interested in Arrow like he was in her. He knew his friend well enough to detect some twitterpatedness, and Arrow certainly seemed to be. He hoped over the next few days things would play in his favor. Maybe this whole accident was meant to be, and that somehow it all would work toward Arrow's meeting a possible eternal companion. She was obviously very interested in the Church. This whole storm, the loss of the raft, and all the things that went wrong might have been the Lord's plan all along. He would bounce this off Jezzy when he got a chance. She was good at finding the hand of the Lord even in the bleakest of situations.

Interlude—
Nephi's Love Story

The rain did not let up. Arrow and LeRoy took turns going down to the little overhang that they had originally sheltered under and watched upstream for another raft. None appeared. It was the beginning of the season, and there were only a few people out on the water this early in the spring—mostly river guides training their crew and scoping the current conditions, but the storm apparently had sent them all running for shelter.

When night came, the two men gave up their watch and returned to the grotto. Everyone was hungry and tired of tea and not in the best mood. Alma Lune was especially put out that Elder Holmberg was stuck without a proper meal. The apostle was not complaining, but he seemed to be stewing with an unpleasant look on his face aimed at no one. Jezzy was trying to pretend she was chipper and everything would be fine, "A boat will likely appear any moment." But as night fell, her optimism was turning into a dark, half-empty despair. Heike had gone quiet, sitting on the sand floor with her back to the cave wall hugging her knees, obviously bored. LeRoy and Arrow were the only ones still soaked to the skin because they were moving back and forth to watch for help from another raft. Everyone was in a bad mood.

Even Nephi. He could not read anyone's mind, but it was clear from his years of experience as both a human and an angel that Heike was even more determined to kill Arrow. Arrow was falling in love with his would-be murderess and was actually glad they were stuck together. Elder Holmberg was uncomfortable, and perhaps even a little agitated and frightened.

LeRoy was slipping into depression because he was the court fool who lost the boat and all their supplies with an apostle of the Lord on his boat. Jezzy felt responsible for everyone's happiness, and since no one was happy she was wracked with guilt and sorrow. And Alma Lune. Alma Lune was not thinking about anyone but Elder Holmberg. Nephi nodded approvingly. There was a man who understood duty and honor. Nephi knew he was a homosexual, but that was not a problem from Nephi's perspective, as the man had repented of any commandments he had broken.

The Goddess Asilah was suddenly standing in the cave. She looked at Nephi, then at the bedraggled group all trying to draw what warmth they could from the fire.

Nephi looked up and rolled his eyes. "Have you come to mock me more?"

The Goddess Asilah said softly, "I have not come to mock you. I would never. It seems we must work together, as our charges have crossed paths."

Nephi laughed, "That is one way to put it."

The Goddess and the angel were silent for a while, watching the lost little group. The Goddess said, "Why don't you plant an idea to help them get to know each other better. They need a distraction. Heike needs to have pity enter her heart for Arrow. Give them some ideas."

Nephi sighed. "I'll try."

Alma Lune looked around at the hapless group and thought that maybe they needed some hope. And what is more hopeful than love?

"Hey, we may be here a while. Let's tell about ourselves. We did this at a ward activity, and it was a very successful thing. So let's tell each other about our first loves?"

Elder Holmberg put his hand on his secretary's shoulder, "I think we are all a little tired, friend."

Regine nodded and said tightly, "I'm afraid we Swedes would have to know you much better before. . . ." She let the thought trail off.

Nephi looked morose, "Well that didn't work."

The Goddess smiled, "Maybe you need to start it?"

Nephi just looked at her and turned away.

"You start. Tell me about your first love. And I'll write their stories even if they don't want to."

"You can't do that. No one can read the thoughts of another. Only God."

"Or Goddesses."

"Nephi looked at her, "I don't believe you."

"Tell me yours and I'll give you theirs."

"How will that help them?"

"By helping you. Maybe you'll see a way to touch their consciousness."

Nephi looked at the Goddess, considering her words, then said, "You know my story."

"I haven't heard you tell it."

A look of anger flashed across his face, then a slow resignation. Nephi looked at Asilah a long time then said, "This is how I wrote it. But the pages were lost. I'll give you this."

It came to pass, that when I was in my seventh year I came to the household of my beloved father's friend Ishmael to be instructed in the learning of the Egyptians. He had many daughters and also had a daughter who was born in the same year of Jehoiakim's reign as I. Behold we became as brother and sister. We did climb the hills around Jerusalem one with another, hiding from the guards her father had hired to watch over us, for yea, the city was dangerous in the years of Jehoiakim's reign. We did not know this then, for we explored and played, but in all things did that which was proper in the sight of the Lord.

It came to pass that many years passed, and behold, on my sixteenth birthday, I planned to ask her father for her hand in marriage that we might be joined in a holy bond of matrimony. Yea, even that we might pass our days as husband and wife, having many children in which we would take delight.

Behold, it was the righteous desire of my heart and I knew that the Lord would not withhold his blessing in this. For I did love Ishmael's daughter with all my heart, and with all my mind, and with all my soul. There was none like her. She was fair beyond the cedars of Lebanon, and verily I say that the gardens of Babylon were no match for her beauty. Her virtue was that of an angel, and in all things she strove to please the Lord in the house of her father.

But behold, in the first year of the reign of Zedekiah King of Judah, my father received a vision in which he saw that the city of Jerusalem would be destroyed and that he should take his family into the wilderness. There was much weeping among my brothers, and in particular I sorrowed much that I would not see Ishmael's daughter again, but behold I inquired of the Lord, and he instructed me that I should not fear to follow the commandments of my father, nor should I wallow in despair over my love, but that I should put my trust in Him and not in the arm of flesh. And so I resolved to follow the admonitions of my father.

However, Ishmael's daughter did not cease to weep, and much sorrow entered into her heart as we made preparations to depart into the wilderness. For she believed that our love would fade and be lost in the sorrows and cares of our departure.

For many days we dwelt in the wilderness, and after many adventures, my father saw the need to provide women to raise up the next generations. Now, at this time I was hated by my brethren. Yea, and much to the sorrow of my father, they did despise me with all the fierceness of their anger, unto persecution of my body, and yea, they did vex my soul.

Nevertheless, when our father did command us to return to the land of our inheritance, and lo, bring down the family of Ishmael, we did all rejoice. And more especially did I rejoice, for behold, it meant that the daughter of Ishmael that I loved would be reunited with me.

So it came to pass that we did make haste to the Land of Jerusalem, and behold we pleased Ishmael with our importuning, and he did agree to bring himself, and his wife, and his daughters, yea and all his household down into the wilderness. But to my sorrow, there was much contention among us as we traveled south into the more fertile parts of the land. Yea, my brothers did contend mightily with me, and they did seek my destruction.

And to my sorrow, they did accomplish their task. For Laman being the oldest did have claim by birthright and by the law of the land and by the traditions of my people to choose first among the daughters of Ishmael to wife. And he, knowing that I did favor one of the daughters of

Ishmael, and indeed did love her with all my heart, did take her unto himself.

And I cried unto the Lord in sorrow. And did rage against my brethren. And knowing my wrath, Laman and Lemuel did flee before me, for I was large of stature and expert at the bow and the scimitar, and yea, I did press upon them with the Sword of Laban. And they fled before me. And in the day I hunted them, and in the night I did fill the darkness with the sound of my rage and mourning. But alas, they did reach the tent of my father before me and did beg him to pacify my anger.

And my father did come to me and spake unto me that the will of the Lord would be done. And that Laman by the inheritance of his birthright had claim to the daughter of Ishmael that I desired. Long he did speak to me, and tell me of the glories that awaited should I give up my hatred of my brethren.

And behold. So it was that I was pacified, and I chose one of the other daughters of Ishmael to wife. Yet I did not love her, and thereby she bore me no children.

Nevertheless I did not cease to love the daughter of Ishmael that Laman had taken. And long after they had separated from us and I had become the king of my people, behold, in the night, I would sneak to their camp and whisper to my beloved the truth of my love. But she did turn away, claiming that she loved Laman, although I knew it could not be true.

Behold, to Laman she bore three children, but I never ceased to love her. Nor will I.

The Goddess Asilah looked at Nephi and said softly, "And I loved you too, Nephi, but never in the way you hoped."

Heike Shoots Arrow
in the Heart—2nd Time

The heart of the void is filled with the nothing of something so nothing-like that no difference between the two can be found. There would still be no relations to frame logic. There would still be no empty set to hold open a place to add elements. It would be undifferentiated, inseparable, un—whatever category of being you wish to add, for this substance of the void of which I hypothesize has all of the properties of nothing.

—Frau Professorin Heike Marquardt,
On the Void: The Theology of Nothingness

The night was cold. Not below freezing, but cold enough to rob a body of comfort. To keep warm, following the same method bees use to stay warm in the winter by shivering en masse, with a slow individual migration from the warm center to the outer edges of the hive, Arrow had everyone lie on their sides and line up front to back and snuggle together forming sort of an ad hoc sardine can. About every hour of the night he had the people on the ends move to the middle. Of course, given his age and position in the church, Elder Holmberg was excluded from taking one of the end positions; everyone noticed that Alma Lune was taking double shifts.

In the morning they found Elder Holmberg shivering and radiating heat like a furnace, his fever belying his trembling body and chattering teeth.

Alma Lune looking lost and despairing said, "We've got to get him to a hospital."

Arrow stepped up, "If I follow this canyon up, maybe ten miles, I'll get up near park headquarters. They can send for a helicopter from Search and Rescue."

Alma Lune said without hope, "There is nowhere to land."

"They won't land. They'll lower a stretcher and hoist him up."

Alma Lune looked at him with wide eyes, "Yes. Get help!" He said letting out a stifled sob.

"I'm going with you," the Swedish woman said.

"It's safer here," Arrow stated it almost like a question.

"I go."

And so into the rain Heike and Arrow resolutely marched, both hunched over, their feet making red divots with every step in the saturated soil, sliding from time to time as they made their way up the valley, trying to keep well above the torrent splashing and thundering below them in a flash flood of such violence that only a few earthly souls have seen the earth in such unmasked sublime rage. So wild and chaotic is a berserking drylands gale, no one can speak about the experience without resorting to overused words that in no practical sense capture the noise echoing from that turbulent water in a furor of elemental madness, as forces manic and frenzied toss boulders— sandstone remnants of the peeling and crumbling canyon's slick rock walls. Which, after eons, have slid to the bottom of the valley and lie in the path of the pillaging creek as the storm unleashes its seething water and runs into the Colorado. Now the easily pried up titanic slabs of sandstone slide loose from the sediments that have so long cemented them to their static moorings, freeing them to be lifted and set adrift into the chaos as if they were leaves flitting helter-skelter in blusterous wind.

Slowly, the two slogged forward between the walls of the canyon. There was a growing sense of danger as they had to cross several ordinarily dry gullies that were now torrential streams. One slip into the stream would carry a body over rocks and boulders into the violent waters storming down the gully, and then on into the fury of the overflowing Colorado River below. It would mean certain death. Soon the pair were covered in red earth due to their repeated sliding and falling on the slippery slope of the canyon running down to the river. They were so muddy that they resorted to going on hands and knees as often as hiking because a slip can mean not stopping until you hit the water. Even so, they made progress.

Arrow was only focusing on the task at hand—picking a path forward, trying to avoid areas that might send them sliding into one of the many streams coming off of the cliffs and rushing into the river. Overwhelmed with a sense of the precarious position they found themselves in, he had no idea that Heike had other things on her mind.

Heike looked at Arrow and thought, 'I should kill him now. It would be so easy just to sever his hamstrings, and then after a bit of recompense I could throw his body into the torrent and no one would be the wiser.' And he would be dead. She considered his form marching a few feet in front of her. She could take the diving knife strapped to her ankle and plunge it into his lower back, but then that would be identifiable as a murder if his body were found. No, she should use a rock and bring it down on his head. But he needs to suffer. I need a stick, someone tumbling in a flash flood could be pierced by sticks easily. Jam it into his kidney, then, as he is roiling around, get his legs to stop thrashing with another jab to his lower back. That will stop his legs, and I can work on creating an hour or two of pain in the upper half of his body. She could start with his fingers, perhaps. Smashing them with rocks one by one until his flanges were dust, then slowly do the same to his arms. She could then slice him open and one by one pull his ribs out like God did to Adam, except she would make no Eves of these ribs. The more she thought about it, the more excited she became.

In the midst of such a storm as this, Arrow exemplified how to walk by carefully watching every step; all of one's attention should be focused on navigating the treacherous terrain before you. Heike's attention was split, however. She slipped. She was trying to cross a small stream that Arrow had just leapt across. He was standing on a rock leaning out, offering his hand for her to grab, but she did not see it, nor even the stream, so she stepped full into the water, which swept her feet away, and in an instant she was sliding madly toward the torrent below. Arrow was leaping after her taking giant moon-steps down the steep gradient screaming for her to grab one of the sage-brush roots lining the side, but she was too caught in the panic of the moment to even hear his words. She went over a small woman-high waterfall that had dug out a small basin with the force of the water's descent, and there she was trapped by a tangle of woody debris scoured from above. The main force of the flooded ravine was only about 30 meters below her.

Arrow reached the spot and grabbed her leg and pulled her out. She was unconscious and bleeding badly from a wound on the top of her head. The rain poured around them. He quickly cleaned the wound. It was bad. There was a bloody dent that meant her skull was crushed. Blood was leaking out of one ear. She was breathing, but he could see a small stick had pierced her between a pair of ribs. Bubbles were emerging from the wound where air was leaking from her lungs. Drawing on basic, barely remembered medical knowledge he received as a soldier and in his training as a vet, he went to work. He had nothing to seal the wound, so took off his swimming suit and pulled the lining off. He fashioned a bizarre dressing around the stick in her lung with the outer part of his suit using the drawstring and the stick itself as an anchor, then he wrapped the lining around her head and tied it like a kerchief as best he could. One arm was broken. He knelt beside her and carefully laid his hands on her head.

"By the power of the holy Melchizedek Priesthood which I hold, and in the name of Jesus Christ, I command you to live until medical help can be obtained. I bless you and set you apart to live until then."

She would die if she did not get help. He picked her up—it didn't matter if her back were broken, he had to act. And naked as Adam he began to run, cradling her in his arms, and sprinting like an Olympic runner. He found a power he did not expect. He slipped a few times, but in every case that he fell, he protected his charge like a mother would a child. At last he came to the end of the canyon, he found a muddy path that led onto the plateau above. In three more miles he burst into the Ranger's office covered in Heike's blood, unable to talk, and after setting her down, he collapsed in unconsciousness.

The two rangers knew their business. They called for emergency transport. Despite the rain, Medivacs were dispatched, and help was on its way. While they were waiting they used an emergency first aid kit to better stabilize Heike. Then after caring for her, they wrapped Arrow in a blanket. In a few minutes Arrow came to and was able to give details about what had happened. He explained about the others down below at the mouth of canyon, suggesting that Elder Holmberg's life was also likely in danger. The rangers conveyed this information to Search and Rescue, and a second helicopter was dispatched.

Arrow relaxed. There was nothing more he could do. The Swedish woman was lying next to him. Her eyes were fixed open, but the gurgling from her chest told him she was yet living. She had a beautiful face he thought, then realized how silly that was to notice that when she might die now. The terms of her blessing had been fulfilled.

The rain on the roof gave a peaceful sound, and he was warmer than he had been in a long time. Not the heat radiating from his chest that the long run up the valley had produced, but warmth on his skin. Warmth all around. He coughed once and fell asleep and did not hear the helicopter land, or the men come in and work on Heike for almost thirty minutes to stabilize her enough for transport. He did not hear the news come in on the radio that Search and Rescue had picked up Elder Holmberg and his secretary, and were taking them to the Church's Primary Children's Hospital. He did not hear their skepticism about whether Heike would live. When they put him on a stretcher, he stirred a little, and then in the roar of rotor-blades, he slipped into another peaceful slumber, but not before thinking, "I'm going to marry that woman."

The Angel Nephi and the Goddess Argue About Their Charges

And why cannot this sort of something be nothing? Or, asked another way, how could you tell if this void of something differed from nothing when they have identical properties? Certainly you cannot add anything to this something as nothing or nothing as something. You cannot cut it into smaller pieces. You cannot find a way into it. Can you name one aspect of the void that cannot be filled with this substance and its aspects? No, the ensubstanced void is identical to the emptyish void. And as we might suspect, if you will let me sneak in just a modicum of logic, of things (or not things) with all of the same properties we suspect that indeed they are the same thing. A void of substance of the right type and the void of emptiness are identical.

—Frau Professorin Heike Marquardt,
On the Void: The Theology of Nothingness

Nephi spat. "Marry that woman! Ha! She was about to kill him in the cruelest way she could think of! She was about to torture him to death. Marry him! My charge has a wry sense of humor."

The Goddess stood beside him watching as the medics tried to stabilize Heike. She turned and looked at the angel Nephi.

"Do you remember the last time you snuck up to speak to me in my tent to try and convince me to follow you back to your village?"

"I was a fool. I repented of that long ago. I find no need to discuss it further. Especially with you, your Ladyship. Those days are passed. Why do you bring it up now? To torture me for my foibles? Trust me, there is no end to them I assure you, so pick another."

"It had been raining for days. Laman was leading a hunting party after a large herd of tapirs in the jungle, spotted a day's journey by boat down the River Lehi. That river, named after his and your father, was treacherous, with several whitewater rapids popping up with regularity. Only two years before, it had taken the life of one of the Omya men whose people had navigated on the river in time beyond memory and with whom we were friendly. I was worried about him. The trip was dangerous, but he would not be dissuaded, as we had had a hard season, and the flood made the fish harder to catch. We were all feeling the need for some animal protein. One of the Omya aunties was sitting with my other children, and I felt a need to walk in the forest. To feel my feet on the soil and make physical contact with the earth. I needed to pray to the Mother, to feel her arms around me. I took a path that wound up to a high space where our village grew corn and beans in the dry season because it managed to pull down a little moisture from the trees when morning clouds drifted low. As I walked, I listened to the birds chattering and singing, the monkeys playing like rambunctious children in the branches above me. I was too worried about Laman to feel completely at rest, but I pulled what peace I could allow close and wrapped myself in its warmth. You came suddenly out of the trees—how you found me I do not know. You grabbed my wrist and began pulling me down the path. Now's our chance, you said. I tried to pull away, but you kept pulling me down the path. You did not let go until I started screaming and fighting you. You were so surprised. I'll never forget the confusion on your face, as if our childhood puppy love somehow gave you rights that transcended ten years and three children with Laman. I started running back down the path, afraid of what you might do."

"I would have done nothing."

"How was I to know that? I'm a Goddess now and recognize you are right, but then it was well known that the Nephites were women-stealers and keepers of large harems. I was frightened you would rape me and drag me back to your camp."

"Never! How dare you..."

"I'm talking about how I perceived you. You had snuck to my camp several times and for several years before my little Ishmael was born and tried to convince me that I should return to your camp with you. You were such a child. And to be honest, I don't think you ever grew up. You held your wife in contempt her whole life because she was not me. Shame on you. How much pain did you caused her for that offense? The cost of her not being me ran high."

Nephi said nothing.

"You chased me down and tackled me, and I fought you like a jaguar. But you were too strong—'large in stature' is I believe how you described yourself. Then you stood me up. I realized then that perhaps you meant not to take me against my will."

The angel looked at the ground chewing his lip.

"You said it was my last chance. To choose you or Laman. You claimed you would never return to ask again. Looking at you I realized that you fully expected me to choose you. Choose you? Over my husband? That you thought I would leave my husband and children and follow you back to that strange kingdom you ruled? So isolated from most of your father's family, from the Omya who had been so friendly to us since we arrived, from even yourself. And your God."

Nephi looked up at the Goddess and whispered, "It's true. I thought you would follow me back. It never occurred to me that...."

"That I was happy?"

"Yes. I hated my brother. I thought you must too."

"No. I loved your brother."

"I know."

"But you never understood, I loved you too."

Nephi looked up confused.

"Not in the way I loved him. But genuinely, and truly I loved you too. The Omya have thirteen words for love. Love has many facets, like shimmering scales of a butterfly wing. I could not love you the way you wanted, but I loved you in many other shades and colors. Can you not return love to me in those hues?"

Nephi bowed and began to glow brightly, "I must go. I leave you to your abysmal murderous charge. And no. No I cannot love you except it includes all the colors. Adieu."

"À tout à l'heure."

"Yes. That's what I meant." And he was gone.

PART II

Sister Beamon's
Primary Class

Sister Beamon held up the picture and asked the class, "What are these people doing?"

The ten-year-olds squirming on their chairs were looking everywhere but at their teacher. So she gently asked again, and a little girl raised her hand and simultaneously answered, "They lost their cat. When our cat got lost when my brother left the door open mama said we should all pray, and so we got on our knees and said a prayer and you'll never guess what but heavenly father heard us and told that cat to get on home and she did and we found her just like that."

Sister Beamon smiled just as the five-minute warning bell rang. She looked at all the children bouncing up and down, poking each other and whispering (and not whispering) back and forth. Smiling, she started to sing. She started softly, then gained strength as she continued,

> *O du fröhliche,*
> *O du selige,*

Gnadenbringende Weihnachtszeit.
Welt ging verloren,
Christ ist geboren,
Freue, freue dich, o Christenheit!

Her voice was beautiful. Clear as a glacial mountain stream flowing over rounded river stones. As she sang, little Morgan Golightly ran to Sister Beamon and climbed on her lap. Sister Beamon wrapped her in her arms and gently rocked her as she sang the Christmas carol.

As she finished Sister Beamon looked up and saw that Sister Williams was standing in the door waiting to pick up her son, looking at her and smiling.

"Oh Regine that was so beautiful. Your voice ... it's like an angel singing."

"Doch ... you are silly, Marcy. I'm not that good."

"No seriously, I love your voice. Are you singing that for the Christmas program next Sunday? I hope you are."

"Yes. The bishop asked, and so I must obey," she laughed.

Rambunctious Kyle Williams ran past his mother standing in the doorway and ran into the hallway. Sis. Williams gave a quick wave and followed him out.

One by one the parents of the children came to gather their children until only Regine and her daughter Gerda remained. Regine thought how lucky she was to be back in Primary to be with her daughter.

"Ready to go home?"

Her daughter nodded, and hand and hand they left the classroom to find her two older brothers and their vater. She found her husband talking with one of the other elders in the foyer. He excused himself from the conversation and followed her out of the rear door to where her boys were waiting.

"Can I drive?" Her oldest son Kimball asked.

"You only have your learner's permit, and you are not supposed…"

Her husband threw the keys to the boy with a shrug. "It's only two miles. He'll be fine."

She clenched her teeth, "*Dickkopf. Warum schwächst du meine Autorität?*"

Her bite took him by surprise. He overcorrected.

"Give me the keys, son. I'll drive."

"Dad! Come on. How am I ever going to learn…"

"GIVE ME THE KEYS!"

On the way home no one said a word. When they got to their split-level ranch nestled in the little housing development off Murphy Lane, everyone quickly got out of the car and ran into the house. Everyone except Regine and Arrow, who stayed sitting in their minivan. For a few minutes they sat in silence staring straight ahead.

"What's up. Something is wrong." Arrow finally said.

Regine owned her mood, "Sorry. I'm upset."

"You've been all weekend."

She sat fidgeting with her hands. Then she looked at him and pulled a book out of her primary bag and handed it to him. He took it and looked down at it, opened it, and slowly flipped through the pages.

He looked up, "You can..."

"Read it. *Ja.*"

"Well... We will just add Greek to your set of language skills."

"German, Japanese, French, English, and now New Testament Greek."

"Where did you find this?" He asked holding up the Greek New Testament.

"At the library. Someone left it on the reshelving table. I was just curious so I picked it up, and I could read it like it was German. I'm fluent. Rusty, but fluent."

Arrow ran his hand through his hair and was silent. She looked out of the front window staring straight ahead. Then her shoulders started to shake, the sobs started in earnest. Mascara ran down her cheeks. He quickly wrapped his arms around her shoulders and pulled her close. She grabbed on to him and held him tight.

"Who am I?"she wept. "Someone please tell me who I am?"

"You are Regine Beamon, wife, mother, and amazing human being."

They were silent. Then Arrow started breathing more rapidly. Then blurted out, "Please. Let's not do this all over again. We've spent years trying to find who you are. We've talked to Embassies on three continents. We've checked missing persons in Sweden, Germany, Japan, and there is no one looking for you. Spent every vacation traveling over there looking for some hint. We've put your picture in the papers all over the world, and no one has responded. Please...." His voice cracked, "let it go. I can't do this anymore. We've tried, Regine, you know how hard we've tried and...I can't do it anymore. You can't do it anymore. When we get into the Celestial Kingdom, we'll watch the movie and figure it out.... But let's not do this all over again. Please? For the children's sake... and mine... and yours. I just can't..."

Her face took a hard edge. Her jaw tightened, and she almost spat out the words, "You still blame me, don't you. You think if I hadn't been looking through microfiche records on German births that...."

"Stop! Stop. You know I don't blame you! That was ten years ago. It wasn't your fault. You've got to let it go."

She pressed her lips together, tears forming in her eyes, and nodded her head, "I know. I know. I'm sorry. I still wake up at night...."

"I know you do. Remember what your psychologist says. When you feel like that, talk to me."

She nodded again. She looked at her husband and grabbed his hand, "OK, let me tell you this then. It was the night after I discovered the Greek New Testament..."

He held onto her hand with both hands now.

"...I dreamed I was in high mountains..."

The La Sals.

"No. Somewhere else. I was in a meadow covered in wildflowers, and in the dream I could name every single one. Butterflies were flitting over the grass, and birds, whose names I also knew, were singing. And suddenly a little girl was running on the grass toward me."

Arrow, put his arm around her and whispered, "Heike."

She nodded and was silent for a while, slight sobs coming from between breaths.

"Heike. She was not an infant, of course. She was nine or so, like she would be now. She came up to me with a small bouquet she had been gathering, and I gathered her up in my arms." She laughed at the memory. She said, "*Du tust mir weh. Halt mich nicht so fest, Mama.*"

Arrow nodded, his eyes glistening.

I asked her how heaven was, and she just smiled. Then a pack of large wolves appeared, and she looked at them and said in English, "I've got to go with them, Mutter." And she ran to them and they ran off together. I was not scared for her. I knew they would take care of her.

Arrow now had full tears in his eyes. "Beautiful dream."

She nodded.

They were silent.

"She is all right. She's being cared for. Like in the dream."

"I know. I just wish it were me caring for her."

"You will."

"*Ja. Ich werde.*"

Suddenly, Gerda burst from the door. "Mom, Jens is breaking the Sabbath. He just turned on the TV."

Jens followed, bolting out of the door behind her, yelling just as loud, "I did not. I was just checking the score, and dad said that was OK. I didn't watch it hardly at all. Like ten seconds."

Arrow and Regine smiled at each other and got out of the car.

Nephi Contemplates
the Justice of God

Here is Nephi. Nephi sighs as only an angel can, that deep existential sigh that would make a Bohemian Sartre afficionado's affected exhalation look amateurish. It is a sigh that reaches the heavens. Deep and magnificent, full of the indignation and sorrow of having lived, lo, these many years, doing task after task with unfathomably uninteresting people who had little hope of exaltation. It had been a long time since Nephi had checked on Arrow. Several years at least. After his charge's marriage to Heike and her conversion to the church, it seemed unnecessary. They were doing fine. Strong upstanding citizens of the kingdom were these two bedraggled souls. One who had arranged things so his own cousin died at the hands of terrorists, and the other a murderer who had forgotten her trade. Fine job for the founder of a mighty nation, babysitting the guilty.

Sam would not have acted like this, Nephi realized in mid-petulance. He thought about Sam. Unable to hear, and with his clubfoot, it always surprised Nephi that Sam found so much good in the world. He would stare at butterflies and water striders when they would go to the falls in the little valley a day's walk out of the little city where they lived near Jerusalem. Because Sam's foot was folded into a ball, the sand and dirt would find its way inside his mother's bindings, so Nephi would take him to the waterfall and let the force of the cascading water clean the folds and crevices of his deformed and twisted foot. Sam with his gestures would show Nephi things he would never see otherwise. A chamois hidden in the bushes. A hive of bees in the hollow of a tree. Sam always found ways to calm Nephi's soul. They were both at their best looking at God's creation. Even the memory of Sam from their mortal life calmed him, and he could use a little tranquility at the moment.

But Nephi was troubled even more than usual. This new Heike was as different from the old as a monarch butterfly is from the bloated caterpillar out of which it unfolds itself. How could someone of such monstrous sins just get a fresh start? Her entire past just rubbed away as if it had never happened? Was sin nothing more than a bundle of neurons woven and braided by a series of bad choices into a character framed by connecting dendrites and axons and other brain structures that can be violently unbundled by a blow to the head? Didn't she have to repent before she was baptized? Wasn't that one of the first principles and ordinances of the gospel? She had crocheted the egregious,

monstrous creature she had become through a series of inhuman and devilish actions. Actions that deserved a clear,
righteous judgment, consignment to the lowest kingdom.
Now, however, she was freed of guilt, shame, and sin by
nothing but a fortunate accident that just barely prevented
her from murdering the man who was now her husband!
How can an injury do what was the provenance of Christ's
atonement? It made no sense.

Arrow had gone to work at the vet clinic. Nephi knew
there would be nothing to see there but Arrow sticking
his arm up a cow's vagina to inseminate the beast, and he
wasn't in the mood for earthy fluids oozing out of bovine
orifices at the moment. So Nephi stayed behind to observe
Heike. It all seemed unjust through and through. He was
a mere angel because, in a moment of passion, as a very
young man, he had killed Laban in an act that saved his
descendants from being unbelievers—all the while believing he was inspired by God. And yet, here was a woman
who had done actions of such horror and evil (he used that
word sparingly, but in Heike's case it seemed to fit), and
yet that person had been replaced by this new 'Regine' as if
this murderess had been born to life afresh, "Oh sorry you
botched that earthly existence so badly, let's try another
round." She got a do-over, as they would say in Arrow's
time. Undeservedly so. Heike was someone redeemed, not
by Christ, but by a storm and a random rock just moments
before she could carry out her deliberate plan to execute a
fellow human being—one of God's children, to whom she

was now married in the temple. A shudder passed through Nephi. This did not seem right. Where was the justice in that? He supposed she would just go on up to the Celestial Kingdom without knowing about the monster she had chosen to become. Nephi sighed again.

Heike was sitting on her front steps putting on her running shoes. After the death of their infant many years ago, she had started running to forget the terror of that death, and now she was training for her third half-marathon. Nephi watched her lace up her shoes.

⊃ ⋉ ⋏ ⋉ ⊂

"Don't you just adore her?"

He should have known that the Goddess Asilah would show up. He did not want to argue. The Goddess had access to much more knowledge, power, and sheer insight than Nephi had at the moment. She would win every argument he could muster. She had the mind and heart of a Goddess. He was merely an angel.

"She takes care of her body." He said noncommittally.

"You still don't like her, do you? She is the part of Heike I always saw. The narrow thing that was the murderess is just a twisted thing curled up and buried within her brain."

"You know what she was. However, she is the wife of my charge; she is not mine to like or dislike." Nephi turned as if he'd apparate to another realm.

"Why don't you take the miracle of her life as it's been graced. You still want justice to bring its hammer down on her, all the while you are flawed in similar ways."

"I am nothing like her! I killed Laban because..."

"I'm not talking about Laban."

Nephi's eyes went wide. Then he said in a quieter voice, "It was war."

Regine Flees the Past

Regine ran. She took off up Spanish Valley Drive running along the road. She was moving at a good pace now, about a 7.5 minute mile. It was early spring, and it felt good to breathe the cool air coming down off of the La Sals. It was faster than she usually went, but she was feeling good, and wanted to push herself. The Canyonlands 5-mile race was only a month away, and she wanted to make a good showing. She passed the Hendersons' trailer, with the lovely cottonwoods providing shade that kept their trailer fairly cool, even on the hottest of Moab's summer days. Their mutt, Catfish, looked up lazily as she ran by. For a second it looked like it was thinking about rising to its feet, but in the end, true to its nature, it settled back down. Regine liked Mazy Henderson; she worked hard to manage her six boys and still had to hold down a full time job as a teacher's aide at the Helen M. Knight elementary school, but her husband was a lazy sot. He sometimes did odd jobs like repairing small engines, lawnmowers, or rototillers, but mostly he could be found sitting on the porch swing reading motorcycle magazines or tinkering with this Yamaha

650cc, which he raced on Sundays, despite it being the Sabbath. Regine frowned. Mazy deserved better, but she never said a word against her husband.

She ran on past a green alfalfa field blooming with purple flowers. Everything was blossoming. Creation astir. The air seemed so fresh now. The sun was still rising in the early morning air. It gave the world a sense of renewal. It made her think life was good. All was right in the world.

Then it wasn't.

She was running up a slight incline when she saw a boy playing with a black lab. He was picking up a tennis ball and throwing it into a patch of grass that fronted their house. The dog would tear after it like a bullet, catching it on the first or second bounce then bounding back to the boy and dropping the ball at his feet. What a good dog, she thought happily. Their dog, Bones, would chase a ball, but to get it back you had to chase her down, wrestle her to the ground, and pry the ball from between her clenched teeth while she shook her head violently from side to side. She didn't know the family that lived there and owned that obedient lab. They weren't Mormon, so she'd never had a reason to stop by, but the boy seemed happy. He looked to be 10... The age Heike would be... Then her thoughts followed her down into the darkness. That place they always tended towards. The hearing. The hearing,

The teenager is standing there. She remembers her face as cold and uncaring, but Arrow remembers it differently. He remembers the kid being scared but she sees her unrepentant face clearly in her mind's eye. She is utterly cold. Aloof. Thoughtless. Regine had stopped at the Library to pick up the microfiche films of the Berlin Zeitung, just for a second. She was looking for news of missing persons in Germany, just for a second. The baby in the car. Just for a second. And the kid. Not paying attention. Playing with the radio. A matter of seconds. A matter of bad timing. It was Spring, just like now. The car sat under the shade of the maples. It was cool. All the windows were down. She left her for just a second. She was gone, what, two minutes? Maybe only one. The sound. The awful sound. The horrific sound of breaking glass and tearing metal and the horn going off and then the sounds of people screaming for help and she knew, she knew right then that something had happened to her new baby, her new baby that had been blessed that last Sunday, and her name on the earth and on the records of the church was to be Heike Shellie Beamon, and she knew she was dead. She could feel that the connection between her and her baby had been torn from the earth. And that kid, what did she say? She didn't mean to hurt the baby. Hurt the baby! She killed it. Because she couldn't pay attention for three seconds and at that moment had adjusted the radio.

Regine stopped running. She put her hands on her knees and tried to focus on her breath. Why did she so often play this in her head? She tried so hard to keep it from coming up, but it did. Too often. By now, she had gotten better at catching it early; she didn't usually get this far down before she tried to stop it.

She breathed awhile. Looked at the world around her. Focused on the red cliffs that surrounded her. She remembered her other children. She remembered Arrow's love for her. She remembered her friends in Primary. She thought about how they were going to take a family vacation to Lake Powell. She remembered her little brick house on Bittle Lane and how good her life was right now. Heike had even visited her in a dream. She didn't need to go to this endless replay of the worst moment of her life. She smiled. Her life was not bad. She had just shy of twenty years of memory, but that was enough. She started running again.

I know how to read ancient Greek, she thought, and started playing with the implications of that. Little Heike slipped away again, although she was never far from her mother's thoughts.

A New Calling

Everyone was coming. Elder Holmberg, Alma Lune, the Stouts and their kids that weren't either off to college or serving missions. It was Arrow and Regine's 15th wedding anniversary and nearly Regine's 16th year as a member of the Church of Jesus Christ of Latter-day Saints. Arrow had baptized her, LeRoy had confirmed her, and Elder Holmberg had married and sealed Arrow and Regine. Alma Lune had been determined to bring all the players together one more time before… well let's be honest, Elder Holmberg was getting up in years. He now had lighter duties in recognition of growing frailties. He quite likely could go at any time… so bringing all the "Colorado River Survivors" together before Elder Holmberg was taken home to continue his eternal work on the other side seemed a necessity to Alma Lune. Elder Holmberg and Alma were flying down on Friday. They would spend a night at the stake president's house, and then the big party would be held in the cultural hall of the Stake Center.

The Relief Society had been commissioned to carry off the entire party—with all details placed in their capable hands. No one doubted it would be spectacular. It was to be dinner (cooked by a real chef borrowed from one of Moab's finer restaurants) and a dance. It would be decorated like a 1979 Disco, and of course the elders would set up the tables and chairs.

It would be amazing.

Today however, the stake president wanted to see Arrow and Regine, and they had to come to his office at precisely eight o'clock. They expected the worst. It could only be a calling, and a big one at that if they both had to appear at his office.

They waited on the efficient couch in the small foyer outside the stake offices.

"I'm guessing High Council," Regine said.

He nodded. A distracted look on his face.

She continued, "I think the bishop hasn't been in long enough for that to be it."

He looked at her hopefully. Then said, "I hope you are right. Me being called as bishop would pretty much convince everyone that the church is not being led by inspiration."

He was not joking. She laughed, then mocked a news anchor, "Ex-prisoner tagged as bishop! News at 7!"

He didn't laugh and she saw his face transition to the deep sorrow too often gracing his face.

"I'm sorry. But to be honest, I don't think people would care. No one thinks about it anymore. Really. You're fine. Remember the book about the bicycle; you have to not only believe in Christ, you have to believe him when he tells you that you can be redeemed."

He nodded, "Maybe." He stared at his shoes needing a good polishing. "People remember my mom's cousin."

She stared at him for a while, then added softly, "That's not on you. You know that."

He smiled, "I know."

Then he laughed and added, "I think I really, really, don't want to be bishop."

She squeezed his hand.

"You'll do what you're asked."

"That's the problem."

⊃ ✕ ⊹ ✕ ⊂

Arrow drummed on the steering wheel laughing with glee.

"Relief Society President! Ha. I should have known it was you and not me!"

He turned his pounding on the wheel into the drum solo of Iron Butterfly's classic *In-A-Gadda-Da-Vida*.

Regine scowled at him. Then looked out the window and after a few blocks said, "I can't do this right now."

Arrow is attentive enough to know that this was not the time to rub it in. He paused in his solo then said softly, "You'll be great. Better than anyone I can think of... I think the Lord needs you there... I think it will help with your worries."

She did not look at him.

"I can read Ancient Greek. I'm trying to figure things out all over again. This isn't a good time."

They passed Milt's Diner and crossed Mill Creek in silence. When they got to Bittle Lane, she said, "Don't tell the kids yet... OK?"

"About the calling? Or the Greek?"

"Either one. OK?"

He nodded, "*Sicher.*"

"I want to ask Elder Holmberg about it. I'm just not comfortable with it."

"You want to ask if it is OK to bow out?"

"Yeah, but not like that. I just want to hear what he thinks about the whole thing, the Greek, the calling, maybe even my nightmares."

"You know he's in his 90s"

"Yeah, but he's still as sharp as a tack according to Alma Lune."

"Yeah. I didn't mean he would not give good advice... I guess I'm saying don't expect too much. He may just tell you to trust in the Lord and do as you're called."

"I know. But that's OK. I don't really expect anything. I just need some assurance. You know?"

"Yeah. It's a good idea. Hey, while there ask him Kimball's question, "Why doesn't anyone ever have the faith to help an accident victim with their head cut off get it restored through the priesthood?"

Regine shook her head darkly then said, "That boy scares me. He is definitely your son."

Both fell silent, pursuing their own thoughts about the changes that lay ahead.

Clarity For Two
in Darkness

Alma Lune helped Elder Holmberg down the aluminum steps descending from the small single-engine prop commuter plane and onto the runway. He held the old gentleman's elbow until he reached the tarmac, then handed him the silver tipped yew cane with its silver lion-head handle. A gift from the members in Switzerland when he visited there three years ago.

Elder Holmberg was elderly, but there was a strength about him that radiated from his thick white hair, his straight back, and his persistent smile. He showed the infirmity of age in the slowness of his forward motion as he clicked forward on his cane supported by his secretary, but there was a solidity to him, a strength of bearing that seemed to radiate from his white suit.

Driving through the red rock canyon that ran into Moab valley, Alma Lune looked over at the sleeping man whose head was softly bobbing to the car's rhythm. They had been together, seeing each other nearly every day for years beyond count. Alma Lune had great affection for the man snoozing beside him. The thought that his time was short upon the earth always brought a feeling of melancholy. When he passed away, Alma Lune would retire. He had it all planned out. He would put in his papers for a mission. He wanted to go foreign. Maybe somewhere exotic like China or perhaps Africa. He remembered when he had once travelled to Uganda with Elder Holmberg on an assignment to assess the potential of opening a mission; he had been struck by the eagerness for the gospel with which he had been greeted. The people there touched his heart in ways that never really dissolved into the busyness of his work with the Apostle. It still surfaced from time to time, and maybe after the elder returned to his heavenly home, Alma Lune would head there. He was quite sure that he could request to go just about anywhere in the world and it would be granted—his years of service were well known in the church.

He looked over and found Elder Holmberg watching him.

"What are you thinking about?" he asked softly, still trying to find his bearings as he returned to wakefulness.

"You know, I've always wanted to serve a mission. I was just thinking about that when I retire."

"You mean when I die," the elderly man said, his eyes dancing with a bit of mischievousness.

"Die? You're still a stripling, you've got another ten years' work in you, I'll wager. And a bit more, I'll be bound."

Elder Holmberg waved his hand in dismissal, "We'll see. We'll see. But thinking of retiring, are you? You deserve it after being joined with me at the hip all these years."

Alma Lune laughed, "I would not have done a thing differently."

"So thinking about a mission?"

"Yeah."

"You choose the place, and I'll see that you go anywhere you want. Hawaii, maybe?"

Alma Lune laughed. "I was actually thinking of Africa, like Uganda. Or maybe China."

The old man smiled. "You'll be great no matter where you go. If you had just gotten married, you could have been a mission president, you know."

Alma Lune did not answer.

"I'll always count it as my greatest failure that I kept you too busy to properly look for a wife. You would have made a first-rate husband."

Alma Lune said nothing.

"Yes sir. There is some woman, somewhere in the world that should be weeping her heart out right now that you never offered her your heart."

Alma Lune's mouth became a tight line.

"I know you are in your sixties, but it's never too late, you know. I know some girls in their forties who would swoon for a chance at a man who has devoted his life to the service of the Lord."

Alma Lune's hand began to shake. He stared straight ahead.

"In fact. I happen to know that Elder Bismuth... you remember, he was just called to the Quorum of the Seventy last Conference, has an unmarried daughter who just turned 51. She works at KSL as one of the writers, and believe me she is passing fair. Fit as a fiddle and works out every morning from what Elder Bismuth says. And if you are interested, I'm sure I could wrangle an introduction out of him."

Alma Lune's eyes were starting to water.

"What's the matter? I know you are bone-shy, but time's a-ticking man. Let me help."

Alma Lune shook his head vehemently and choked out something indiscernible.

"What's that my boy? Speak up. My ears aren't those of a seventy-year-old you know."

Alma Lune composed himself. "I'm not interested. I've told you that again and again."

"Why not man? You know..." and Elder Holmberg lowered his voice into conspiratorial whisper, "...people are starting to wonder if you are unnatural or something, if you take my meaning."

Alma Lune spun his head toward the old man.

"Don't worry. Don't worry. I always set them straight. I tell them you aren't a fag in the least. That you are just extra shy of the lady folk."

They were passing the entrance to Arches National Park on the left. Alma Lune's face was a study in agony.

"You aren't one of those are you? You know, a homo?"

If Alma Lune had looked back over, he would have seen that Elder Holmberg had a strange scowl on this face.

"You're not. Right? I mean, I've never asked because well, my hell, man, you are one of the best people I know. Not some pervert. Speak up. You are worrying me."

Alma Lune's cheeks ran with tears.

"You've been a son to me. Say something."

Alma Lune could no longer drive due to the tears filling his eyes. Near the turnoff to Potash Road he pulled over, covered his face with his hands, and wept.

Elder Holmberg got out of the car and tried to start walking. His face. It was a devil's mask through and through.

⊃ ⲝ ⲫ ⲝ ⊂

So here was the weeping Alma Lune following God-hated Elder Holmberg down 191 just before the Colorado River bridge. The old man is shuffling in front of the rented Honda Accord as fast as he can cane. After about a 100 yards, Alma Lune pulls beside him and lowers the passenger side window and calls out to the old apostle, who is currently ignoring him thoroughly, "President Holmberg, please get in the car."

The apostle keeps walking. Eyes fixed in front of him, a vision of determination and pluck. However, his breathing is becoming labored, and sweat is now running down his face in little rivulets of perspiration tracking the arroyos of his jowls.

"Please! Elder, you cannot do this in this heat! Please get in the car."

The younger man notices a slight pause in the older man's step so tries to press the matter, "Please get in the car. It makes no sense for you to keep pressing forward. We need to talk about this."

The old man glances his way, but his face is twisted in a strange grimace that, even after all these years, Alma Lune is not sure whether he'd ever seen before.

They get to the bridge spanning the silt laden Colorado. The highway narrows here to two lanes, and there is no shoulder to speak of in which to walk. As the old elder enters onto the bridge, and Alma Lune continues to follow slowly behind, cars begin piling up behind them. Alma Lune sticks his arm out the window and tries to wave cars stalled behind him forward whenever the road clears, but horns are starting to honk, and even the loud foghorn-like sound of a semi-truck trailer blares from several cars back. Alma Lune shouts loudly out the window with all the fury and frustration he can muster.

"Elder Holmberg! Get in this car. You are making a scene. How does that serve the interests of the church? Do you want a reporter to discover you causing a traffic jam because you are being as stubborn as Balaam's ass?" The old man stops and turns to him and stares, his mouth moving, but nothing comes out. His anger has not relented one whit.

Alma Lune adds, "Do you really believe there is no forgiveness for me? That Christ died for nothing?"

That shocks him out of his petulance. "No of course not. Christ's atonement is absolute. But…but… a faggot?!"

"Get in, Elder Holmberg. I'll take you to President Lock's house."

Amid the honking horns, Alma Lune exits the vehicle, runs to the other side of the Accord, and helps his longtime friend and leader into the car. The old man is breathing heavily, so Alma Lune runs back around, jumps into the driver's seat, and speeds toward the stake president's house. The entire way he can tell Elder Holmberg is praying.

⊃ ≍ ⨯ ≍ ⊂

Nephi watches this scene with a scowl. Lady Asilah, the Goddess, is beside him. It is important to her that Elder Holmberg make it to the party—no, not the party, to the interview with Regine before the party. After that he will be ready to pass into the next life. It may take a while, or it may happen soon, but she is there just in case. His little stunt of walking down the highway greatly disturbed her.

Nephi is there because he's bored watching Arrow. He suspects Asilah is up to something with her attentions to the upcoming events. She's been hovering over the planning, putting her nose into things that seem like trivia, like what kind of ice cream to serve or whether to have a chocolate fountain at the dance.

They are both now flying behind the car, cautiously moving through the streets of Moab with the apostle and his secretary, carefully making their way to the stake president's house.

"Do you think he'll ever change?"

Asilah looks at her companion and narrows her eyes. Finally she shrugs, "Does it matter? Who knows what the future will bring?"

Nephi considers the elder and says, as if intuiting something within, "Of course it matters. We all want to think we are beloved of God. I know that God hates some, and it's hard to say who, and, obviously, he never tells. But if God can't change some aspects of himself, why should we act like some people can't ether. Sometimes I wonder if he hates me."

"Nephi, Nephi, God treats everyone as if they were beloved. It hardly matters in the scheme of things how he actually feels. He..."

"It would matter to me. It would explain so much about why I've been treated like a criminal since I died, rather than getting the opportunities that Moroni, Moses, and other prophets have had. I'm beginning to suspect he might feel that way toward me." Nephi tried to say this nonchalantly, as if he didn't really care, but he choked a little as he completed the sentence.

"Nephi. He's not going to tell you if he loves you or not. But be assured that, if he hates you, you'll never know."

"So he'll lie and say he loves me? Even if he doesn't?"

Nephi knew the answer to these questions, as every angel did, but he just felt like playing the petulant child.

"He loves all his children, either by inclination or by choice. Just because he's inclined to hate some doesn't mean that… Why am I bothering? You know all this."

Nephi turned away and went back to watching the automobile conveying President Holmberg. Why was life so complicated? Alma Lune had lived a good life, but still, why did the inclination to love other men exist at all? God was inclined to hate Elder Holmberg. Alma Lune was inclined to like men. Nephi had been inclined to love Asilah his whole life, and nothing could be done about any of it. Everyone went around doing differently than they felt. Something was wrong with heaven and hell.

⊃ ⋈ ⊹ ⋈ ⊂

Nephi gave up chasing the apostle and went in search of Arrow. He found him reclining in the hammock strung between two eucalyptus trees in the backyard reading a science fiction novel. Nephi stared at his charge. This man deserved less than he had been given. His wife deserved far, far less than she had been given. Where was justice? Where were the laws that were supposed to govern the universe? The righteousness inherent in things? Nephi floated down the draw downhill from Arrow's house and into the willows that lined Pack Creek. He stood above the river brooding. Slow water slipped down this ancient meander. It calmed his soul and clarified his mind. Nature had that effect on the ancient prophet. It always had. He thought back to his time on earth when the Lord had caught him up to a high mountain and taught him from on high. He remembered the cold air blowing wild over the wastelands below him from that height. The feel of giddy trust as he realized that there was no way down from these craggy heights save the Lord brought him back across the desert. There were high peaks all around him, covered in snow save where the hurricane force winds had scoured the snow away exposing the bare rock. He had been instructed from on high. From on high! What had happened that he now was a mere angel, had not been lifted up like his brethren? His brother Jacob? Enos? Alma and his son? The great captain and champion Moroni? Mormon and his son Moroni? All were Gods. Resurrected to the highest degree of glory. But it was worse than that. Laman was a God. Laman! How could that be? His brother had rebelled at every turn. He had murmured against his father Lehi! It all made no sense. And Asilah. A Goddess. And he, Nephi? Left behind. He felt like an unfinished resurrection. A transitional form. He was nothing more than a decision left pending by the eternities. A stymied metamorphosis. Asked to follow a stunningly uninteresting person who had done terrible things and then been rewarded. He'd likely be a God before Nephi. His wife, someone who properly belonged in the basement of the lowest degree of kingdoms for her unimaginable crimes, was likely to be dining with Asilah soon. Two pestilent souls somehow raised up and blessed with children bursting with potential and promise. How could all this be? Where was justice? And what was he supposed to do to earn the grace of the Lord and stand again in the place reserved for the righteous?

Nephi stared into the water, slow here by the willows. Water striders scurried here and there, standing still for a time, then for reasons only they understood bolting to a new position in the quiet water where they again sat patiently among their fellows. What was he supposed to do? What was he supposed to learn?

These facts existed:

1. Nephi had not been given any assignment but Arrow.
2. There was little to do.
3. He did not know what his Heavenly Parents wanted him to do.
4. Justice demanded certain ends.
5. Neither Nephi nor Heike had satisfied those.

"Perhaps," Nephi said to the willows, "despite Asilah's constant jabs, my purpose is to help bring about those demands. Enact Justice."

Then in a flash it came to him. Recompense was needed. He had been given this assignment to restore order and balance to the universe.

For the first time in a long time Nephi's heart felt light. This was the spirit. He could tell. It felt so good and right. And liberating. He knew what he had to do. He picked up a rock and tossed it into the still waters, sending the water striders scattering. Yes. He knew what he had to do.

Ministering Angels

Regine nervously tapped the steering wheel as she drove to her interview with President Holmberg. At first she had turned on a recording of the Mormon Tabernacle Choir to help prepare her spirit, but it was not helping calm her nerves at all. She pulled up to the Stake President's house and looked at the well-manicured yard with its nicely shaped lilacs siding the two-story frame house. The house was painted a lovely Alice blue that contrasted nicely with the red rocks surrounding the Moab Valley. It was reminiscent of a New England saltbox house, giving it a slight whaling village feel, but off enough to make it belong amicably in the Canyonlands. Boxwood hedges lined the sidewalk and the path to the front door, and a small cement birdbath, which sported a fountain coming from a frog's mouth, added a sense of luxury to the home. President Barnhart was the local orthodontist, and two of her own children had braces. Given the cost she and Arrow were paying, she was sure they must be doing very well financially.

She was a little early, so she bowed her head and whispered a prayer for help. She felt a little better after. She got out of the car and walked to the door. She rang the bell, which played some snippet of classical music she recognized but could not place. In seconds Sister Barnhart answered the door. She was dressed as if she were going to church in a lovely teal dress, with a modest pearl necklace ringing her neck—no doubt real. She was also wearing heels. In her house? She was wearing heels? In her house! Heels! She realized that the presence of Elder Holmberg must be driving formality, and it made Regine even more nervous, as she had not dressed nearly as churchly. She had not even worn a dress, but rather a set of dressy black slacks with a pretty white muslin cotton blouse. Sister Barnhart did not seem to notice her indiscretion and hugged her warmly.

"Regine, come in. I'm so glad you are here. I mean, I'm glad to see you. Come in, come in. "

It occurred to Regine that it must be pretty stressful having the president of the Quorum of the Twelve Apostles staying at your house.

"It is good to see you too. How are things? Is there anything I can do to help out?"

Sister Barnhart smiled, warmly sensing the empathy in what Regine was asking, "No, I'm doing OK. But thank you."

She led her to the front room. There was a fire burning despite it being in the middle of a fairly warm day. The place was immaculate and smelled strongly of lavender and cinnamon.

"The president is sitting in the kitchen having a glass of milk and a piece of bread. I'll let him know you are here."

Regine sat down on the leather couch and looked at the painting on the wall. It was a picture of the savior with a group of children gathered about listening in rapture to his words, although his mouth was closed and he did not seem to be saying anything really. And he was not looking at the children at all, but rather between them, as if there were someone standing nearby that he was actually attending. It bothered her for some reason that he was not looking at the children. She squirmed a bit on the sofa, trying to force herself into a posture of comfort, then sighed deeply, nervously trying to realign her breath. She was about to meet the president of the Quorum of the Twelve Apostles. As her belly seemed to be moving to her throat, she reconsidered. No, he was not just his title. He was a friend. He had been with her from the beginning on that fateful river trip. They had shared a hospital stay together for a few days recovering from pneumonia just two doors down at LDS Hospital. They had visited often. He had sealed her and Arrow together. He and Alma Lune had visited them in Moab, and they had had dinner with them for years. He had even come to Kimball's baptism, although he had been on assignments for the other children. Why was she so nervous now? She knew why. She was afraid he would not help her. She did not want to be the Stake Relief Society President. She sighed again, and so did her soul.

President Holmberg came into the room supported by Sister Barnhart's arm. He looked up and smiled, somewhat sadly she thought. He was maneuvered adroitly and efficiently to a large recliner turned slightly toward the couch so they could have a comfortable conversation. Sister Beamon stood up and warmly hugged the old Apostle in his chair.

"President, it is so good to see you. You are looking well. Did you have a pleasant flight down?"

He looked uncomfortable, but Elder Holmberg smiled and said, "Yes. Fine. A fine trip. I'm still a little worn from it all, but fit as a fiddle as they say. I'll be OK for this evening's celebration. All is well."

She nodded, "Where is Alma Lune staying?"

He had a look of surprise on his face, and tried to say something, but she could not make it out.

"I'm sorry, is he not staying with one of the members?"

"No. No. I've put him up in a hotel. I changed it. You can't be too careful with these. There were children in the home you know. The Littlewoods. You know?"

Regine nodded. President Holmberg was right. Alma Lune needed rest as much as the president, and children can be so noisy.

"How are you sister Beamon? It's been too long. Are your children doing well?"

She smiled. "You should see them! They are so grown up. Our oldest is learning to drive. Can you believe it? How the time passes."

The old gentleman smiled back. "Indeed. As Jacob says, 'Our lives passed as if in a dream.'"

Regine reached out suddenly and took both of the Apostle's hands and held them for a heartbeat or two. "That's just it. Half of mine is missing. I woke up in my thirties, and I don't know who I am. I've woken up in the middle of my dream. I don't know what to do. I just discovered I can read Greek. Fluently. It seems so strange. Who am I?"

The Apostle patted her hands but did not say anything in response to her flowing tears.

Things started pouring out of her. "They've called me to be the stake Relief Society president, and I can't do it right now. I'm so scared. My mind is too full. I've started having dreams of little Heike, and I can't seem to let go of the anger and hate I feel towards the teenager that killed her. Now I learn that I know yet another language. Who am I? I can't add this to the pile."

"German, Japanese, French, and English as I recall."

"Yes. And now Greek."

"My dear, Regine Beamon. Haven't you learned by now that the Lord qualifies who he calls? Do you think your stake president uninspired?"

"No not that. It's just he likely doesn't know...."

"Does the Lord?"

"Yes. Of course. But…"

"Trust your leaders. They might not know everything you are dealing with, but I assure you, for I have experienced it many times, that when the spirit speaks, it is aware of what you are going through. My dear girl. Trust in the Lord, and lean not unto your own understanding and it will be well with you at the last day."

Regine did not say anything but had ceased crying. President Holmberg patted her hand kindly.

"Now you listen up. Don't worry. If it becomes overwhelming, you just give me a call and I'll rearrange things for you. But try it for a time. Will you? Just for a time. See what blessings unfold. Maybe the answers to your doubts and fears will make themselves plain as you lose yourself in the errand of the Lord. Will you give the calling a go? I have a feeling you may find it suits you better than you think. No, I feel it stronger. I feel the Lord speaking to my soul that this will be a joyful service for you. There is something waiting for you that will answer many of your questions. Doubt not. Fear not."

Regine nodded and stood and hugged him again, then sat back down.

"I'll try. I really will. Thank you. Thank you for taking the time with me."

"Oh dear, Regine. You are like a daughter to me. I'm glad to do what I can for you any time."

"I'd better let you rest for tonight's party. I suppose Alma Lune will pick you up right before?"

Elder Holmberg looked strangely uncomfortable.

"Is everything OK?"

"It's just… awkward… You see, I've released Alma Lune as my secretary and well… He'll be there I suppose?"

"What? Of course he'll be there. He's a dear friend too. He's been your right hand for years. What's going on? Did you two have a falling out?"

"Yes. That's just it. We had a falling out. Yes, that's right, we had a falling out, and I'm no longer comfortable with him as my secretary."

Regine stared at the old man then shook her head and started a mock scolding. "Now you listen here, President. Whatever the source of your tiff, you've got to make it right again. I seem to remember a certain General Conference talk last April called, 'Forgiveness, A More Righteous Way.' It touched me deeply—do you remember who gave it?"

Elder Holmberg looked sheepish, but did not say anything.

Regine looked at him and then her eyes misting again, said, "Forgiveness is hard."

Elder Holmberg nodded, "Yes. I'm sorry. You are trying to forgive someone who wronged you deeply, and here I am…." He too started to weep.

"Alma Lune. It's just… How?… He's been a part of my life… and now?"

"Of course. You must…."

"But what if he's the one who gave my son the sickness? That's where I met him… you know. It all makes sense. He was with my son. Maybe he was the one? But he's never gotten sick. And it doesn't go away, does it. So he couldn't have. But what if he did? Or what if he opened the door through which my son slipped. He's served me all these years so faithfully, but what if it was guilt?"

Regine moved back, wide-eyed and confused.

"What are you talking about? Elder Holmberg… Are you OK? I'm not sure what you are saying."

He looked up suddenly and became very formal. He tried to get out of the chair but could not quite manage it given how deeply he had sunk into it. She rose and helped him up. He said, quickly,

"It's nothing. I'm just tired and starting to ramble a bit. I must rest before the party. Will you call Sister Barnhart? Accept the call. You won't regret it. I promise in the name of the Lord that you will find unexpected blessings as you faithfully fulfill your calling."

Sister Beamon exchanged goodbyes with Sister Barnhart and walked to her car. She shuddered before starting the car and driving home to make preparations for the party. She knew, however, she would accept the calling.

⊃ ⋈ ⋆ ⋈ ⊂

The party was a few hours away and Regine had to rest. She hadn't been sleeping well, and her visit with President Holmberg had not left her with the peace she expected to find. She felt wrung out. He had not really seemed interested that she could speak Greek, or that she had only half a life of memories. She felt so tired. The kids, the new calling, the party, her strange dreams of Heike, so many things were weighing her down and pressing her into such nebulous shapes. She just had to rest. She picked up the new Jack Weyland novel Arrow had gotten for her on a recent trip to Price and lay down on the couch to escape from the world for just a little while.

⊃ ⋈ ⊁ ⋈ ⊂

The angel hovered over Regine lying on the couch lightly sleeping, a novel lying face down, open on her chest. She was breathing softly and steadily. Perfect for the work at hand.

Nephi shrank. He smalled and smalled until he was as small as a grain of sand. Then, as tiny as a bacterium. And then to a size smaller than a water molecule. With his smalling complete, he entered through one of the pores on Regine's check and made his way deep into her brain. He spent a long time looking at the damage her fall had done to her cerebral structures. The wreckage was complex. He studied it a long time, carefully analyzing the pathways that had been damaged. There was general damage in many areas, but these had been repaired by neural growth and by rerouting critical functions to new areas of the brain. He found that most of the relevant damage to the current state was in a small part of the temporal lobe and lower portions of the frontal lobes. He then surveyed the mechanical function of her entire neural net, up and down, back and forth until he kenned both where things stood, and, more importantly, where things needed to go to restore justice to the world. It had to be done carefully. If done clumsily, or in a way that lacked finesse and nuance, the repairs he effected could overwhelm this damaged person.

He was somewhat surprised, but pleased, to find a region, detached from the rest of her brain by the trauma of her injury, still functioning, still rolling in ways that suggested cognition. Heike was still alive, and by all the neuronal activity he could detect, still in command of a great store of neural resources, despite their being detached from much of the brain.

He observed and calculated. He traced the workings of this complex being until he was sure he understood at least enough to suggest how these neural leanings might inform the mind. And when satisfied with his explorations, he pulled a bit here. He snipped a thing or two there. He wiggled and jiggled certain structures, fused together others, and all in all made sure everything was fitly arranged.

Justice would be served. Let mercy then work its magic with ALL the demands of justice standing in their proper place, exposed to the light where it could be fully satisfied with nothing masked or hidden due to accident or caprice. This was why he had been called to be Arrow's guardian angel.

The Party

Regine looked radiant. Arrow thought she moved like a Goddess, speaking warmly with nearly everyone there—moving from group to group with grace and elegance. Why someone so splendid and refined would be married for seventeen years to this kid from Moab was beyond him. The cultural hall was decorated with beautiful roses, hearts, and flowers. A table with a red punch fountain was splashing merrily under one of the basketball baskets at one end amid an army of red plastic cups, and on the other a table loaded with presents, a pink book for the guests to sign, and a display of framed pictures of Regine and Arrow's life together. Soft music from a jazz band was playing through a sound system (provided by Brother Ortega, a professional DJ). President Holmberg was seated in a folding chair at the terminus of a line of people waiting to shake his hand or to get him to sign his book from many years ago, *Fear Not But Be Believing* or his latest book for youth, *What's Your Thirty Pieces of Silver?* He seemed tired, but was managing to smile as each person took his hand and warmly exchanged pleasantries.

Arrow wandered around with a drink in his hand smiling ear to ear. This was what the Celestial Kingdom must be like—friends, children, laughter, a joyous sense of familiarity and comfort. He heard snippets of conversation. Brother Gleason was telling a story about his neighbor's calf getting loose in his corn field and the devil of a time they had getting it out. LeRoy was telling Alma Lune about how Regine could read Greek like a classical scholar. Penny Coll was telling a group of the sisters about how, since she started using lavender in her new oil infuser, the number of her migraines had been cut in half. All was right in the world.

Brother Ortega cleared his throat in the microphone and tapped it a couple of times to get everyone's attention. Once obtained, he said in his best DJ voice:

"It's time for dancing!"

There was a great cheer and a hearty round of clapping.

"First, let's give a round of applause for our honorees this night, Regine and Arrow Beamon!"

The room exploded in calls and cheers, hoots, hollers, and an applause vigorous enough to content a rock star.

"We are also honored to have in our presence Elder Holmberg, president of the Quorum of the Twelve Apostles."

A more calm round of applause as Elder Holmberg stood and waved his white handkerchief over his head in a small circle. He then sat down and mopped his face with the device, a big smile beaming from his face.

The DJ's voice echoed over the dance floor, "Is everyone having a good time!?!"

The crowd exploded with cheering, clapping, and stomping.

"Now, before I play the first dance, there is the matter of an anniversary present for Brother and Sister Beamon."

Arrow, who was standing next to Regine holding her hand, looked at her and shrugged his innocence. He knew nothing about this. She returned the gesture.

"A lot of people have gone in on this, but well... let's just get to it... Open the curtain! The lights were dimmed and the curtain fronting the stage of the cultural hall began to open onto a fairly dark stage, and as Arrow and Regine watched with some concern and perplexity on their faces, the room went absolutely still. One could just make out two large white objects on the stage. Suddenly, a single stage light illuminated the scene. Standing there was a complete set of large kitchen appliances, refrigerator/freezer, a new gas range, and a dishwasher.

Regine just stood there staring around stupidly. Arrow seemed both pleased and embarrassed. Suddenly Regine covered her face with her hands, and went down on her knees shaking and crying.

"It's too much. Too much. *So viel. Mein Freunde! Wie habt Ihr Das getan?! Danke. Danke schön.*"

Arrow went idiotic in his thank yous. Although he made a good bit as a vet and had his university pension, in taking on Regine's hospital bills and her numerous surgeries, they lived very frugally to pay off the debt they had incurred.

Everyone clapped and encouraged them onto the stage where they looked over their new appliances with Regine bawling like a baby. Arrow tried to gather some of his dignity and formally thanked everyone involved, gave a small lecture on how badly they had needed these things, but with all the needs of hospital bills and the kids, they had put off getting new ones year after year until their appliances were on the verge of being nonfunctional—except their old dishwasher which had not worked for three years but had kept its place of honor because no one wanted a big hole gracing their kitchen. Then Arrow got all teary-eyed, and Regine looking at him just started laughing. Everyone joined in.

They climbed up onto the stage with their children and inspected their new treasures. Arrow, with a heave, picked up Greta and placed her on the washing machine. She said in a soft voice, "*Wunderbar!*" Everyone clapped and laughed, but not as hard as when Kimball said in all seriousness, "I'll never have to wash the dishes again!"

Brother Ortega saved another round of embarrassing gratitude by announcing it was time for the dance and asked that the honored couple lead the way by moving to the middle of the dance floor. They did.

"I have it on good authority that about seventeen years ago this song was playing the first time they kissed." With that, Foreigner's "I Want to Know What Love Is," started playing through the speakers. Regine looked at Arrow, who was smiling mischievously. She shook her head smiling and then kissed him hard on the lips. The people let out a long ahh and applauded again joyously. And the dance started.

⊃ ⤬ ⤩ ⤬ ⊂

Elder Holmberg looked at Alma Lune with displeasure. He was dancing like a mad man. Smiling. Wiggling around to the music like a teenager. He should have known the man was a homo. He had fired him that same day, and Lune didn't look the least bit apologetic or even unhappy. He was on the dance floor smiling, having fun, and not in the least maintaining the quiet dignity of a man in his position. Or the position he used to be in. Still. A little decorum seemed warranted given his age and his long association as the secretary to the president of the Twelve Apostles. He was showing his true self. He had never acted so flippant in all these years of service, yet now so recently released that he was still trailing clouds of responsibility, he was bouncing around like one of that Dick Clark fellow's teeny-boppers. Shameful. He found nothing inappropriate in the behavior of his fellow saints dancing. Brigham Young had encouraged the early pioneers to dance. Yet as a servant of the Lord, he had always maintained the dignity of his office, as he expected of Alma Lune, or had expected of him, but he supposed now that he had been released he could fall back on his old ways, well not all his old ways hopefully, but he had not expected him to become so unleashed quite so quickly. First, he had danced with the Beamon children, and now he was dancing with sister Stout, and Brother Stout was laughing hilariously watching them do a 1950s sock-hop dance to an Elton John song. "Elton John," Elder Holmberg thought, "A known homosexual."

Finally, he could not take it. The music was much too loud, and Alma Lune's conduct was repulsive. He had to go. He sent someone to fetch Sister Barnhart, who came with alacrity, and explained he was tired and thought it best if she took him home. She helped him to his feet, and they walked over to Regine and Arrow who were standing near the punchbowl taking a break from the dancing.

"My friends, I'm going to have to retire I'm afraid. My old bones wear out much faster than they should. I hate to miss the festivities, but I'm going to have a glass of warm milk and go to bed."

Regine took both his hands. "Dear, sweet President Holmberg. We are so honored you came. We have been greatly blessed."

Arrow joined in. "Indeed. Indeed. This meant the world to us. Thank you so much for coming. You are like a part of the family."

The old apostle hugged them and patted Regine's cheek. "Remember what I said. You've got some sweet blessings coming."

She put her hand on his and inclined her head as if to enjoy his touch more deeply. He pulled it away, and on Sister Barnhart's arm walked out of the building.

つ × ⼂ × ⼂

Regine was standing outside looking at the moon and cooling off from the dance when Alma Lune walked out of the door on the way to his car.

"I was hoping to see you! I said my goodbyes to Arrow, but I could not find you."

"You won't get away without saying goodbye, I assure you, Alma Lune."

"I should have known."

"It was so good to see you having a good time!" She said, then remembering, "I'm so sorry about what happened between you and Elder Holmberg. I'm sure he'll change his mind. He told me he had released you as his secretary. But I can't see him doing anything without you."

A shadow passed across Alma Lune's face, but he smiled and said, "I'm sure you are right."

They stood silently together looking at the full moon just rising from the rim of the Moab Valley. The white orb seemed so pregnant with life and meaning. A sense of the sublime seemed to infuse the air as the red rocks around their little town lit up under the lunar glow, creating a patchwork of light and shadow through the complexity made of the boulders, cracks, ravines, and crevasses of the surrounding red rock cliffs.

"The world is so beautiful," Alma Lune suddenly exclaimed.

Regine took his hand and kissed him on the cheek. "Alma Lune, I love you. So does Arrow. You are very dear to us. Don't let the old man's moods spoil things for you. It will change. I'm sure."

Alma Lune looked at her sadly, "Yes. Of course. Thank you. I love you too." He then added, looking at the moon above, "I wish I were as pure as that light from the moon. I wish I were like an angel. Pure and right."

Regine looked at him, "Oh my dear, sweet, man, you already are. Don't you see?"

Alma Lune smiled at her sadly, "This human body and all its wants and needs seem so much of earth. I'm not an angel at all. Perish the thought. I'm so much of the mud God created us humans from. I know it's an unrighteous wish, but I'm looking forward to it all being cleaned up in the resurrection. I just have this beautiful desire to be good. Better than I am. Really good inside and out."

Regine reached out and took his hand. "You are good Alma Lune. I have no doubt about that.... I'd better get back to the party—Arrow will wonder where I am. But promise me after we sit together at a meal in the next life, and THAT party starts, that when the music begins you will give me the first dance."

Alma Lune smiled at her and kissed her on the cheek. "I promise. Thank you. You and Arrow have been one of the Lord's tender mercies in my life. I glory in what you and your family have given me. I have been greatly blessed."

They watched the moon for a moment more. Then Alma Lune said, "I think I'll take a drive out in the canyons tonight and get a better look at this moon. It is so lovely."

"Be safe and don't stay out too late."

He gave her a kind smile, and they gave each other a hug and each went their separate ways.

What Have You Done?

The news of Alma Lune's death did not reach them until three days after the accident on Dead Horse Point Road. Elder Holmberg had flown back early the day after the party and assumed that Alma Lune would follow in two days when they were scheduled to return. The County Sheriff who investigated the accident could find no next of kin, and knowing only that the car had been rented by the Corporation of the Church of Jesus Christ under the name of President Holmberg, had called Salt Lake and been referred to the people in charge of handling insurance claims. Finding that a death had occurred, they had called the managing secretary of the Office of the First Presidency and found, to their relief, that Elder Holmberg was hale and hardy because he had attended a meeting of the Twelve that very morning. Checking further, they found the death had been his secretary, Alma Lune. No one of consequence, so they relaxed (they should not be faulted for their seeming callousness; they dealt with death claims among the Saints at a rate of at least one a day, often more). However, the next day, because there had been a death, they called

Elder Holmberg's office secretary to see if the driving records of Alma Lune could be obtained, seeing as how he
had no significant other or next of kin to request them. She
was devastated and told Elder Holmberg the terrible news
of his death. Elder Holmberg was so distraught as to be
almost non-functional, and he was admitted to the hospital
because of heart palpations. He told his office secretary to
let Alma Lune's ward know and also asked her to call the
Beamons, whom he knew would be devastated as well. This
is how they found out. Elder Holmberg died two days later.
The saying went abroad that Alma Lune, his nearly lifelong
secretary, had gone before him to prepare for the Apostle's
greater work to continue in the spirit world.

⊃ ⋉ ⊀ ⋉ ⊂

Arrow lay in bed, his heart sad over the death of Alma
Lune. In the morning, they were driving up for the funeral
in Salt Lake City. His ward was handling all the details. He
was beloved in the ward and had served as elder's quorum
president, second counselor in two bishoprics, and was
well known as a generous and capable man. His loss would
be felt in many ways. He touched many lives. Arrow had
just come from his daughter's room—he had gone in after
he overheard her weeping over Alma Lune's death. They
talked about the things they remembered, how much fun
he was. He was like a beloved uncle. They would all miss
him terribly. He'd gone to bed after suggesting she think

on all the good things he'd taught her and try to remember him by living a good life, following his example of love and service. She had finally gone to sleep.

Tears were never far from his eyes these last few days. The loss of both Elder Holmberg and his secretary seemed too much. Regine had been particularly distraught. She walked around as if in a daze. He understood that. But she had also been moody and distracted. Sometimes even laughing in the middle of one of the children crying over the loss of their friend.

She suddenly sat up and looked at him lying next to her in the bed.

"I had the strangest dream." She was speaking German. "I was in a forest, and an angel appeared to me. She wanted me to find her. Isn't that strange, James?"

"James?"

"I mean Arrow. I don't know why I said that. Good-night." And with that she plopped down and turned on her side and started breathing heavily.

How strange. What was stress doing to her? And who the hell was James?" That was not a name she had ever mentioned.

⊃ ⋉ ⊀ ⋉ ⊂

The drive up to Salt Lake was tearful but uneventful. They had visited Alma Lune almost every visit to Salt Lake, and he stayed with them often when he came to visit the canyonlands he loved. His funeral was this afternoon. Elder Holmberg's was tomorrow.

The ward had learned of their friendship, and at the insistence of Elder Brinkleton of the Twelve, they were seated in an area roped off for family. Since Alma Lune never mentioned any, and none could be found, the Beamons and their children were given the privilege of sitting there with the members of the First Presidency and the entire Quorum of the Twelve, save Elder Ambrose, who was away on assignment.

It was a beautiful service. Elder Brinkleton conducted. Alma Lune's favorite song, "All Creatures of Our God and King," was played by a quartet of string players from the Utah Symphony. Beth Rosenblatt, a singer from the Denver Opera whom Alma Lune had been instrumental in bringing into the Church, sang "Holy City," another of Alma Lune's beloved hymns. The Prophet himself stood and told a number of stories of his remembrances of Alma Lune, some of them funny and all of them heartwarming and meaningful. Elder Brinkleton stood and asked if anyone would like to say a few words about this beloved man. His bishop rose and talked about his service. He broke down as he described the deep love that Alma Lune displayed to everyone he met.

Then Regine stood. Arrow looked up in surprise, but smiled knowing how much he meant to her. He had been a part of her life as long as he himself had. She looked sadly at the casket, then said,

"I was probably the last person to see him alive. We were standing outside the ward building in Moab looking at the moon. It was so beautiful as it rose above the rim of the Moab valley; we were struck with an awe so profound... we were filled with wonder. He mentioned how beautiful the world was. He loved the area in which he perished. He loved the red rock country, its canyons, its arches and formations. I think more often than not when he claimed to be visiting us, he was really visiting the landscape. He knew how to breathe the air there, how to let it run into his veins and fill up his senses with meaning and beauty. There was a grace about him. A joy. A childlike wonder that was infectious whenever he was around. My children will miss him, as will we. So the full moon over Moab will now always remind me of his too short presence in the world. I have always loved the moon, and now it will mean even more. I remember my mother waking me late at night. We were staying in our cabin high in the Bavarian Alps, and she insisted that I come outside and look at the moon. It was bright and full like the last night of Alma Lune's life. The moon lit the mountains and fell like daylight in the meadow that fronted our little cottage. It was magical. The world is full of magic. May it always be so. In the Name of Jesus Christ Amen."

After the interment, Arrow was shaking as they drove to their hotel provided by the Church. He did not want to think about this right now, but his oldest son, Kimball, brought the reason home when he asked, "Mom do you re- member your mother? I've never heard that story. I thought you did not remember anything before you met dad in the hospital?"

Arrow noticed she was leaning against the window holding her head as if in pain, but she answered. "Of course I don't remember my mother. Why would you say that?"

"It's what you said at the funeral."

"Don't be silly." She answered with some impatience, "I don't remember anything about my mother. You know that."

Arrow signaled with a backward glance for his son to drop it. Which he did.

Then Regine, gave a soft moan and said, "My head really hurts."

"Greta and Jens started an argument about which burger place was better and where they should eat tonight.

Regine gave another moan and said, "Kids, kids, let's not argue right now. Mommy's head hurts so why don't we all shut the fuck up for a little while, OK?"

⊃ ⋉ ⋇ ⋉ ⊂

"What have you done?"

Asilah appeared before Nephi in all her glory. She was radiant. Bright as the sun and as terrible as an army with banners. Her body celestial was revealed in all its splendor and power. Nephi was taken by surprise. He had never seen her like this, but he did not question what this was about. It was his act to bring righteousness back to the world. He stood by his decision.

"I have brought again the justice that was taken when the Heike creature was unmade by a rock. Not the atonement of the Holy One. But by a rock. That cannot be."

"Nephi, who were you to decide that? You have broken our most fundamental rules. You have manipulated matter without the right or insight. You have played with someone's salvation? How could you? How dare you take on God's most sacred powers?"

"I was inspired by the spirit."

"You were not. You were inspired by your own self-righteousness. The Spirit? Isn't that what you claimed when you slew Laban?"

"I will not hear your mockery any longer." He tried to leave, but found himself bound. His powers of transport taken.

"What is this?"

"Nephi. Nephi. I have pled on your behalf. Though your crimes against me were many, I forgave you."

"Crimes against you! Are you mad? I did nothing to you."

The sadness in Asilah's voice was palpable.

"I will tell you. You would have found out eventually. I will tell you now."

"What are you talking about? I remember earth life as well as you do..."

She interrupted him, "In your life you feared too much. You hated that we had joined the Omya. That we had begun to live among them. To learn their ways. That our children began to marry their children. You were filled with hatred for them because their skins were dark, their language was strange, their ways were different."

"I didn't hate them…"

"We did not bother you. We taught the Omya, our friends, our new brothers and sisters, not to bother you. Other Omya attacked you. But you never bothered to learn the difference between the different groups, between the peoples; they were all one to you. You hated them all. You hated them indiscriminately. And you taught your people to hate them. And you stirred up those who stayed with you. And you told them that it was your brothers Laman and Lemuel who were causing them to attack you. And so you came against us. You made swords like the sword of Laban. And you attacked us without warrant. Without finding out who your enemies were, or who you were fighting against. Your heart was filled with hatred."

Nephi stared in horror, "We were the ones hated. Laman and Lem…"

"Silence! You attacked us in our village. You killed many of the Omya. And you came upon a young man, Hebrew like yourself. You slew him. You cut him down without thought. Filled with a misdirected rage. You killed my son, Nephi. Do you hear me? You didn't know. No one told you. You killed your nephew. His name was Lehi. After his father's father, who was beloved of my husband Laman. You killed my son."

Nephi stared. He was trying to say something. But no words came.

"I forgave you. It took years. But I did. While I was still alive. I knew your heart. I knew there was goodness there. This was an act of malice and war, but somewhere in there was a good man. I pled on your behalf."

"You were led to believe this was about slaying Laban. We thought if you could accept that, your culpability for the greater crimes enacted as you hated and raged at others might help you repent. You were given this assignment with Arrow to learn forgiveness. To learn to love him, and Heike, two very lost souls. Like yourself."

Nephi looked at his hands and shrank back in terror at Asilah's words.

"But you have instead added to your crimes. And so much damage has resulted. I'm sorry. You could have been one of the most blessed and loving souls, but you chose it not. Now all things will come before your remembrance."

"But I loved God with all my heart!"

"Oh, Nephi, my beloved brother, that was only ever half of the requirement."

And suddenly, Alma's description of the pains of a damned soul descended on Nephi in their fullness, and he recognized them. He saw how he had treated his brothers, Asilah, those who called him king, and all those whom he had filled with fear and hate. He found his murders placed at his feet. And he saw Heike, whom he had poisoned and corrupted with his fear. He fell to his knees. An angel in the grip of pain and sorrow he was never prepared to face.

Holding On

Regine knew with whom she wrestled. And for the moment, she had it cornered, but how long could this last? The phantom from her past appeared from time to time. When it did, Regine could not remember what happened when the beast took over. Arrow claimed that when the thing came out, Regine never appeared to be out of control or dangerous. She would say odd things, refer to things Regine had never spoken of, like her comments during the funeral service, or behave in ways inconsistent with her nature. Regine, however, could feel her down there, buzzing around like a bumble bee trapped between the window and a screen, trying to find the crack that would lead to its freedom. She could sense her malicious presence. A demon—searching, prying, trying the boundaries which caged her. She did not tell Arrow; she did not want him to think she was losing her mind, even though she was. Who was this woman whom no one had tried to find? Who spoke so many languages with such felicity? Why had she come to Moab? How had she become trapped so deeply inside Regine?

Occasionally, Regine would get a glimpse of a fragment of memory that she knew was owned by someone else. This was infrequent, but when it occurred she almost vomited as if to purge her insides from the presence. Last week, she had been sitting with ward choir when she had a memory of singing in a beautiful cathedral. There were candles burning everywhere. The building was cold, and the people all around her were wrapped in furs and soft wool clothing. She was holding a hymnal, and there was an organ accompanying the choir. From where she was singing, she could see hardwood benches stretching back toward the entrance where a massive hardwood double door hung. Suddenly, it opened and other singers entered. She could see it was dark outside and snow was falling, dusting the entering singers. They marched down the aisle and joined her and the choir singing in the front of the chapel. Another time she had been sorting laundry and she remembered standing in a packed subway in Japan. There was a slight feeling of claustrophobia and being trapped. She was holding onto a hand strap trying to keep from swaying into the people beside her.

She wondered about her previous life, but she felt a strange reversal. She knew someone had been watching. All this time, her previous self had been stuck somewhere in her mind watching all of it as it unfolded but unable to influence anything. And she knew without any doubt that this person hated her. Hated Arrow. Hated every single aspect of her life, from her marriage to her service within the church to each of her children—individually. She was scared of her. Her presence was as palpable as a lump in the throat or a toothache. There was something infernal about the shade within. More like a possession than a set of memories trying to find their way out.

⊃ ⨯ ⭍ ⨯ ⊂

Arrow looked over at Regine sleeping against the window as they passed the turnoff to La Sal. What was happening to her? She seemed so strange the last few days, but today at the temple had taken the cake. Before it had been little things, like occasionally uttering profane words in front of the children in ways she'd never done during their entire time together. Sometimes she would lose her bearings for a few seconds, but when it happened it was like someone else was looking through her eyes. His mind thought of episodes in the scriptures where demons had taken over someone's body. It made him frightened, but she always came out of it quickly and returned to herself. But today at the Monticello Temple, things had taken a much more alarming turn. It was time to take her to Doc Mayfield to see if there might be more to this than met the eye.

It had all seemed so normal this morning. It was the third Saturday of the month, and the whole Moab 4th ward (or those members inclined to take temple work seriously) were going to the temple to do work for the dead. Regine loved this. Their time together alone was always precious. Kimball would watch his younger brother and sister while they made this monthly pilgrimage. After doing a couple of endowment sessions, they would stop at Butch Cassidy's Burgers and Shakes for a hamburger and pastrami sandwich and a blueberry shake. Then they would drive back, often stopping for some elk jerky or pine nuts sold from the back of pickups just outside of town. Best of all, they would talk. Work through problems. Discuss the kids. Worry over the state of the world and other topics that would knit them just a little closer. Going to the temple was the best day of the month for both of them.

Today it started just as it always did. A mad dash out the door. Kids arguing but promising they'd listen to their brother. The two of them running late and wondering if they would get there in time for the nine o'clock session, when most of the ward would be there too. Finally breathing a sigh as they hit the highway southbound. By the time they were descending the big hill about ten miles outside of Moab and passing the Hole in the Rock tourist trap (years ago, a local fellow had dug out a house into the red rock cliff face, and now it was a place to stop for a little local color and to pick up some souvenirs and other Southern Utah kitsch), they had turned on the car stereo and listened to some soft rock. Regine did seem a little more agitated and on edge, but when he asked her what was wrong she denied anything was the matter. She said she was just tired and not sleeping well. He knew that was true; she had been particularly restless the night before. So most of the way they just listened to an old Michael Jackson album. But it was not that out of the ordinary except in retrospect, when everything preceding the event was scrutinized in fine grain detail to see if some hints of what was coming were haunting the things going on beforehand.

They met a couple from the ward going in and chatted about how nice it would be if Moab ever got a temple. All four gave the smiling temple worker their recommends and headed to their respective changing rooms to change into their white temple clothes. They met again and walked to the chapel, where they waited for the session to start. They spent a quiet moment in the waiting area reading the scriptures and praying until the workers announced it was time to go to the endowment room. They were walking hand in hand when Arrow leaned over and whispered, smiling, "We are entering sacred space." Suddenly, Regine stopped and looked strangely at him. The people behind them in the hall paused, when suddenly Regine ripped her hand out of his and said, dropping to her knees, "In Çatalhöyük, to enter the sacred space, people had to crawl through a porthole and down a long tunnel." She began crawling on her hands and knees toward the endowment room.

"Regine please get up."

People were looking at her in concern, and all had abandoned making their way to the room where the work would be done. A matron rushed over and tried to help Regine to her feet, but she would not budge.

"I've been there, you know. To Çatalhöyük. It's in Turkey. Over 10,000 years old, and we climbed down. Just like the ancients. James started singing 'I feel the earth move under my feet' by Carol King and James Taylor, remember that song?" And suddenly Regine was crawling down the hall belting the lyrics at full volume.

Arrow held her in his arms and rocked her gently, whispering softly into her ear and hushing her. She seemed to calm, but she did not seem to be aware of where she was. The matron moved the people behind them into the endowment room and closed the door quietly behind them and then came back to Arrow and Regine. She squatted beside Regine and stroked her hair.

"Are you all right, Sister?"

She asked Regine, but was looking at Arrow to whom the question was directed. He just looked back at her with wide uncertain eyes reading nothing but calm in her face. He did not know what to do.

Regine shuddered and looked around.

"What are we doing on the floor? Arrow?"

Arrow burst into tears.

"You went away. You went totally away. I didn't know what to do. Are you OK? Do you remember what happened? Oh, Regine."

Then she was holding him. The matron helped them back to the dressing room and went in to assist Regine changing into her street clothes. She met Arrow again in the foyer. They got back in the car to head to Moab. Arrow told her the story of what had happened, and the rest of the way they cried, trying to work through what might be wrong. They both agreed they would drive straight to the emergency room.

⊃ ⋉ ⊹ ⋊ ⊂

The doctors had been of no real help. They did an MRI, but there was nothing they could see from the scan that indicated a change from her post-accident MRIs from Primary Children's Hospital in Salt Lake City. The doctor made an appointment with a psychiatrist to see them on Monday and gave Regine a sedative to help her sleep, suggesting that a lack of sleep may be affecting her and causing her strange behavior.

The kids, learning that their mother was sick, rose to the challenge magnificently. Arrow explained that she needed a break, so the kids rallied, took over all the chores, cooked the meals, and everything they could think of doing. Regine thought all the fuss was overblown, but enjoyed it anyway. It allowed her to curl up with a book and read. They all skipped church on Sunday and rented the Wizard of Oz to watch on TV. It was a nearly perfect day.

The next day, they took her to Marin Coburg, a new psychiatrist who had moved to Moab after retiring from a Boston private practice. She had opened a limited mental health practice only a couple of months earlier, focusing on just a few patients she found interesting and who might provide cases for a book she was working on. She claimed that she retired in Moab to enjoy the landscapes and live in beauty, but could not stay away from the work she'd loved for thirty years. When she heard about Regine, she jumped at the case—an amnesia patient, who was showing a personality disequilibrium seventeen years after the accident. Regine and she hit it off, and Regine spent most of their time catching the doctor up on her life. Regine had no trouble expressing the extreme fear and panic she was experiencing.

ꓳ ⤬ ⼂ ⤬ ꓔ

Asilah hovered over the pair listening and weeping as she realized the extent of Nephi's damage to Regine's brain. She tried to assist the doctor in calming and helping Regine by bringing sweet memories of when her children were little. But suddenly she realized that the doctor was trying to get her to detail the death of little Heike. Regine started off speaking of it with a matter-of-fact attitude, but she melted down as she got to the part about her rushing out of the library at the sound of the accident. Asilah just held Regine as she wept uncontrollably. Asilah was glad Regine was getting professional help but wished she could communicate to the doctor what had really happened to Regine's brain.

The doctor handed her a handkerchief and explained that her feelings were natural, but the trauma of all that she'd been through would have inclined her to sublimate many of the things she should have worked through. She would be there to help. She gave her a prescription of imipramine, explaining that it would probably be a few weeks before she would feel its effects, but it would likely help her sleep a little better. The physician then scheduled an appointment for the next week but told her to call immediately if she had any more episodes.

Asilah could feel the relief Regine felt just from the fact that someone was watching out for her and would help keep an eye on where these strange thoughts and feelings were coming from. The Goddess watched as Regine and Arrow, who had stayed in the waiting room, climbed into their car and drove home. Asilah started weeping again. She could not seem to stop.

⊃ ≍ ⊹ ≍ ⊂

Two nights later Regine was sleeping while Arrow lay awake lost in thought. Regine had had no more episodes since the temple, and he was hoping that the medicine the doctor had given her was helping. What would he do if she… he could not think of a more appropriate clinical word… went crazy? Lost her mind? Entered la la land? How would he cope without her? She was everything. She was his anchor to reality. She had handed him back his life. Could all that be taken away? He slid out from under the covers and knelt beside the bed. He poured out his heart and pled with God to heal his wife. His life. He expressed deep sorrow for all his faults and promised he would do better if only He would help Regine recover. He felt good as he crawled into bed. His Heavenly Father would be there come what may.

He had just started to drift off, when suddenly Regine sat up leaning against the backboard. She just sat there, eyes open and staring straight ahead.

"Regine," he said and tentatively looking up at her from where he lay, "are you OK?"

She turned her head and looked down at him. Her eyes were wide and glassy. He was lying on his back without covers, and she grabbed the top of his round-necked garment and pulled it down violently to expose his chest. She poked her finger hard into the old bullet wound he received in Ethiopia, and looking down on him said viciously, "I did that to you!"

Then she sat back up staring straight ahead. She gazed back down looking at him quizzically and said, "Goodnight Arrow," and turned on her side and went back to sleep.

Arrow started shaking. He got up and filled a glass with water from a jar in the refrigerator. She had heard

the story of his being shot many times—was she project-
ing herself as the shooter? Was she mad at him? He was
shaking, his breath coming fast, in almost little gasps as he
returned to bed. There would be no sleep for him until just
before dawn.

Can't Let Go

Regine's whole body began to convulse violently as she stared at the young mother bending down to help a little two year old tie her shoes. Kate Little, the young teenager who had killed Regine's daughter, was now an adult with dyed blond hair, black fingernails, a pierced nose, and a kerchief tied around her hair. Even after ten years, she knew her instantly. And there. There. Standing in a grocery store aisle was that teenager's own daughter. A little girl who was alive and present. Who could be seen. In the world. A little girl who had a body, with feet, wearing shoes that needed to be tied. A toddler alive. Unlike Regine's baby, who had not lived long enough to ever need shoes that could have become untied. Regine could not speak.

The young lady smiled up at Regine apologetically, thinking her shoe rescue was blocking the aisle, but her smile twisted away as recognition dawned on her. She stared at Regine in terror for a full complement of several long, breathless seconds, then snatched her child, and literally ran out of the store, leaving her shopping basket full of gathered food behind.

Regine could not stop shaking. She sat on the floor. An older woman asked if she was OK and put her arms around her, and Regine clutched at her like a drowning woman.

"Should I call an ambulance? You don't look well, Honey. Here, take some water."

The older woman took a bottle of soda out of her cart, opened it, and helped Regine take a few small sips.

"Thank you. I'm sorry. I don't know what happened. I just saw...." She could not finish. A manager came and took them both to a small breakroom and let them sit down. Regine was calming and asked if she could borrow a phone to call her husband.

Arrow was there in just a few minutes.

As they drove home, Regine explained she'd seen the woman who had murdered their baby.

"And she has one of her own now. A little girl."

Arrow was silent. She had not used the word "murder" for the accident in a long time. Regine cried hysterically beside him. He could not make out her words, but it was like the months right after the baby's death. Regine would weep like this. At that time, Arrow would join her in her tears, but now he was just scared. Her strange behavior over the last couple of months had him wondering if her weeping was a manifestation of something deeper. He pulled off of Main Street to head up the river road. They needed a drive. They passed the sloughs and moved west along the south side of the Colorado River. This seemed to calm Regine somewhat, and she began to quiet as she watched the tamarisk lining the river roll past her window. They drove beyond Moon Flower Canyon and on until the pavement turned into a dirt road. They pulled off to the side near where Kane Creek emptied into the River. They sat for a while watching the river, listening to a hidden bird singing in the foliage.

Regine turned to Arrow and said, "I'm sorry."

Arrow nodded and started to say something, then backed out recognizing that Regine had more to say.

She did. But it took a while to let the words find the air. Arrow waited patiently, letting the slow work of the river bring calm and balance.

"I know I have to forgive her. I know that. I've tried, but it won't come. Every time I think about her, I want to let it go. I know she was just a teenager then, doing what teenagers do with radios. I know she must recall it with a kind of anguish that she killed a ba..." Regine choked but did not lose herself, "...Heike. But I still feel rage. I know it is poisoning me. I can't let go of the rage. I feel rage at myself too, for running into the library and leaving her behind in the car. How much more is the crime my own? She was inattentive a moment, I was negligent..."

"Regine, we've talked about this a thousand times. The bishop has counselled you again and again. You must stop blaming yourself... and the girl."

"I'm trying. Or I was trying. I was doing pretty good until the last few weeks. Oh, Arrow, it's haunting me worse than it ever has. More so than it has for years. And... I'm thinking terrible things." Regine went silent, biting her lip. Arrow recognized the look in his longtime wife—it was anger.

"Tell me."

"I picture me killing her."

"Regine, you're the gentlest person I know. You would never kill her."

"But it's in my mind. I picture myself with a knife, and stabbing her again and again. I'm breaking, Arrow. Something is wrong."

"Did you tell Dr. Coburg?"

"Yes. She told me that such ideations were not uncommon in trauma victims. And, oh Schatz, I had such thoughts... even in the temple, and it happened just before, before I disappeared."

"You thought of killing the girl?"

"More than that. It was an image of such clarity it seemed real... and Arrow, I could smell the blood. I could smell it thick and iron-y. I could almost taste it. That's what was going on in my head as we walked to the celestial room. When I collapsed and lost my memory. Arrow. I'm damned. I know I'm damned. How can I forgive her? And when I saw her at City Market. When there she was. Arrow, I almost threw a can of pumpkin paste at her. I could have hit her child, but I almost did it anyway."

"But you didn't."

"I know, but just barely. What if it happens again? What if these violent feelings come out again with our children? What if I'm losing who I am? I did once before, you know, and that woman is lost forever. Or what if I'm turning back? What if this woman is the one appearing, singing, calling you James—all those times that I can't remember what happened? I'm so scared. So angry. So filled with rage. I don't know what I'm becoming. And I know you don't think I'm capable. I know that. But what if I am? What if I start hurting the children?"

"You won't."

"How can you be sure?"

"Regine, whatever you were. Whatever is underneath all the complexity that is you. There is a Regine in front of that. And I know Regine. And Regine will never, ever, under any circumstance, let anyone hurt her children. She will mother-bear anyone, or anything, or any demon, or ungodly thing from the past. Regine is stronger than anyone I know. She is fierce. And her children will never be taken by darkness while she has air to breathe. I know this. I know Regine."

Regine burst into tears, but not the kind that had brought them down the river. She reached over and wrapped her arms around Arrow who grabbed her tight and held her close.

"I'm glad I have you." She said still shaking.

"You do. And I'll never let you go."

⊃ ⤬ ⤙ ⤬ ⊂

When Regine typed Katherine Little into the search engine, she did not expect to find her address so quickly. She knew she was doing something iffy. She would be embarrassed and ashamed if Arrow discovered her at it. And she sensed that if her therapist walked in on her, she would have received some disapprobation. Even so, she knew she was not doing anything really wrong. She told herself she was just trying to find out where the young lady lived to figure out how likely she might be to see her again. For example, if the girl lived near City Market, she would just spend more time at Millers, and vice versa. By knowing where she lived, she could lower the risk of encountering her. Interestingly, she found that she lived in Green River, the first city you'd run into after leaving Moab, about fifty miles north. That meant it was unlikely they would cross paths often enough to worry about. She had probably come into Moab for a day of shopping. How unfortunate they'd met.

Regine was still struggling with crawling back from the brink of disaster when she broke down a couple of weeks ago among the canned goods. But she was crawling back. The medicine seemed to help, as did her talks with Dr. Coburg. She was just checking where this murderous girl lived to make sure she could minimize her encounters. She scanned herself and found that looking up the address had not induced any panic, nor did she find that she was upset in the least. This was a good sign. She relaxed. She went into Kimball's room and gathered a rather substantial pile of laundry and took it down into the washroom. She loaded the washer, poured in the detergent and fabric softener, and turned it all on. Her decision to go to Green River that afternoon seemed to come out of nowhere, but as she thought about it, it made sense because it might be nice to see how the girl was living to get a sense of how far she had come since killing Heike, and maybe that would help Regine forgive her. She grabbed the large butcher knife out of its wooden holder just in case she had time to run it by the cutlery store, which would sharpen knives for free any time after their purchase. Why not slice two birds with one stone since she was going out anyway, and the knife had become so dull that it more pinched the tomatoes she'd cut for last night's salad than sliced them. A quick run to Green River, then to the cutlery store, and home in time to start the dinner before everyone came home. Perfect.

She did not put the knife in her purse or in a separate bag as she might have normally. Instead, she put on a pair of high-top cowboy boots that she would only wear when she and Arrow occasionally went line-dancing. The brown decorated leather didn't really go with the capris she was wearing. In fact, they looked absurd, but the knife slid easily into the boot, which seemed like a fine place to store it for now. No sense letting it rattle around in her purse and likely allow it to pierce and slice up the handbag.

She pulled onto Highway 191 and headed north. She started thinking about Elder Holmberg and Alma Lune. She could not get over their deaths. Alma Lune in an accident, and Elder Holmberg of old age, perhaps sped up at his sorrow at the passing of his beloved secretary. Why did such good men have to die? It made no sense. She thought about the last time she saw him. How she and Alma Lune had looked thoughtfully at the bright moon. He'd seemed so content. So peaceful and calm. How strange to think that in just a few hours, he would be dead. If only she could have known he was so tired he would fall asleep at the wheel. There had been no skid marks as the car hurtled off the cliff's edge. In fact, the police estimated that he had to have been doing over seventy miles an hour when he hit the guardrail in order to break through it. That winding road was too dangerous to go that fast. What was Alma Lune thinking? Then it dawned on her.

Instead of going to Green River, she turned off and headed up to Dead Horse Point, about fifteen miles outside of Moab. She wanted to see the site of Alma Lune's crash. She drove up the winding road to the place where he had rammed the guard rail. The rail was still not repaired, and she could see the gap where he had gone through the railing and pulled a long piece of it over the embankment; it still dangled over the edge like a black snake hanging from a tree. She got out of her car and walked to where the ragged gap now showed the last place her friend had breathed. Then she remembered that Elder Holmberg had said that he had released Alma Lune. So much had been going on, she had forgotten about what the apostle had said about that, so cavalierly. As if it were natural to let a man go who had devoted his life to your service. Then she knew without a shadow of a doubt what had happened to her beloved friend Alma Lune. What he had done. In shock, she sat on the ground and cried out in loud ear-splitting anguish.

⊃ ⋉ ⚹ ⋊ ⊂

When they found her that night around midnight, she was wandering out on the sage flats bordering Highway 191 about three miles from the Dead Horse turnoff. She was confused. Dehydrated. Blood was pooling in one of her boots where a kitchen knife had sliced her foot several times. Search and rescue had joined the hunt following Arrow's 911 report of a missing person, and the Dead Horse Point State Park people had called about an abandoned vehicle, at which point the police put two and two together. Once she was located, EMTs took her to the Moab hospital. Arrow was waiting at the emergency room when they brought her in at nearly 1 AM. Arrow rushed over to the gurney and grabbed her hand on the side without the IV loading her with fluids. Her eyes seemed clear, and she tried to smile a little for his sake.

"Sorry," she said.

He smiled at her and stroked her hair, "You gave us all a scare. Are you OK? What do you remember? Anything? Do you know why you parked near where Alma Lune crashed? That's where they found the car."

"I'm not sure. Arrow. I'm scared. And my foot really hurts."

"I bet. They say it's cut pretty bad. I'm scared too, but we'll figure it out. I called the bishop. He's on his way to help me give you a blessing."

She smiled and patted his hand gratefully.

The medical staff moved her off the gurney and helped get her onto one of the available beds. The only other patient in the emergency room was a boy scout who had crashed on a mountain bike during a moonlight ride and broken his arm and a couple of ribs. They set Regine up with a warm blanket, and checked her IV and gave her some medicine. A doctor came shortly after to give her an examination. He checked her head carefully, looking for signs of a concussion. He seemed tired, but professional.

"So you just decided to wander out into the flats, without water, and a knife in your boot?"

"She's been having memory problems. Episodes."

"How long have they been going on?"

"They started a few weeks ago. The place they found our car parked was where a close friend had an accident."

The ER doctor turned to Regine, "Do you remember what you were doing there?"

Regine shook her head, "No."

"Do you know why you had a butcher's knife in your boot?"

"No."

He unwrapped the bandage the EMTs had placed around the wound and examined the slash in her foot. He opened it and looked at the damage.

"It looks like a good 8–10 stitches will take care of this. Doesn't look like it severed any tendons or did any major damage. A nasty cut to be sure, but not one that will leave any more than a scar. We'll have it fixed up in no time."

They brought in a surgical kit, isolated the wound, injected the area with a local anesthetic, cleaned the wound, swabbed the area with Povidone, and then efficiently stitched up the wound.

The doctor then left them alone for a while. Regine just laid back with her eyes closed. Arrow watched her. He could not turn away, but his mind was working through some anxious prayers for her safety and return. The doctor came back in and said they wanted her to at least spend the night. He wanted a neurologist to look at her, and run some tests to see if they could get to the bottom of what had happened.

The rest of the night was a blur. They moved her to a room. The bishop came, and they gave her a blessing. She was given something to help her sleep; then when she had drifted off, he returned home. It was after four in the morning. All of the kids were up still. They had all talked to their mother on the phone and knew that she had been found and was fine and that she was worried about them all. But they all stayed up waiting for dad to get home. He gave them a quick rundown, then sent them to bed with the promise that they would all see her tomorrow. And yes, they could skip school to go to the hospital. And no, he wasn't sure how long she would be there, but likely not long, just long enough to run some tests. Then she'd be as fit as a fiddle. He collapsed onto his bed and wept until he finally fell asleep.

In the morning, he told the kids they could visit her in the afternoon, but he wanted to see how she was doing this morning before he brought them just to make sure she was up to it. When he arrived at the hospital, Dr. Coburg was just leaving and she stopped to chat with him.

"I'm not sure there is anything physically wrong that we can see. We did another MRI, and it matches the first one we did after her collapse in Monticello, no changes, no causes that we can identify. Her bloodwork seems normal, except for some signs she is under stress. She only has fragments of memory about yesterday. She doesn't know why she drove up there. She doesn't know why she started walking onto the flats. She has no access to the reasons for any of it. The butcher's knife she had in her boot is concerning. It suggests she thought she needed to be armed for whatever she was going toward. It is obviously a weapon. Why she needed to be armed with deadly force is what I'm mostly worried about right now."

Arrow looked at her, his breath coming in rapid bursts. "What should I do?"

"There is nothing we can do until we know more about what is happening, but I want to start more frequent therapy sessions and start her on some new medicines. Your role is to be supportive. Don't try to figure out what happened, let her talk if she wants, but don't try to pull it out of her. Just be there for her. Can you do that?"

"Of course. Oh yes. I can do that."

"Good. I'll stop by tomorrow morning. I want to keep her overnight until… at least for a couple of days."

"Can the kids come and see her?"

"Yes. It's even important they do. What she needs now is a sense of normalcy. I think the kids would be a great idea."

"OK. Thank you, Dr. Coburg."

He went to the room. Regine smiled up at him.

"How's our patient this morning."

"Good. I was just talking to Dr. Coburg, and she is optimistic."

"I ran into her too, just outside your door. She does feel we can get you back in the pink."

"How are the kids?"

"Great. Dr. Coburg said they can visit you today."

"Wonderful. Thank you. This must be hard on you."

Arrow only smiled.

"So how do you feel this morning?"

"I think I could go home right now. My foot doesn't even hurt, and I feel pretty good.

"Did you sleep good, what little you got?"

"I had the best dream. I was running on Spanish Valley Drive when a glowing messenger appeared in the road above me. I stopped and talked. Chatted, like we were old friends. We talked about kids. She said she remembered how hard earth life was, is. Then she said, 'Existence is hard.' And we both laughed. Like hilariously. She was beautiful. Deep brown with gorgeous black hair. She just radiated calm and confidence and told me not to worry. That God was with me. She was so full of love and glowed like, well, an angel."

Arrow nodded and suddenly lost his voice as his eyes filled with tears. She reached out and took his hand.

"I believe her," was all he could get out.

They chatted about things of no consequence, then against his instructions and instincts, Arrow asked, "Any clues about what you were doing? They said you parked that car where Alma Lune crashed."

She looked very sad, then looked up at him and said, "I don't remember much. It seems like the whole day is gone. I…" She suddenly grabbed Arrow's hand tighter and pulled him closer whispered, "I do remember why I was there. I think Alma Lune killed himself."

Arrow stared at her.

"Why would you think that?"

"He and Elder Holmberg had a falling out. He fired him."

"What? He was like a son…"

"And the apostle was like a father. There were no skid marks. He was doing at least 70. That's not someone falling asleep."

Arrow sat on the bed and grabbed her hand. He could find no words to say, but he began to suspect that she might be right.

"He was not wearing a seatbelt."

"He always wore a seatbelt. He was fanatical about...."

She interrupted, "Yes. He was."

They wept and spent the rest of the morning sharing memories about Alma Lune. When Arrow brought the kids that afternoon, the remembrances of their beloved friend continued. Of course, they did not tell the kids their suspicions about his death, but talking about his life was healing as it had the effect of allowing Regine's recent episode to slip out of the present. And it even seemed to Arrow that the spirit of Alma Lune entered the room as they talked, reminding him of the love his beloved friend had radiated.

⊃×⚡×⊂

The explosions outside the house sounded like multiple bombs detonating next to the bed. Arrow had not heard a sound like that since his Army days on the tank firing range when the A1s were target practicing. He leapt to his feet and began to spin in circles. He had to find his shoes; no, he needed to get the kids. No first the shoes. Why were the lights off? Had the house been hit with lightening? Where were his shoes? He spun back to the bed. He thought Regine was out of bed, but she was just sitting there confused and staring. Seconds after he got to his feet, four men burst into the room. They were all shouting things, and he just stood looking at them trying to understand what they were saying. Nothing made sense. He was knocked to the ground, and someone had bound his wrists in seconds. He could hear Regine screaming for them not to the hurt the children.

Things began to dawn on him slowly. These were police. He kept telling them they had no drugs. They were Mormons. He started asking about the children. After only a few minutes, which passed like hours, they stood him up and guided him to the front room. His son Kimball was bound like he was. Arrow was seated next to him on the floor. Three female officers were comforting the other two children, who were sitting on the couch crying.

"Dad, what is happening? I didn't do anything, I swear. I only tried dope once, but it was months ago. I promise I didn't bring any into the house. Dad what are they going to do? Where's Mom?"

"I don't know. This isn't about you. I think there has been a mistake. I think they are not at the house they think they are."

Suddenly he recognized one of the SWAT team members. He was the Boy Scout leader in the 2nd ward.

"Shane. What's going on? You know me. We've been camping together. What's this about? I think there's been a mistake."

Shane came up to him and squatted in front of him.

"I can't say anything, Arrow. The Federal Marshall will fill you in soon."

"Federal Marshall? What do they think I did?"

"Sit tight, Arrow. I'm sorry. It will all be explained in a few minutes."

He reassuringly patted Kimball on the head, muttering something about everything being all right, then joined his comrades to help comfort Jens and Greta.

After what seemed like half the night, but could not have been that long, two men came into the room leading a handcuffed and shackled Regine. Bound not with the giant zip-ties he and his son were bound with, but with handcuffs and leg restraints. She shuffled into the room, her face a carnival mask of terror and confusion. They sat her down in Arrow's big leather recliner. The kids let loose with a mourning wail of questions to their mother. She looked at them helplessly but said nothing.

One of the Feds signaled to one of the SWAT team to bring Arrow into the kitchen, where a chair had been set aside for him. They forced him into the chair and stood by while one of the Marshalls pulled up another across from him.

"Your wife, Heike Marquardt, has been indicted for the murder of five German citizens. Because she is a citizen of that country, she will be extradited under agreements and treaties between the United States of America and the Federal Republic of Germany. We are aware she is also at this time an American Citizen, under the name of Regine

Beamon. Because she was naturalized under a false name, her US citizenship will be revoked. Do you understand the charges against your wife, sir?"

Arrow just stared trying to form the confusion in his mind to a thought.

"Regine would not hurt a fly. You've made a mistake. She's Swedish not German."

"No, Sir. The German authorities have enough evidence to make an arrest, which we have matched with the priso… your wife. It is unlikely there has a mistake, but the German court system will ultimately decide that. Our job is simply to get her safely there. We would, however, now like to ask you some questions to ascertain your own involvement in hiding and abetting a criminal. Be aware, sir, anything you say at this time can and will be held against you in court if such should become necessary. We understand that Ms. Marquardt allegedly lost her memory about 18 years ago just prior to your marriage…."

The Beast Probes
the Limits of Her Cage

Here is the neural bundle we recognize as Heike. Round
and round she broods over the face of the deep. Circling in
the void. Longing to escape its borders and leave an emptiness of such profound nothingness that every apophatic
expression would be inadequate. In no slice between time's
discrete flashes of existence could there be less purchase.
A hole in which no concept could dwell, no phrase in any
language of heaven or earth could voice its description,
no gap in that realm of infinite smallness could be used to
serve as metaphor. She broiled in her hatred. She raged in
her plots for revenge. She watched every scene that entered Regine's eyes. She considered every voice Regine
heard. She felt every touch Regine felt and tasted every
morsel Regine consumed. Round and round she circled the
void, brooding on her revenge. That which Regine loved,
she despised. In the usurpers' children she found disgust.
In the mannequin's faith she found moldy rot. And her
husband? Her husband she hated with the flaming energy

of a hundred million suns. He had killed her only love. Her James. He had killed not only the instantiation of her love, but the very possibility of loving anyone. Ever. And so she circled the void, waiting like a lover to flower from her prison. Or to fall into non-existence. Either was preferable to her current condition.

Yet still she probed. She probed each neural bundle she could feel. She licked at every hormone that crossed her path in the hope and desire and lust that she could have back the body which was taken from her and given to this fragment of her fullness in which she was made to dwell. There must be a way. She had faith. She would find a way to come back. And when she did, she would wreak such vengeance on all she hated that nothing would survive the black hole she would create. The man, his children, his friends, his church, his city, even his dog would not escape the fiery explosion of her wrath. There must be a way out. When she found it she would unleash terror.

Nephi's Lament

Nephi sat on a rocky outcrop on a Pluto-sized dwarf planet in the outer reaches of the Kuiper Belt. He wanted to get as far from Earth as possible. Rules were rules, of course, so he couldn't leave the solar system, but at least this was a long way from earth. The darkness of the sun-leeward-side of the rocky body was complete so he sat in a house-sized divot weeping. Hiding his face, wanting to burn up in the pain he felt. The sorrow. The shame.

He recalled the moment he killed Asilah's son. Vividly. The war had been bloody. The boy, Lehi, was much like Nephi had been when they fled Jerusalem. Large in stature. Fearsome. A warrior like his father and his uncle. What Asilah had said was true. Nephi had raged through the battle, fierce with righteousness and certainty. He had mowed the boy down without giving him a fighting chance. The very sword with which he had slain Laban rose and fell among the combatants without mercy. That sword, in his hand, killed many that day. Most of them were relatives, he knew. All of them had become strangers, who Nephi and his people thought were going to attack their little troop hiding in the edges of the wilderness. The rain forest. The promised land. These strangers they had imagined threatening all that they had built and sacrificed for. Nephi was sure they deserved to die because of that threat. He had to slaughter them before they came upon Nephi's subjects in the night—get, before being gotten. What had he wrought? War. Only War. Why had he not done what the people of Ammon had done? Why did he not try harder to reconcile with his brothers? How had it come to the point where they were killing, attacking, slaughtering each other with such ferocity?

And why hadn't the Lord stopped him?

He had killed Asilah's son. His nephew. His own brother Laman's son. He had known God's help and blessings so often in his life. How had the conditions in what was supposed to be the promised land become so unpromising? So filled with hatred and anger? Nephi crawled deeper into the divot. He wanted to hide for the rest of eternity in this icy rock so far away from the sun.

PART III

In the München Psychiatric Ward

Regine was bathed in delicate moonlight that cast a portentous glow on her face. It smoothed her features with calmness belying the reality she was facing. The window of her south-facing room in the prison-like mental hospital was tall and spacious, giving the room a fin-de-siècle Habsburg air despite the austerity of the decorations. The blue cover of her bed was patterned with a filigree of moon shadows from the naked tree branches of a dead purple beech softly swaying in a light wind. The glow from the window also framed the stark dark line of iron bars casting more deterministic shadows. These did not move with the wind.

Arrow was exhausted. It had been a day of meetings with lawyers, reporters, psychiatrists, doctors, and others. Some were trying to make sure Regine and her family were getting assistance. One of the München wards had also rallied around them—making sure they had everything they needed. He had been reluctant to call on the

Church members, fearful that when they found out that his wife was the Red Army Faction Murderer, and that he had done time in prison for helping the Baader-Meinhof Group, they would be disinclined to help. But they were Saints in every sense of the word. It made him proud to be a Mormon.

He had been interviewed by what seemed like hundreds of papers in the month since his arrival in Germany with the children—*Die Zeit, Süddeutsche Zeitung, Frankfurter, Berliner Morgenpost*, the list went on and on. American papers including the *Washington Post*, the *NY Times*, and the *LA Times* had all run detailed stories. Arrow had been interviewed for multiple television spots and radio talk shows. In every interview, he defended the position that his wife was not the same person who had committed the horrible crimes. The same body, but she was something else. Something new in the world. Many thought Regine faking. Many did not. Many thought the story was made up. Others thought it a fairytale romance with the murderess falling in love and marrying her intended victim.

The extended families of the five people Heike had murdered were vocally demanding justice. Appearing repeatedly in the press, even more than Arrow, to argue that she deserved life in prison for her crimes. So far he had protected the children, but just this morning he had seen the paparazzi cameras gunning from a van across the street from the facility that took care of his kids. The children were in a state of traumatized confusion. There was no hiding the fact that their mother was thought to be a notorious murderer. And their father was an accomplice to murder. He'd told them everything. He'd told them of the power of Christ to heal such hurts. Even so, everyone was lost and floundering in the waves that had broken over the little family.

They had been in Germany over a month, following Regine there about two weeks after her extradition. Getting to Germany had required a series of miracles. Angels had to have been involved. The kids had no passports and his had expired, so they had to expedite the process at great expense. There were bureaucratic log jams at every step of progress he made, but they were solved with improbable ease. There was so much to do. He had to arrange for the only other veterinarian in the town to take over a good part of his practice and ask the veterinarian down in Monticello to come up once a week to see some of his ongoing patients. He made arrangements with his children's teachers to let them do their homework over the internet in Germany with no sense of how long they would be there. If not for LeRoy and Jezzy's help, he was sure he would have gone mad. But they were there every day after Regine's arrest, taking care of the kids, shopping, calling people who needed to be called, finding airplane tickets for the five of them, making arrangements for them to stay in Munich where Regine was staying in a high-security psychiatric facility.

Arrow talked to her on the phone every day. The Germans apparently were very liberal with making sure that she was not only getting good care physically, but that her mental health needs were being met. Through it all, he tried to be upbeat and positive, but inside he was a mess.

These facts existed, or at least seemed plausible enough that he was unable to reject them outright: His wife was named Heike Marquardt. She had brutally and notoriously tortured and then murdered five people, all connected to the Red Army Faction's bombing of the Frankfurt American Officer's Club. She had come to Moab to kill him. She had shot him in Africa. She held a doctorate in Theology from Tubingun University and had been teaching in Berlin when she had begun her killing spree. No one knew any motivation for the killings, and Regine could not help shed light on the matter. If she were convicted, she would spend life in prison. If convicted of being dangerously insane, she would suffer the same duration of punishment but in a secure mental institution.

Each day he talked to her she seemed to grow more despondent and depressed. She was becoming lost in despair. The harder Arrow tried to bring her some hope, the more she resisted. She was slipping away. There was no other way to put it.

Now, looking at her in the moonlight, he was sure that she had gotten worse. She was staring straight up into the ceiling.

"Regine, are you OK?," he asked.

Her eyes shifted over to him, but she did not answer. Her gaze drifted back to the ceiling. At night, she had to be restrained in her bed to ensure she didn't hurt herself or others. She was a notorious serial killer, after all.

When he first brought the children, she was ecstatic. She hugged and kissed them and sat with them for as long as they could visit. But as the weeks progressed their interaction seemed stilted and forced. The last two days she'd asked Arrow not to bring them.

He came over and kissed her on the forehead and whispered in her ear that he loved her.

"I'll be back tomorrow after your interview with Dr. Chang. He wants to talk to me too. But hang in there, sweetheart, I know this is so hard. I'll give the kids your love. OK?"

She managed a quick hug and a nod, but still she was silent. This was not a good turn.

⊃ ≍ ⊀ ≍ ⊂

Regine could see her. The Heike creature inside her was a narrow thing. A small thing. A bit of neural bundle that she could wrap her mind around and squeeze. A thing with access to her memories, but not to her soul. Still the monstrous freak frightened her. Sometimes Heike would talk to Regine. Just cruelties. Hatreds.

"I will kill your children and eat them while you watch."

"I will fuck your husband and then cut him open and watch him bleed onto the floor and lick the blood up with my tongue."

"I can feel it. I'm getting loose. I will escape and own this body again. I will let you watch while I throw your children into a fire. You will watch them burn and sizzle."

And Regine knew she was right. She could not keep it up, and she was slipping away. Heike would come out and do all the horrors she promised. There was nothing she could do to stop it.

⊃ � ⸴ ⸴ ⊂

Dr. Chang looked at Arrow with calm, penetrating eyes. Then shuffled through some papers on his desk and cleared his throat and said in Chinese-accented German, "Thank you for meeting with me. We are concerned that Heike is…"

"Her name is Regine. Regine Beamon."

"Yes… Of course… her former name is written all over her charts, and I slip into that… my apologies."

Arrow nodded.

"As you've likely noticed she is falling into deep depression. This is concerning. She is on several drugs to help counter this, but she is not responding. We also have not been able to find evidence of damage that would explain her amnesia."

"It was a long time ago. It seems to me you are reaching. Just because you can't find damage in the deep regions of the brain does not mean it does not exist!" Arrow was feeling hot and annoyed.

"No doubt. I'm not saying we don't believe her. In fact, I do. Believe her. But we must establish medically whether she is mentally stable in order to determine the future course of her life."

"She's not insane."

"I understand, but we must work within the terminology of the system."

"She is not insane. She's a new person." Arrow would not bend to their attempts to dismiss her as simply mad.

"Nevertheless, we would like to try something more radical. Her treatment team is concerned with her growing depression. Dr. Aygun is an electrotherapist. In severe cases of depression, she has had success in bringing people back from their darkness. Also, there are cases in the medical literature in which electrotherapy has been effective in restoring memories from those suffering from post-traumatic amnesia. We would like your permission to move forward on this treatment option. Because she is mentally incompetent to sign a consent form, and you are her husband, we need your consent."

Arrow thought about the changes occurring in Regine. Would shock therapy help? For the next two hours, he learned as much as he could about the procedure. Because he was a veterinarian, he could read most medical journals, so he asked Dr. Chang to provide him with several technical reports about the risks and benefits of this electroshock therapy. The physician gave him two meta-analyses and several review papers. Some leaning to positive benefits, and others that suggested it was not as effective as claimed. He spent the next two days reading. There was hope that, given the severity of Regine's condition, this might be helpful. Nothing else was working. It seemed time to try something else. "Something more radical," as Dr. Chang called it.

He called Dr. Chang and told him to go ahead with the procedure.

"I think this is the right move," he said.

⊃ ⋈ ⊹ ⋈ ⊂

Arrow did not know who he would find, so he peered into the room quietly. Whoever it was, she was asleep. He slipped into the room and quietly tiptoed to the bed and looked at the sleeping figure. At least she was at peace for the time being. It had been three days since the shock therapy. Arrow had such high hopes. The doctors had been so optimistic. But her first act upon waking up had been to slash his face with her fingernails and scream that she would kill him for what he had done to James. Arrow had foolishly brought the children. She swore at them violently with vile filthy language. He was grateful that his children's German was too poor to catch what she was saying, but they could read the rage on her face and had been pulled from the room by the staff quickly. It took four orderlies to restrain her. Even when she was shackled to her bed, she looked like the creature from a demonic possession film. They sedated her.

Everyone worked to understand what had happened. In the last three days he had seen Regine, Heike, Heike pretending to be Regine, and sometimes such a confused mess he was not sure who was talking. But there was little mistaking when he was talking to Regine. The real Regine. There was something about the way she looked at him when she was present, absent when any of the Heike manifestations were in control. The staff could not tell them apart, and sometimes the fake Regine got them to do things the real Regine would never have done—like get the staff to give her cigarettes and allow her to go to the smoking room in a wheel chair. But he could tell. The psychiatrists were diagnosing multiple personality disorder, but Arrow knew that that was not what was happening to her. He knew Regine was there somewhere in her entirety. He just had to bind Heike and let Regine out. He had no idea how to do that. He tried giving Regine a blessing, but in the middle of the blessing Heike burst out and took control.

Sometimes Heike tried to appear rational.

"I have all Regine's memories. I just want to be free, so learn to let her go. Right. I was her first. I'm the original person. The real person. This person you've known was like a veneer over the top of me. It will soon be gone. Get used to it."

But Heike seemed a narrow, one-dimensional thing. Even the doctor said she seemed hyper-focused on revenge and retaliation. Regine seemed as determined as Heike to assert her will. However, he could tell Regine was losing. Yesterday she was appearing less frequently. He was scared.

He stared down at the sleeping woman and started to cry and pray. As he had so, so many times in the last few weeks. He was tired and lost. Where was God? Where was He?

Suddenly the woman opened her eyes and stared at him. Startled, he stepped back

She said, "Arrow. I'm losing."

It was Regine. He stepped over to the bed, took her hand, and kissed her cheek softly.

"You've got to hang on. I need you. The kids need you." He let out a sob, "Please Regine, don't let her win."

"A Goddess has been visiting me."

Arrow wasn't sure what to do with this. Was this a sign of growing instability?

"What do you mean?"

"Her name is Asilah. She's praying for me. She helps when Heike tries to take over. She has trouble stopping her too." She smiled at Arrow and softly rubbed his hands.

"I'm glad she is there for you." He didn't know what else to say. Whatever helped suppress Heike he was going to support. Imaginary or not. Real or not.

"I don't know what Heike does when she is in charge. I have no memory, but if she is hurting you or the kids, I'm so sorry. It's not me. She is evil. When we talk…."

"You can talk to her?"

"If you can call it that. She torments me. Right now, she is telling me the terrible things she is going to do to you and the kids. I can't bear it."

"Oh, Regine. I'm so sorry." It was a lame thing to say.

"Sometimes Asilah can quiet her. But she is not here now, Arrow." She took his hand in hers despite the restraints, "listen to me carefully. I can't bear this. I cannot stand the thought of this creature taking over. Listen to me. I mean it. If she wins, you may have to kill me. Say I attacked you and it was self-defense. Administer too much of my medicine, or accidently leave it on the table. Please. Do this. Please. Don't leave me in this creature the rest of my life. I don't want to wake up and find myself trapped with this thing. She is in me. Right now I have no memory of when she is in control, but I don't know if it's because I don't remember it—like, I'm awake in there until I get control, and then I forget when I'm me again… or if I'm unconscious in some way. Does that make any sense? Please. If she wins, you must end me. Please. Please just kill me."

"I'll never kill you."

"I'll never kill you," mocked a singsong voice. Then the woman on the bed tried to scratch the hand she was holding with her fingernails.

Heike is Freed

The next day was Saturday, and Arrow decided to take the kids out for a walk in the Maximiliansanlagen Park along the Isar River. Summer was ending. There was that feeling in the slant of the sun and some subtle change in the green of the leaves that portended seasonal change. The day was beautiful, cool, mostly sunny but with outsized lazy clouds boating by, providing occasional moments of shade. Abundant thick-branched trees scattered in the short grass of the park along the river made it the perfect place to spend late morning adventures. They strolled down the path along the river, passing students reading, old men playing chess, young mothers pushing strollers and carriages and chatting with others similarly festooned with small children and babies. It was idyllic. When they reached the edge of the river, Greta and Jens started a game that involved throwing sticks as far as they could into the mellow river, then racing the ersatz boats until they reached an agreed-upon finish line marked by an old beech. Then they would race back to start again. Kimball left his brothers and sisters and sat next to Arrow. He had that look that meant he wanted to talk. Arrow had learned a long time ago not to try and force it—just sit quietly until he was ready to speak.

"They said there are two people in Mom's body." His son tried to look nonchalant, but his trembling hand gave him away.

"You overheard that?"

"I heard two orderlies talking," he said quietly.

"It's not quite that simple. I think it has to do with the memories Mom lost, when… you know the story."

"Yeah, the raft trip with Elder Holmberg and Uncle Lune." His eyes watered at the mention of these men, now gone. Heroes bigger than life who had been a part of his whole life.

"Well, it's not like there are really two people. Two personalities maybe, but your mother is fighting the bad one off. The one that did the terrible things. I'm sure mom is going to win."

"What if she doesn't?" His son choked as he said it.

He couldn't answer. He just yelled to his other children to not get too close to the bank.

He didn't know how to answer Kimball's question. It was his greatest fear too. His son did not press on.

"Whose spirit is real? When Mom was born on the river, did Heavenly Father put a new spirit in her? If he didn't, don't you think Mom will go to the Terrestrial Kingdom for killing all those people? She spilled innocent blood."

"Where did you hear that term?"

"At scout camp last year. Brother Wilks said that if you spill innocent blood, you could never go to the Celestial Kingdom. The other kids don't know, but a kid at school showed me the newspapers telling about what Mom did. I cannot believe it was her. I think a new spirit was put in her body."

Arrow thought about it. How could the Regine he knew and loved be the same woman? What would God do? Heike deserved the lowest kingdom. But Regine? She loved unreservedly. She was the best mom he could imagine. She was the best person he knew. She was filled with the spirit of Christ. She served everyone. Almost the stereotype of the perfect Mormon. Yet, she was also a serial killer. Not only that, but one of the most notorious and cruel murderers that he had ever heard of. She had shot him. Left him for dead. What would God do? Could his son be right? Could she have gotten a new spirit? Maybe Heike's spirit had been pulled out and a new one put in? That made more sense than that the woman who had tried to kill him, and then came to finish him off, could now be so completely new. His best friend. His eternal companion. Heike had not repented. She'd just ended. And Regine emerged. It did not fit into anything he believed about repentance. Or Christ's atonement.

His son was looking at him, waiting for an answer. Arrow just burst into tears. He couldn't help it. His son moved forward and hugged him tight. As he had so often over the last weeks, Kimball had to be the comforting adult to both his parents and his brother and sister. He was weeping too as he held his father. By the river. In the park. Far away from home.

⊃ ⤬ ⚹ ⤬ ⊂

"Ready for your second treatment."

"What?" Regine was confused. The orderly standing with a clip board was smiling knowingly, her voice with the abject authority and force that all mental hospital staff adopted—no nonsense kindness.

"You are scheduled for three electric therapy treatments. It's time for the second."

"I don't think my husband knows about this. You have to contact him."

"He's signed the order here at the bottom." He pointed to a signature at the bottom of the form.

"I don't think he read it carefully; he even said something about being glad it was over after the last one. Please will you contact him?" Her voice was frantic in alarm.

"No. Everything is in order. Come. Don't make a fuss. It will only hurt at first, then everything will be better. You will see."

⊃ ⤬ ⚹ ⤬ ⊂

Heike was laughing. Regine could hear her... no, feel her... almost dancing, her disembodied feet moving in a jubilant expression of ecstasy. Regine gave in. What did it matter? She felt herself being half lifted, half guided into the wheelchair that would take her to the room where she would be electrocuted. That was the only word that made any sense for what was about to happen. Electrocuted.

"You are hanging by a thread my dear Regine." Heike sneered, "One more jolt and that thread will disappear. Poof, and you are gone. No more Regine. Just like that. Whatever bang in the head brought you into being is about to be unmade. To the void with you."

Regine didn't care anymore. Heike had won. Why bother. She couldn't bear this anymore. It had been too much. Heike's incessant voice in her head. Mocking everything she loved. The constant vigilance against her. The crippling anxiety over Arrow and Kimball and Greta and Jens. The relentless hurt it caused all of them. It was over. She was letting go. Whatever was left of her, when the electricity hit her neurons she would just let them go. Heike would go to prison. Arrow would take the kids back to Moab. They would all mourn her, but better this than to keep trying to fight the forces bent on her destruction.

She could hear Heike describing in detail something about how she had mapped out the neurons that constructed them both and how, with a snip of one area Regine would be cut off from the rest of the brain. Somehow, she could control the flow of electricity, and she would direct it to that area blah, blah, blah. Regine quit listening. She knew she had lost.

⊃ ⋈ ⊁ ⋈ ⊂

Arrow rubbed his son's back and gained a measure of control. He checked the kids playing by the river. They were still having fun. It was good to see them distracted from the things they were facing.

Arrow turned to his son and spoke softly, "I don't know how it will work. All I know is your mom is real and good and loving and filled with all the holiness that is needed to get into the Celestial Kingdom. I don't know how that came out of the Heike monster, but I know she is not her. I know it."

His son nodded. They turned their attention and sat in silence for a while and watched the twins playing. Arrow's cell phone rang and he picked it up.

"Herr Beamon?"

"*Ja.*"

"Your wife will be taken to the recovery room in a few minutes if you want to be there when she wakes up."

"Recovery room!? Recovery from what? What happened?"

"From her electroshock treatment this morning."

"What? Why wasn't I informed? Who authorized this?"

"You did, Mr. Beamon. You signed the form for three treatments. I have it right here in front of me."

"I did no such thing."

"I'm afraid you did, Mr. Beamon. It is all in order I assure you."

"Has the procedure been done?" Arrow was breathing in a panic; his son looked at him in terror.

"Yes. I'm afraid it is all finished. As I said; she is being taken to recovery and if you would like to be here you should arrive in the next twenty minutes."

Arrow hung up the cell phone and yelled, "Everyone get in the car. We have to go—now!"

There was no time to take them to where they were staying. He herded them quickly into the car and sped to the hospital. They were shuttled to a waiting area. No one spoke. A feeling of dread was palpable in every electron in the car. He knew. It was over. He could feel it, and it felt as real as his love for his kids. Or the reality of Regine's death.

⊃ ⋉ ⊬ ⋉ ⊂

Regine could feel Asilah stroking her hair. She knew she was weeping.

"Heike has won." Regine said.

Asilah said, "I don't know how to stop it."

Regine wished she could see the Goddess and thank her. Her thoughts turned to her little family.

"Will you send comfort to Arrow and my darlings? I'm worried they'll never give up hoping I'll pop out again. They'll spend their lives wondering. They'll constantly try to visit Heike. They don't know what she is. Please. Please. Help them understand I'm gone. Please."

"Yes. I'll try." Asilah could hardly speak.

Regine looked over her life. The part she remembered had seemed so short. She thought about camping in the La Sals. Fishing at Warner Lake. The stars spread out over the night sky with the Milky Way burning across the sky so cold and clear. She thought about canning peaches in the late summer and running along Mill Creek. She thought of singing with the choir and her primary class. Suddenly, she remembered another Heike. The daughter who died too young. But unlike in years past, she didn't feel obsessed about her, maybe because she thought it not unlikely she might meet her soon, or maybe she could see that she was never hers in some sense. Strangely, her thoughts turned to the young teenager who had in a moment of distraction ended her daughter's life. How unfair she'd been! To blame a child just starting her life for what was clearly an accident. It was just that. Not the kind of intention of the monster who was now baiting her with cruelties. It was an accident.

"Asilah! Please help the young lady who caused the accident that took my baby. Please. It was just an accident. Help her forgive herself. I do. I do forgive her. With all my heart I'm sorry for the way I treated her in my heart. Please help her."

Asilah squeezed her hand in affirmation. But it was not enough. Regine, as if in vision, saw the pain the young girl had felt. She saw the terrible burden of guilt she bore. She felt the unforgiving spirit that surrounded her every day, made worse in some ways by the birth of her own little baby. And Regine saw she needed her to forgive her. In person. She raged. She could not leave this undone. She could not leave that teenager to Asilah. And as her mind groped to escape from what she saw, her vision expanded. She saw Heike and her narrow schemes moving to and fro among the nerves of her mind, directing neural impulses this way and that sending up paths for the electricity to follow that would utterly destroy Regine. Suddenly, Heike looked up at her as if she saw Regine looking down at her. And she laughed.

"Say goodbye Regine! You are about to disappear into the void. Forever. You will be burned from my brain like you never existed. You will be ended. Say goodbye."

"No."

"Ha! You can do nothing."

"I'm not finished yet. There are things I have to do."

"Like die?"

"No. Live."

And suddenly Regine's mind expanded. She saw Asilah weeping beside her, but her perception expanded outward, like she was growing to fill a great space. She saw the workings of the universe, like Jared or Moses. It was beautiful. Rich. Expansive beyond her dreams. She became filled with wonder and light. She saw the great Mother and Father and the love they shared with each other and with her. And she understood something then fully and clearly. She had access to their priesthood and their power and facility. She was a daughter. Like Asilah, a deity and force and power. Fully light. She looked down into her mind and saw Heike. A tiny thing. A thing without consequence or power. A little scheming thing. Demonic. Empty of compassion. A void in truth. She was a kind of emptiness. Her existence had somehow become so narrow, that she had shrunk nearly to one single dimension. To a single point.

She saw doctors attaching electrodes to her head. She saw them throwing a switch. And as if in slow motion she saw the electric current flashing through her brain along the course Heike had laid out to destroy her. It tracked pathways Heike had signposted throughout her brain, concentrating and directing the electric pulse like a Canyonlands flash flood coursing through ancient river channels, gathering and forcing the destructive power of the raging waters to ends that cannot be gainsaid or diverted. A force of electrons raging to everything Regine had become out of the flotsam that Heike once was. A voltage charge with all the deterministic force necessitated by the demands and laws of physics.

And at that Regine despaired. She had no power that could circumvent what was about to happen. As much as she felt the power of priesthood, there were limits to faith. She remembered Kimball's question about why no one ever tried to reattach a head lost in an automobile crash through faith. Not even God could gainsay the laws that determine certain outcomes of the physical universe. Some things were permanently non-negotiable. Not even Jesus could gainsay the crucifixion, and even his father could not bear to look when his son was nailed to the cross in a Roman execution.

As she watched the current voltage descend, she lost all faith that she would not enter the void. She saw Asilah beginning a scream, her eyes wide in terror or surprise. There was a flash of light as if some great presence had suddenly entered her field of consciousness obscuring everything in its light. Then darkness. And the emptiness of the void.

⊃ ⤫ ⤸ ⤫ ⊂

From millions of miles away, Nephi saw what was about to happen. Something awoke within him. Something beyond his self-doubts, his sense of guilt and shame for what he had done, something that resided at the core of who he was and who he had become and always been. And he was beside Regine instantaneously. The contact between the connections with the switch had been made, and the electric current was speeding toward the brain of the prone woman at something approaching the speed of light as it wended through the wetness of the material brain. He knew what he had done, and now what he had to do. And what it would cost. These are the things he knew:

1. He could reach in and redirect the current into
    A. the creature called Heike
       or

    B. into the blockage that would reconnect the two parts of the brain

2. He knew he could not take a life ever again. He had killed Laban, and the justifications—even if the spirit had justified his actions—never felt satisfying or right. He had killed Asilah's son. His nephew. He could not kill Heike. Even if she were the most deserving soul on the face of the earth of death.

These are the costs he would bear:

1. Certain sacrifices left physical scars, even after the resurrection. Like the spear wound in the Savior's side. Like the imprints of the nails in Christ's hands and wrists.

2. He would be willing to bear those scars.

In a motion as fast as the speed of light he thrust his hand forward to intercept that descending arch of electrons racing but slowed because of the resistive capacity of the nerves toward the part of the brain dedicated to processing the bulk of what made up Regine's neural core. He knew where he had manipulated the nerves to release the Heike personality into the space of total consciousness. He placed his little finger in front of the electric current. He placed his thumb just so into the mess he had made of Regine's neural blockage—the blockage created by a blow to the head by a red sandstone rock so long ago in a Canyonlands' thunderstorm just before Heike planned to kill Arrow. He knew what would happen. In part. Regine and Heike would no longer be separate individuals. Their brains would be one again, and what exactly the result of that melding-meddling would be he could not guess because the complexity of emergent consciousness was algorithmically incalculable, even for a deity, let alone an angel. No one could know. Not even the highest of High Gods or Goddesses. But he knew what would happen as the electric arc formed between the little finger and thumb of his resurrected hand—it exploded in a flash of heavenly light and energy in the dimension in which he existed at that moment. He knew with perfect clarity and complete certainty, and with his full approbation, that for the rest of eternity everything below his wrist would be gone—never to be returned or repaired or made right. He could live with that.

⊃ × ⚡ × ⊂

From the crater in which he had ensconced himself, Nephi looked at the Milky Way burning across the blackness of a sky that mirrored his abyss. He thought about his life. The preexistent excitement of the possibility of his becoming thick matter. The leadership role he took in defeating Satan. His earthly sojourn, with highs that brought him the chance during his mortal ministry to converse with angels. His derangements that brought him to disastrous actions and attitudes even to the point he murdered someone, perhaps without necessity. Laban. This was certainly true of his nephew. And now he had broken the fundamental vows of a guardian angel by trying to rearrange Heike's neurology. He bowed his head in shame and tried to tunnel deeper into the crater into which he fled. He wanted to look again at Regine and see how she was faring in the mental ward. He wanted to comfort Arrow and send him help and support. But he had failed those two—not only by not warning, encouraging, or guiding them—but by being the cause of their distress and undoing. The. Cause. Of. This. Entire. Mess. And now the abject feeling of fallenness, his mistakes with Heike. He wept and wrung his hands together in misery. He wanted to call upon Christ. He wanted to be redeemed again—like he had been so many times in mortality. Christ's atonement was infinite, he knew, but his ability to sin infinitely often seemed inescapable. Nephi stared skyward again and tried to frame a prayer, but none would come. No words seemed possible to one who had failed so utterly. So completely. He thought about Alma, whose angelic credentials were beyond reproach, though in life he had been worse than Nephi. Nephi wept.

His resurrected eyes were blurred by the tears meeting temperatures near absolute zero, but still he seemed to make out a figure walking toward him. He could discern it was a spirit, not an angel, but one whose countenance radiated love so clearly and brightly Nephi was strongly tempted to worship him. Nephi, with an act of angelic will, cleared his eyes of frozen tears and saw the person approaching him clearly. It was Alma Lune. The friend of Arrow and Regine's he had failed to appreciate during the good man's lifetime. But now. All of Nephi's superiority and self-righteousness had melted away.

Alma Lune stood beside Nephi and laid his hand on his arm.

"I've never seen you without Elder Holmberg," Nephi said, not having anything more insightful to offer.

"He's listening to the story of my companion's life—" Alma Lune said smiling, "his son."

Nephi nodded, "As the saying goes, Zion will not be Zion, nor the Celestial Kingdom the Celestial Kingdom, until we've listened to each other's stories."

"Spirit Prison." Alma Lune said flatly, "Until we've redeemed each other by sitting side by side and listening, really hearing who we are by embracing each other's story. I look forward to hearing yours, Nephi. I know it a little."

Nephi nodded, looking sad.

"I've been sitting with Elder Holmberg. He's been through more than I ever expected. He's a wonderful son of God."

"I do not doubt you are right," Nephi observed. "He had a good character."

"Yes. He did," Alma Lune observed. "What about yours?" he said, holding more tightly onto Nephi's arm.

Nephi turned away.

"I came to tell you," Alma Lune began hesitantly, "you do, too."

Nephi said nothing.

"I came to tell you, you can be redeemed."

Nephi said nothing, but he placed his hand on Alma Lune's.

"You know it's true."

Nephi looked at Alma Lune and stared at him for a long time. Weighing his words. His eyes moving back and forth, not examining Alma Lune, but scanning his own soul, considering what he knew and what he did not know.

"I'll have to pay a heavy price." Nephi said.

"No you won't. It doesn't work like that, and you know it. You can make choices. You can do good. And continue doing so. You know this, likely better than I do. The things you've done? Just based on Earth mortality alone, let's see. Leading your people to a promised land. Taming a new continent. Building a temple. Planting new kinds of crops in soil far outside of your ken, culture, and people back in Palestine. Trying to manage the weight of believing that the fate of future nations depended on your righteousness and ability to tame your brothers' lack of enthusiasm for the entire project. The question of more import is, what things you will do in the future? How will you spend your eternities? You were not made an angel because you lacked in righteousness, you know. It was because you refused to believe you were ever good enough. You were. Of course you were. But you never believed it. You refused to honor even your humanity."

"But I…" Nephi stopped the sentence. He looked hard at Alma Lune.

"People are complex," Alma Lune said. "No one. Ever. Is beyond redemption."

Nephi nodded.

"There are things you need to work out. And I think it's going to start sooner than you think. It looks like you have visitors."

Nephi looked up and he saw the last people in the universe, literally the whole field of existence, that he wanted to see: Asilah and her son, Lehi, now a man of stature and glory, walking toward him. And Sam. Up from his work in South America. The clubfooted angel was becoming famous among the poor. All were walking across the asteroid as if it were Earth. As if it were 2500 years ago in a rainforest in coastal lowlands and they were out for a stroll, even though they were really walking across a small planetoid in the Kuiper Belt.

Nephi watched as they approached. A void opened in his heart. He did not want to face his Asilah, and especially his nephew. They looked awkward and nervous too. Nephi started shaking. Like on earth. Things were happening inside him.

Nephi stood. And ran. He could not help himself. It all was too impossible. He just ran. He ran with all the speed his resurrected heart could muster. Right into the arms of his nephew, who retuned his embrace with vigor and laughter. They pulled awkwardly away.

"Well, Nephi… I didn't know what to expect. Not that, I suppose. Last time we met, you killed me." Even though the words were harsh he was trying to smile.

Nephi stepped away, then looked over at Asilah, whose eyes were bright, shining against the midnight darkness above them. She was hard to read. No words were exchanged between them. The silence was full of meaning, conveying some things more fully than words.[*]

---

[*] The silence conveyed that Nephi's soul was rank with sorrow for his actions during their stark earthly sojourn and especially that he had taken his young nephew's life in the heat of battle and how he stole the youth's life and how terrible and devastating that was to someone whose mortality was ripped away robbing him of so much and how he would do anything to manipulate things back to restoring his rightful place in time again and how it was of a piece and parcel of Nephi's great mourning about so much and so many things but that he was willing to try and incorporate and integrate both he and his mother Asilah and his father Nephi's brother Laman into his everlasting life that they might be linked together bound as a family for the unfolding and uncertain eternities in the great priesthood chain binding and granting access to bonds of love and trust that might be reestablished throughout time as they learned to forgive each other framing a new unfractured facticity learning that the great and last atonement would offer a space for them to become again family with all of Adam's children and this great network would forge new worlds and novel possibilities in ways that not even the Gods could predict but through love would allow them to become more than anyone dreamed or dared dream or even could imagine because it would create new situations instantiate nascent opportunities and initiate motive forces that would create abundant topologies evolving to forms of being able to face the chance and caprice that were part of the fabric of all that was and all it meant for existence and the existence of Gods and families of Gods held to-

And the silence finished its discourse.

gether by the one force that has proven beyond all other forces that of love and the meaning that comes thereby and by which all universes at the base are held together if they are to hold together at all to resist the void at the heart of the world always threating dissolution chaos and the undoing of what love holds together by the forces it forges in bonds of meaningful togetherness for as long as those linked bonds can be maintained and forged in such a way the nothing breaks them among those who act in deep freewheeling agency yea those who are willing to love unfeigned such that not even the void can pull them asunder nor allow them to be unwound or undone or dissolved by agents of covenant and connection who have pulled themselves together refusing the centripetal forces that act as a force of separation and denial of love eating away at the immanent being of those who do love and act in love and work together for love and that though such love an ascending lifting might form in which other entities of the great all there is provide a basis for memory and time and space and of which this universe is just a part of a greater and more glorious patch where creativity can flower and bring forth the diversity of entities that can and do and might exist and thereby make a vibrant and more wondrous and vivacious universe where artful beauty reigns and goodness unfolds and love and mercy counter the void limiting and containing the emptiness and its attempt to keep such care from emerging into the world through the appearance of agents who have learned what wisdom and knowledge can offer in this space of being if given the chance to direct their energies in combination with other such entities of power having learned through and again and again the power of love captured through endless cycles of concern that infect those who understand how much love might give face if given voice in hearts that cannot be gainsaid by even so great a force as the great sea of chaos which hovers below the world and is always in motion trying to pull down those agents and forces of love determined to never let their creative charity be damped or moderated or squelched or dismissed because it will not abate its power as it is surrounded by those who together in love find ways that make the demonic chaos tremble with

This silence was broken when Alma Lune was suddenly distracted, as spirit personages often are, by something happening on earth. He directed their attention to Regine and the imminent danger that she was about to be destroyed.

"I must go to her." Asilah said and disappeared.

Nephi looked terrified.

"I've done this." His voice resolved and determined rather than accusatory.

"Lehi, I look forward to getting to know you better again. We will try to grow to love each other in this phase of our existence. I'm sure we will. And Sam, it is so good to see you again."

Then Nephi, too, disappeared.

---

tremulous fear because it cannot abide the light created by such emanations as such beings create because they have learned and directed their love to others as Jesus so well exemplifies on the cross.

Epilogue:
An Emergent
Redemption

And so we come to the end of our tale. Elder Holmberg (whom God Almighty hates) was welcomed by the Lord into the highest kingdom, where he and Alma Lune were again reunited as bosom friends, without the complications of power, of course. LeRoy and Jezzy's river running business thrived to the point that they were able to secure a college education for their children, all of whom became leaders in Blanding. Nephi sans hand was better than his word. He became a friend to his nephew and mentored and supported him for millions of years. They were friends for the rest of eternity. And Sam? No one is sure. Some say he is limping among universes, helping the poor and downtrodden and assisting anyone who feels slighted or left out of larger narratives.

As for Heike/Regine: For the first month she screamed. She screamed when they force-fed her meals. She had to be strapped to her bed, and she screamed in the restraints.

They submerged her in medicines, therapies, and care. Arrow was not allowed to visit her at first, neither were her children—she screamed as they entered the room. She was no longer Heike. She was no longer Regine. She was a cloud of memories untethered to any ground on which she could stand. She sometimes screamed in German. Sometimes in English. Sometimes in Greek. She spouted phrases that seemed to be no language whatsoever, yet contained some disgruntled grammar that verged on the edge of sense but descended into chaos. Leviathan and other monsters of the deep seemed to swim and sport just below her surface, great shadows that showed and formed horrors that could be glimpsed but not grasped. She prayed. She cursed God and wished to die. She seemed to have lost both the powers of sensible speech and of awareness and coherence. She shat and pissed in her diapers and did not complain more or less than usual when they were soiled. Sometimes she wept like a child, and at other times laughed deliriously without any context. What she was, no one knew. Neither the Gods nor angels that watched over her and prayed endlessly on her behalf could reach her. Her eyes wandered to and fro over the face of the room. She was and was not a plant nor an animal, neither human nor monster; she was lost to being, neither an agent nor a thing. She was not anything recognizable, and as the doctors scoured the excellent research that was brought to bear to attempt to help her, they found nothing. She was two spirits striving over her body, and yet the two spirits were singular. Lost. Empty. Both, matter unorganized. Perception without concepts. Concepts without perception. A cantering horse as a song of colors. Hexapod eyes in a metamorphic structure of unwillingness. Slippages of undoing framed around a matrix of mathematical solidity and oversight. Reckless xylem floating over wrath. She was connected to silence by a machine of lightminded taste and photosynthesis.

Then one day, an orderly came in to change her diapers and found her calm and watching a pigeon pecking outside her barred window. She looked at the orderly, and calmly said, "Did you know these are all descendants of the wild rock pigeon?"

It was a beginning. A toe hold. And she began to enter into the common reality of a shared world.

She was not void. She was a thing that could be loved. A life. A grace. And slowly. Something began to emerge. A pocket of stability. A modicum of sense.

⊃ ✕ ✦ ✕ ⊂

Arrow cried for three days as, for the first time, he dared to hope again.

Then these. Said in the psychiatric ward—as she wandered into connection and light like a mushroom fruiting through the forest leaves:

"I feel frightened when he comes in the room. I know who he is and that I both once hated him and loved him. I remember both shooting him and making love to him."

"I feel nothing when I see the children. And I feel guilty for feeling nothing."

"I remember the Goddess from both disconnected histories."

"Yes. I remember the murders. I feel so sad. So undone. At one level they seemed to deserve what I did to them, but I can't feel that anymore. I feel a draining despair. I disgust me."

"Must he visit every day?"

"Please will you give this card to the woman who hit my car and killed my baby? I want her to understand something about guilt."

"Yes. Please. I would like to see my mother again."

"Thank you for taking me to the park today. I have not seen a nuthatch for many years."

"Aren't the children coming today?"

"Please close the curtain. I am not in the mood for sunshine."

"Ha! And remember that time in St. Thomas Church, when the organist farted and the entire choir broke out in a fit of laughter in the middle of Bach's Cantata 243?... Did you ever resolve your question about Aquinas and substance? About the reciliation of God's being and aseity?

"He's very kind isn't he? He comes every day... I knew you would like him, mother."

"I'm not sure who I am. I don't know if I will love you again, but I like your visits."

"We took a field trip to the Schwarzwald. And we saw a badger! Not too far away! She was so handsome and pleasant with the white stripes running through the black fir of her face. There is such beauty in the world that sometimes I cannot bear it."

"I know it was a dream. But it seemed so real. An angel came and did something with the electricity. Strange to remember it so vividly. But more important, and I know as an analyst you will try to pigeonhole this into whatever is current in your circles—Freud, Lacan, whoever—but I've encountered the divine in my life before the accident and after. She, and it was a 'she,' manifest herself as a woman of power, a Goddess, someone who radiated light and authority, who held an earthy delight in the networked ecologies of this planet, a care for me. She was the embodiment of a deep embrace of creation. This earth was hers, and she loved me even though I had lost myself completely in the terror and pain of my loss. She loved me."

"Call me Khôra. It means vessel. Or the void in a vessel."

"It is so kind of you to visit me, Professor, after all I've done. I don't know what to say. I've disappointed you and all my committee and both male and female colleagues. But I thank you for visiting me and bringing to mind my paper on the void... I think I've been there, or near enough to its edge to see into its heart, and I think I can see it being the source of being—including Becoming-Goddess.... No I haven't changed my mind about that... yes, we will argue about that on your next visit."

"Christ is the event that gives me hope. A resurrection of a new me. Why is his cross so bright in my mind and yet my heart so dark?... I understand. And don't. I'll just leave it at that."

"Kimball, I do remember giving birth to you... and from that moment until now... l love you.... Your German is improving!"

"Please hold my hand. I feel so lost today. Remind me of the time you took me to the dance at the sandbar along the Colorado River. Remind me of the sunsets we saw."

"I thought that about Alma Lune too. He was the best of us."

"Jens please don't get so near the window! Are you trying to scare me to death?"

"No. The Book of Mormon is not my kind of theology. Don't cry. It's still a wonderful work of literature. I love so much about your faith, the possibility found in a Heavenly Mother. That earth and matter, matter. But its theology needs development. Maybe in a thousand years it will be ready for what I see as its potential.... Please don't cry. You are so much more than you think through the lens of your Moab Mormon faith. It's that that I've grown to appreciate."

"Why do you love me? For the last year I've done nothing but hurt and confuse you. Can't you just see that I'm not that person anymore?"

"Why didn't you come for the last week? I missed you so much. Please come here. Please?"

"I think Christ dwells everywhere. He can't be confined to a church. He was an event that launched something into the universe that cannot be contained. He defies categories of limit and reaches back to the void from where God emerged and to all endings when all becomes one whole assemblage... but he is not just male... not just creaturely human... in becoming Christ, he transcended all life. He is woman, wolf, nuthatch, beech and birch, and even tardigrade and aspen. She is an osprey."

"Close the curtains. I don't want to feel anything today."

"I cannot see a future anymore. I'm just glad to take a step each day. To watch the birds and feel the wind. To drink my coffee and see to my rounds visiting the patients who can use a kind word or to hold their hand. But no. I don't want you to go, but I understand. But… If you can stay… I would be most grateful. No more than that. Please stay if you can?"

ᗡ ⋈ ⚦ ⋈ ᑕ

After serving a three-year sentence for criminal insanity, Khôra moved to Moab to be near her children.

And Arrow.

THE END

Ø

References Used

From the Heart of the World: The Elder Brothers' Warning.
Documentary Film. Director: Alan Ereira; camera: Bill
Broomfield; editor: Horacio Queiro; sound: John Wills.
1990, color, 87 minutes VHS-NTSC. English narration
and subtitles. Distributed by BBC Enterprises, London.

McGinn, B., and M. O. C. Walshe. 2009. *The Complete Mystical Works of Meister Eckhart*: Crossroad Publishing
Company.

Schelling, F. W. J., J. Love, and J. Schmidt. 2010. *Philosophical Investigations into the Essence of Human Freedom,
SUNY series in Contemporary Continental Philosophy*:
State University of New York Press.

Storm, R., J. Ray, and Society Folio. 2003. *Myths and Legends of the Ancient Near East*: Folio Society.

Acknowledgements

I thank the wonderful people at BCC Press. They have been a constant blessing and support in my life. Steve Evans and Michael Austin have been vital to this book just by believing in it. Andrew Heiss's amazing typesetting needs to be put in context. I've known Andrew since he was a toddler in my sons' playgroup, and we have published an important ecological theory paper together—he has been a force for good in my life. Christian Harrison's cover has been so well-conceived and executed, not only in this book but on all of my books published with BCC Press. Kristine Haglund is one of the few people on the planet who can edit me. And I feel lucky that she consented to do this, knowing full well what a challenge it would be! She is a wonderful soul and has been a blessing in my life. Lori Forsyth played a vital role in editing this book. I have worked with Lori on academic projects, and her work is always phenomenal. She was crucial in making this a cleaner work that reflected my voice and intent.

Becky Roesler played a significant role in the book. She read an early draft and noted that Nephi seemed like a two-dimensional character. Her knowledge of the Book of Mormon helped me see him in a new light, and Nephi developed into a lead character thereby. She also helped me make the book more coherent and pointed out that the original ending did not work, so I completely restructured it, which vastly improved the novel. She read through several drafts, and I owe her a debt of gratitude—this would be a mediocre book without her influence and help.

In all mentioned above, I feel blessed to have such friends in my life. Despite all the help, all the mistakes I own. My mistakes are both subtle and occult, and no one can find them all. Someday, when powerful AIs can be marshaled to mine my work for errors, there will be a chance that many more will be found. Never all. Even the Library of Babel is insufficient to hold them all. If in the next life you stand before a great demon who tells you to slot the volume of Peck's errors into the wall—Despair. All is lost.

Note: In the Baader-Meinhof Gang bombing of the Frankfurt Officer's Club, my mother's cousin, officer Paul Bloomquist, was killed. I borrowed the details of the bombing for the context of the story. The character James in this novel bears no resemblance to the actual man killed. On the contrary, Paul was a genuine Vietnam war hero who was happily married and died in service to his country. See details about his life on his Wikipedia page.

Steven L. Peck is an ecology professor at Brigham Young University. He has published over 50 scientific articles in evolutionary ecology and the philosophy of biology. He has also published four literary novels, including *A Short Stay in Hell*, published by Strange Violin Editions; the magical realism novel *The Scholar of Moab*, published by Torrey House Press—an AML (Association of Mormon Letters) novel award winner and Montaigne Medal Finalist; and the AML novel award winner *Gilda Trillim*, Shepherdess of Rats. His climate change fiction book *King Leere, Goatherd of the La Sals*, published by BCC Press, was a semi-finalist for the Black Lawrence Press Big Moose Prize for a literary novel, short-listed for the Hoffer Award, and received a starred review from Publishers Weekly. He also won the AML short story award for "Two-Dog

Dose" published in *Dialogue*. In addition, he has published many short stories and has two collections of short stories, *Wandering Realities* by Zarahemla Press, and one self-published collection, *Tales of Pleasant Grove*.

His poetry has appeared in *Cold Mountain Review, Flyway, New Myths, Pedestal Magazine, Prairie Schooner, Red Rock Review, Whitefish Review,* and numerous other publications. His poetry collection *Incorrect Astronomy* was published by Aldrich Press.

For the body of his literary work, he received the 2021 Smith-Pettit Foundation Award for Outstanding Contribution to Mormon Letters.

For more information see his Wikipedia page https://en.wikipedia.org/wiki/Steven_L._Peck.

Made in the USA
Monee, IL
04 December 2022